T0126035

FRANKIE STYNE
AND THE SILVER MAN

KATHY PAGE

FRANKIE STYNE
and the Silver Man

BIBLIOASIS
WINDSOR, ONTARIO

FIRST EDITION

Library and Archives Canada Cataloguing in Publication

Page, Kathy, 1958-, author
    Frankie Styne and the silver man / Kathy Page.

Originally published: London : Meuthen, ©1992.
ISBN 978-1-77196-038-0 (paperback)

    I. Title.

PR6066.A325F73 2015   823'.914   C2015-903740-9

Edited by John Metcalf
Copy-edited by Allana Amlin
Typeset by Chris Andrechek
Cover designed by Kate Hargreaves

Published with the generous assistance of the Canada Council for the Arts and the Ontario Arts Council. Biblioasis also acknowledges the support of the Government of Canada through the Canada Book Fund and the Government of Ontario through the Ontario Book Publishing Tax Credit.

PRINTED AND BOUND IN CANADA

MIX
Paper from
responsible sources
FSC® C004071

ANCIENT FOREST ™
FRIENDLY

CONTENTS

CONTENTS

PART ONE

PART ONE

LIFE WITHOUT TV

L iz was waiting. She sat in her bed upstairs at the back of 127 Onley Street, leaning against the party wall with the covers drawn up to her waist, her head slightly upturned, her eyes open and unblinking in the dark. The argument next door always seemed to begin in the same way, about now, with a woman's voice, low: 'Tom . . .'

She'd seen them from the window: Tom, tall, his face all jaw, was close shaven, with a tight helmet of black hair. In her mind's eye Liz could see him sleeping with his face crushed determinedly into the pillow, his hands to either side of his head, almost covering his ears.

'Tom—please—'

The woman was called Alice. Her voice rose a step each time she spoke. Liz guessed that Alice too had been awake for the past hour, lying in the dark with her eyes open. As the minutes ticked wakefully by, the wardrobe, the kidney-shaped dressing table with its padded stool and the billowing shadows of the curtains would have come gradually clear, then painfully, unbearably sharp.

Liz didn't have curtains. Onley Street was a good two hundred miles from her last official home, the Black Swan, though in three and a half years she had been much farther from it than that. She had been to Stonehenge, to Brighton, to Wales and almost to Scotland. She had travelled for free in lorry cabs and the backs of vans, helmetless on the pillions of motorbikes, bolted in the toilets of InterCity trains—but mostly she had walked. She had lived in many derelict houses and several tents and once each in a cave and a railway carriage. She had wanted to go abroad, but that hadn't worked out. Circumstances had brought her here, to what people called a proper—a permanent—home. It was almost a week since she'd moved in.

She had grown up. She had dyed her mousy hair purplish red with henna powder. She had pierced her ears with a red-hot needle and a cork. She had had a baby, Jim, now sleeping beside her in the bed. His name had slipped out when they asked her in the hospital, and in the space of a few hours it had been written in waterproof ink on an armband fastened around his wrist and probably typed on half a dozen forms as well. She didn't use it when they were alone. She just called him 'you', and thought of him that way too.

127 was a terraced house. The walls were thin. It was one among many of the same, spreading across town, across Britain, side to side and back to back; one huge dwelling under a long narrow roof. The party walls, the variation of numbers and a little decoration above the window arches marked one unit from the next. In the dark, the carefully different colours of the painted doors didn't show. Even so, Liz's house stood out: no curtains and no car outside; inside, no fridge, sofa, vacuum cleaner, washing machine, no telephone, not so much as a single dining chair, and, despite the aerial on the roof, no television set. The house stood blind and disconnected, but sound travelled easily through its walls.

'Tom! Wake up!' Alice was tiny and smart. If someone had made her portrait it would have had to be from fine clay, kept moist and painstakingly smooth, carefully teased to show how a thousand angles can be softly graduated into curves. Making Alice's likeness would have been hard work, the artist bending close to move from detail to detail—compelled to reproduce as exactly as possible in the attempt to understand; never satisfied, losing sight of the whole, developing eyestrain and crickneck, having to take rests—just as Alice herself did when she bent and peered, removing hairs with tweezers, rubbing in oil, filing her nails, pressing at the pores around her nose and in the crease of her chin, faithfully rubbing in cream every night before she slept.

Liz was very different. She had a long straight back; she had wide shoulders, hips and thighs. Seen from the side she was narrow, but from the front everything about her was broad: the planes of her face, the span of her hands and feet, the stretch of her mouth. She could have been painted with a thick brush in two or three colours in oil paint or acrylic. Just two reddish strokes for the hair, parted in the centre—no highlights, no shine—the rest in cream. Bold. Few shadows. A flat, wide body, strong, and, but for the now swollen breasts, inherently stark and rather unapproachable. It could do anything—or it could just sit there, doing nothing much. Physically, at least, she took after her father, who must have taken after his—the one who widowed Grammy, who had tended to fat herself.

'Tom! Please . . .' Even through plaster and brick, Alice's voice caught at the nerves in Liz's neck. Of course, Liz would have heard less if she'd moved her bed to the other side, or even to the other bedroom at the front. But the nights were long. Listening was something to do—waiting, along with Alice, for Tom to wake, raise his head an inch or so and say, bewildered, 'Ally?'

Beside Liz in bed, Jim stirred and drew the sudden breath that preceded a cry. 'Sssh . . . Sssh,' she said as she reached for him, lifted her T-shirt, then settled back against the wall. The voices from next door were very clear—very likely they could hear her too, if they had a mind to.

'No, Ally, not now,' said Tom, as if he were busy and talking to a child who wanted to play. 'It's after midnight.'

'I don't believe you've really made your mind up.'

'I have.'

'You've seen her. You saw her today.'

'No, I didn't. I've told you. Please, can we go to sleep?' Then a light switch sounded, close, almost as if it were fixed inside Liz's ear, and Tom's voice grew suddenly deep and masterful, reminding her of the kind of voice used for God in the biblical films she and Grammy had used to watch on TV in the afternoons.

'Alice—turn it off!'

'I want to see your face,' hissed Alice. 'Someone saw you. So don't waste time telling lies.'

'Who? Who saw me?' He would be looking, Liz decided, at the ceiling and Alice would be propped on one elbow studying him, biting her lip. She could see them, Alice and Tom and their room, behind her eyes. It was almost as if she were there—even though she never had been—as if she were a camera, or as if they were on a television screen inside her head. If so it would be good, she thought, to be able to change the programme for something more exciting, with murders and space ships, aliens, time warps, ghosts.

'But it's better than nothing,' she whispered to Jim, moving him carefully to the other breast.

'Who saw me?'

'That girl who's moved in next door, the one with the baby. She saw you.'

Now, that's something, thought Liz, which doesn't happen on the television; they don't all of a sudden mention you, as if you weren't there watching them. Much less *lie* about you.

Tom said nothing. Liz imagined him, staring straight ahead at the wall, rock-still, weighing the information for plausibility, deciding on his tactics. It was Alice's voice she heard next, muffled: 'I'm sorry!' Tom, Liz thought, must be holding her to his chest. He must have flicked his eyes round and shaken his head ever so slightly. Now Alice would pull away, her face crumpled. She'd wipe her eyes, swallow . . .

'Answer me this. Just this,' Alice said. 'If you had an absolutely free choice. If it wouldn't hurt anyone, her or me, what would you do? Would you go to one or the other, or neither, or would you stay or want to leave me? Or would you want to see both, and if you did that where would you want to live? Tell me, please.'

'That's ridiculous,' said Tom. 'You.'

'Even though—?'

'It may not even be mine.'

'I hate her,' Alice said.

'I do too,' said Tom.

This was how it had always ended, so far. Tom's face, large-featured and normally open to the point of blank, would be tight, the light shaming and relentless.

'Off?' Tom asked hopefully, reaching across Alice for the switch. After a few moments Alice would press herself next to Tom so that he could feel her and smell her. She would change position a few times, wait a little, reach down . . .

'No—'

'Sorry—' Tom added, as Alice began to sob and gasp.

'What's wrong?'

'Nothing. I want to really,' he said. 'Really. But we must get some sleep.'

On the other side of the wall Jim sucked slower, making small wet noises, breathing hard. Liz listened to Alice's speechlessness. The light switch clicked again. A door, flung open, banged against a wall; there were footsteps on the stairs. Liz could still follow them in her mind's eye—Alice in an embroidered kimono perhaps, Tom in a crumpled track suit picked off the bedroom floor—but although she could hear their plumbing squeal and their boiler coughing itself into life, the faint mumble of their voices scarcely carried upstairs.

She patted Jim's back the way she had been shown. 'We have to guess what will happen next,' she said. 'He might go for her with a kitchen knife, and sever the carotid, not meaning to. But after, to make the best of it, he'd joint and freeze her. Then eat her slowly, over a year or so, everything, keeping up his normal life just the same. But he'd save the heart for last . . .

' . . . and roast it. But it'd choke him.' She wrapped Jim up and settled him back in the bed. 'Couldn't tell an *ordinary* baby stories like that.'

'First thing I'll do,' she told him, 'as soon as I've got the lie of the land, is get us a decent TV set.'

In 125, which joined Liz's house at the top but was separated at ground-floor level by a passageway, Frank Styne—born John Green—was also awake, despite the sleeping pill he had taken to make sure that the girl and her baby didn't keep him awake. If there had been a constant stream of sounds it would have been easier to ignore or to complain about. But there was only the other-worldly cry of the child, the soft sudden mumble of the girl's speech, not loud enough to follow, not frequent enough to anticipate. He often found himself listening to the silence between sounds. Oh, sleep . . . Being a big man, he thought, perhaps he should have taken *two* of the tablets. But where would it end? He mistrusted the yellow, metal-smelling pills. They were to be just a temporary measure. The house next door had been empty for a long time before, then workmen had come, then her . . . Presumably, he told himself, I will grow used to it in time, adjust.

He sat in his pyjamas, banked with pillows, in his single bed. An aluminium reading frame supported the book on his lap; a tiny halogen lamp peeped over his shoulder illuminating only the page and his hand. Frank was an author. He read from one of his own novels every night. Constant re-reading ensured a consistent style. There were nearly twenty to choose from now. *The Killer Gene,* written ten years ago, was still in print and earning—less, but steadily.

Sleep was a necessity, but Frank loved and savoured it like a luxury; the way it pushed him down, obliterated him. Complete conquest. Absolute nothingness. He didn't dream pictures or words. He sometimes dreamed a feeling, a feeling of hotness and fullness and want and fight, an aching dream, restless as wind, half dangerous, half safe—a dream, almost, of wakefulness—then lost it, mercifully, at dawn. It was best, he believed, to live as much as possible in the present, which was quite bearable, even good.

And, at last, the key turned. The words before him tumbled in slow motion to nonsense. He lifted the reading frame from his lap and gratefully extinguished the light.

HIDE AND SEEK

The early morning sun painted Onley Street bright, though by afternoon it would be swamped in shadow. If there had not been bollards sealing it at one end, the street would have been an ideal shortcut between two of the eight major roads which converged gradually until they reached the centre of town. Even so it was busy, filled morning and afternoon with a tide of schoolchildren, a steady procession of shoppers winding their way back home. Delivery vans eased around the sharp corners of its tributary streets; market researchers, postmen and leafleteers moved, heavy as summer bees, from door to door.

Frank's alarm was set for seven, and even having taken the pill he woke the usual two minutes before it sounded. He made himself espresso coffee with a specially imported Italian machine. He preferred to write by hand and to cook on a real flame, but otherwise he was drawn to gadgets, provided they worked; things automatic, cordless, remote-controlled; things which timed or cleaned themselves, had memories; the cunningly concealed, the multifunctional, the miniature . . .

A wad of mail slapped onto the floor. Apart from bills and the small blue envelopes that came occasionally from his dead mother's friends, now living in retirement homes, the bulk of it was professional. There was always a great deal of routine publishing correspondence, including at the end of every month a padded envelope of fan mail forwarded by Cougar Books. Periodically he would enter into correspondence with a willing academic or specialist of some kind. For research purposes, he subscribed to over a dozen journals, ranging from *The Lancet* and *Military Hardware* to *Modern Interiors*. He never neglected research and prided himself on the accuracy of his descriptive passages.

His current novel, *The Procreators,* had a suburban setting—a four-bedroomed house on a Barratt housing estate. One of the bedrooms was done out as a nursery: Beatrix Potter wallpaper and curtains, a cot with ruched linen, a changing table and associated paraphernalia, a cheerful mobile of ducks hanging from the ceiling, a baby bouncer—Frank had spent two whole mornings at the shops getting the stuff just so.

The living room was based on the careful examination of several show houses on luxury estates on the edge of town. It was carpeted wall-to-wall in a soft wool of a pale pinkish beige called Oyster. Framed prints—rural landscapes, vases of sweet peas on windowsills—hung on walls papered a slightly richer pink called Blush, and the suite was upholstered in a tapestry-like print which, in a lighter weight, had been used for the curtains and pelmets as well.

The small circular tables with tooled leather tops bore vases of flowers and magazines stacked neatly in piles. Light came from shell-like fittings mounted on each wall and from the large television, on without the sound . . . It was ghastly, truly revolting to one who preferred clean lines and simplicity, but Frank had described it without detectable rancour; a matter of taste, after all. A log effect gas fire had been set in an exposed brick fireplace, and in front of it lay a white fur rug. On this the action of the main scene was to take place.

He carried the bundle of mail to the kitchen and extracted a cream bond envelope from his agent, Katie Rumbold. The envelope was thick—it must contain, he thought, at least two pages of 90-gramme bond paper. Katie Rumbold always addressed him as Dear John or even Dear *Jon*. This was how, at the age of eighteen, he had signed his first letter to her predecessor at the agency. Ever since he had used Frank and ever since she had refused to notice—not that he had actually told her how much it irritated him, because doing that might involve explaining *why*. How, for instance, a black and white photograph, framed in silver, used to stand on a small cabinet next to his mother's double bed. It showed a fair-skinned man whose face looked smooth and lean beneath his military cap, whose broad shoulders reached firmly out of the frame. A six-foot man with features often described as 'chiselled' and eyes which could be no other colour but ice-blue. There would never, ever, be another like him, Frank's dead mother had often proclaimed: not on this earth. The photograph was gone, but sometimes a print of it appeared behind Frank's eyes—and soon after would follow the rest of the room: the pattern of roses on the walls, the thick maroon carpet, the white candle-wick bedspread, the single light hanging from the dead centre of the room.

A humpback clock ticked quietly. A dressing table was set in the window bay. It had two drawers either side and a space between for his mother's knees, if she ever had time, between him and her book-keeping job at the garage, to sit at the stool. The dressing table blocked the netted light and made the room uncomfortably dark, but still its mirrors—one huge expanse of glass, arched at the top, with two smaller panels, hinged, on either side—absorbed enough light to shine. It was the only mirror in the house and in it Frank, then John, had seen himself for the first time, one afternoon long before he went to school. He had pushed open her bedroom door, which stuck slightly on the carpet and made a noise somewhere between a grunt and a sigh, and walked carefully across, avoiding the mirror's eye until he was right in front of it.

There were the lace mats, the cut-glass jar containing face powder and a smell, and the white china dish made to look like a basket, containing two crumpled hairnets. There were the lipsticks in scratched gold holders, the hairbrush, an atomiser of perfume, and the cake mascara with its clogged brush—all finely coated in pinkish powder-dust, all standing there in the silence and looking just like themselves. Behind was a hugeness of wallpaper, like some kind of patterned sky. Between the table and the wallpaper sky was him: a thick-necked child, with a large crimson birthmark spreading across his right cheek and dipping into the socket of his eye. Like a magnet, it affected everything else: the eyes seemed to be different sizes, the brows to be at cross purposes; the forehead hung; his lips, just licked, reminded him of worms. Frank, then John, gripped the edge of the dressing table. There he was, his mother's own and only. He wanted to believe that it was some kind of mistake. But everything else was copied perfectly.

Of course, the ugly duckling became a swan. But the ugly sisters envied and were punished twice over; he had seen it on the stage. Mirrors on the wall always told the truth.

He turned away from the mirror, realising the worst thing of all: that this discovery could not be kept secret, because everyone else already knew. *She* already knew. As he pushed her bedroom door softly to, it was this that made him want to cry—and remembering it could, too—and once started it would lead on to more as well, one memory dragging out the next like a conjuror's handkerchiefs.

Katie Rumbold wasn't the kind of person to do something without knowing why. 'But why, John, why?' she would ask, all smiles. Just thinking about explaining it all he could feel the past's sharp edges pressing cruelly at the tolerableness of the present . . . No. He couldn't. He just signed his letters Frank, and hoped that one day she would notice. He set her letter flat on the table next to his cup.

Dear John,

I'm writing with some very good news—do you remember me mentioning the Hanslett Award when we met before Christmas?

Christmas? No, he didn't. These days her letters were typed by a machine that made them look virtually published. The clear black type, absolutely even, made it difficult to believe that anything she wrote was less than definite or could ever be wrong. Misspelled words had an authority which made them unsettling and difficult to challenge with any confidence. Frank abandoned the letter and went to replenish his cup of coffee, standing by the machine while the dark liquid leaked fitfully out. He adjusted the kitchen blind to make the light softer. The blind was very pale yellow and made from extremely narrow slats, with a rod at the side. It was the best you could get. Frank had a special attachment for cleaning it. In his mother's day the window had been covered with a plastic gingham curtain. She said it was practical, but in fact it had attracted mildew at the bottom, and it felt dreadful to the touch, damp and smooth, like a sick person's skin.

He had waited for eighteen months after her death. Then he had gutted the house. The floral wallpapers were replaced with simple stripes, pinstripe-fine; the textured ceilings were plastered smooth. He had spotlights and wall lights and dimmer switches, integral shelving; he installed a new kitchen, heating, a shower, the blinds. He stayed with his mother's friend Marjorie while it was done, and came back to find the place unrecognisable, as he had hoped. He had lived it out day by day and he had been loyal to the end—what choice, after her faithfulness? But after, he had wanted to forget; and to be only, and thoroughly, Frank Styne.

Returning to his chair he forced himself to read on:

It's a new and substantial prize, likely to carry a great deal of publicity. The prospectus says it is intended for

The type slipped effortlessly into italics.

—daring and experimental work at the cutting edge of contemporary fiction.

Of course, no one knows what that means, especially first time around! But I must confess that although I've long felt your work to be underestimated, it never occurred to me to press Cougar to enter *To the Slaughter* for the Hanslett! I have it from P. Magee, however, that a member of the judging panel is a great fan of yours and has called for *TTS* to be considered. And of course the kind of post-modern, ironic horror you are so well known for is certainly at the "cutting edge"!

Cougar are delighted, though not sure quite what's hit them. Naturally, if you win, it may in the end mean some kind of deal with a more literary house. The shortlist (rumour has it that you are on it) will emerge this week—coinciding almost exactly with publication of *TTS*—and the result comes out in early May. Even at this stage I think there could be *considerable* interest from the press. I'm sure you'll be as delighted as I am. I may well be able to give you further information when we meet for lunch next Wednesday, 3 April. Fingers crossed!

He'd never much cared for the loose generosity—or was it arrogance?—of the way Katie Rumbold could fill any available space with her signature, and now, suddenly, he detested it. He had never, ever, thought of—let alone wanted to win—a literary prize. Postmodern? Ironic? I don't even want to be in the running, he thought. I write *pulp*. The plot of *The Procreators*, for instance, was nothing but, though it did differ in one respect from his previous work. His editor at Cougar, Pete Magee, had recently told him that it was time he included detailed sex scenes in his books. Times were changing. Television was to blame. It was, he had said, virtually obligatory nowadays to include some sexual action, and he expressed his complete confidence that Frank could take it on. But if not, perhaps just an outline, and someone in the office could do it, and slip it in? Frank could just tidy it up and make it blend . . . 'Only trying to make things easy for you, old chap,' he said when Frank asked him why didn't he dispense with authors altogether. 'Just so long as you get it in, I don't care how, that's all.'

As a result of this discussion Frank had roughed out *The Procreators*. The Barratt-house husband's desperate and humiliating attempts to produce viable sperm—spurred on by his belief that his beautiful wife Sandra was already unfaithful and staying with him only for material reasons—had culminated in a visit to a Dr Villarossa. From her he had learned that his infertility was the result of hiding his true nature. For too long he'd suppressed the virile part, the beast in himself, walking on soft carpets, bringing his wife flowers, busying himself with home improvements and gardening. Dr Villarossa had given him a series of injections to change all this. He would, she said, become what he truly was, and then a child would be conceived.

As a result of the injections, Mr Barratt-Homes began to change physically. His shoulders broadened, his skin became greasy and then flaky. He perspired constantly; his sweat had a terrible odour like cat's breath and left dark, ineradicable stains on his clothes. Sandra—at first concerned—had grown utterly repelled and rejected him. He had suffered terrible physical pain and grown even more miserable than before but Dr Villarossa had reassured him that everything was as it should be.

Eventually he had taken to one of the spare bedrooms and locked the door. Finally, he emerged, creeping up on his wife in the sitting room while she watched TV and drank Martinis.

Frank had already described this: his Barratt-Homes husband was man-shaped for the most part, but had grown unevenly, his buttocks, shoulders and feet huge, his arms long, his legs short. His jaw had grown larger, his forehead receded. Where a human skin would be soft—the lips and fingertips, the palms of the hands, the insides of the thighs—so his was scaled and hard, and elsewhere covered in a terrible eczema, a crust of flakes concealing the soft putrescence underneath, like pastry on a pie. They would have sex on the rug. Pete Magee was pleased.

This is what I do, Frank thought. Pulp. Junk. I do it well. It's not daring or experimental but I want to go on doing it *in peace.* No publicity. No people coming around and wanting to find out about the real me or what it all means deep down . . . But it was there, in his hand, typed: the future, the shortlist, the result in early May . . . Publicity, which meant, of course, television. It was as if a skewer had slipped through his flesh.

'Beauty is in the eye of the beholder, John,' his mother had said, returning with custard creams and gold-top milk. The next day she had bought him the snow-storm paperweight. She found a wooden box so that he could stand next to her in the kitchen as she worked. But glass truth was truer than mother truth. The mirror had nothing to gain and nothing to lose. 'Being bad is far worse than being ugly,' she also said. But when school came—playtime—they had all run away.

Liz possessed neither watch nor alarm clock. And there was no point, she believed, in getting up as soon as she woke; a waste of warmth—also, and more importantly, a waste of the special freedom that lingered after sleep, when she couldn't quite remember what it felt like to be who she was, where she was, how she got there, nor how long it was that she must stay. A square of buttery light fell in ripples over the crumpled bedclothes and she moved her hand into its warmth.

She set herself to imagine that she was a visitor from another planet, waking to her first dawn in the body of a human. She looked out through the borrowed eyes and asked: What kind of place is this? If she didn't like it, she could always go somewhere else, or far back across the galaxies, home . . .

So: the place that contained her was roughly a cube, with the four vertical planes smooth and white. The surface beneath her was made up of dark stripes, not quite regular; the one above was patterned with a kind of white stubble, as if something had once dripped from it and all of a sudden frozen: she must not forget to take a sample home. In the centre of this hung a small transparent globe, peppered on its upper curve with dust (perhaps it was an eye?) and at the corners between the vertical and upper horizontal planes bundles of fine greyish threads (some kind of primitive plant?) had gathered and moved gently in the atmospheric tides. A large framed panel made of something hard and reflective had been set into the vertical plane to the right of the bed. It displayed an image which, when examined very closely, seemed also to be moving, just. It was pretty clever, she admitted grudgingly. It seemed almost as real as the space she was in—

A hammering at the front door reverberated through the empty house. Liz kept her face loose and still, her eyes fixed on the window. They'll go away, she told herself, half statement, half spell. They *will* go away. She proceeded to examine the faint steam rising from the roof tiles visible through her window: what was this substance? She must remember to mention it in her report . . . (And it couldn't, anyway, be Purvis who would never knock like that: hard and fast, four rapid beats then a pause, then again, and again the pause growing shorter each time.) Police? she thought, without much conviction. I wonder, she willed herself to consider as a tabby cat eased itself onto her windowsill, what kind of being that could be a picture of? The knocking stopped then and silence pushed through the house as aggressively as sound had done the moment before.

Liz sighed, swung her legs over the edge of the bed. The mechanism was crude, she noted; generally, the earth-body was rather poorly designed and the need to empty it of liquid poisons three or four times a day was its crowning indignity. Still, seeing as it was only a short visit, the creatures being (not surprisingly) so short-lived, she'd probably manage to bear it. She glanced back at the bed, observing that it contained a small human being with a disproportionately large head covered in silver-white down, sleeping. So: she must be what they called *female*. She made for the stairs (very awkward device), catching her foot on a small round-headed tack protruding from the boards; a pretty-coloured liquid, she observed, the brightest thing I have seen here so far . . . and the sensation also most peculiar.

The knocking recommenced as she reached the bottom of the stairs. She stood frozen, unable to decide, then changed direction and opened the door just a little way. She had a duty; it might be of interest.

'Mrs Meredith?'

'Mrs Nothing,' she said. The stocky man standing on her doorstep was wearing a tightly belted all-in-one garment, made from synthetic fibres; blue, very smooth, with a faint sheen. It was too clean and smart to be called a boiler suit and too practical for a leisure garment. The pocket, emblazoned with a yellow 'T', bristled with pens. He was holding a clipboard, also yellow. They have come to greet me, she told herself—the custom is to smile.

'Phone,' he said, twisting the clipboard around so that she could see a tiny laminated photograph of him. He had only knocked, he added, for such a length of time because the neighbour had said she must be in. He nearly went away, and then she'd've had to wait another three weeks, so she should thank her lucky stars.

'What for?' she asked. She was wearing only a large T-shirt, milk-stained across the breast—not that she cared about that—and her legs were crinkling in the cold. Earth has a *most* unpleasant climate, she thought, and then realised that she was probably stuck there for good.

'Telephone. You asked for it.' The man tried to step in, pushing the yellow clipboard forward ahead of him like a shield.

Liz stood her ground, holding the door. 'I never asked for a telephone. It's a mistake.'

He stuck his foot forward and leafed through the papers on the board. He was calmer when he looked up. 'It's free,' he said, 'the installation, that is.' He added in a lowered voice, 'Social Services. Because of the baby. Okay?' He handed her a thin blue paper covered in faint carbon marks. Liz held it just long enough to see two signatures: her own—faint, as if written by a ghost, and certainly she couldn't remember writing it—and another, very firm. *A. Purvis.* She screwed it tight in her hand. Purvis. Purvis was tying her up in little knots, stitching through her skin with a flat-ended needle and nylon fishing line. It hurt. The scarlet blood was bright and real.

'I don't want one,' she repeated, pushing at the door just enough to keep it where it was. The man pushed back.

'But it's free,' he said, grunting slightly as he increased the pressure. He lowered his eyes as he pushed, and his face seemed all skin; freckled, the soft lids fringed with pale lashes.

'If you don't use it except for emergencies it won't cost you a thing—'

'But I don't want a phone!' I do want a television, she thought, but I bet no one's going to knock on the door with one of those . . . Another inconvenient feature of human design, the tears lurking just behind her eyes. 'I don't want one!' she repeated and suddenly the man stopped pushing. The door swung a little between them, as if to say, What next? Liz's T-shirt had ridden up her hips. The man took a step back and coughed, glancing briefly at the stiff fringe of hair that showed beneath its hem.

'You'll have to sign a declaration then.'

'No,' said Liz, 'I'm not signing anything.'

'Please yourself.' The man turned on his heel, walked stiffly towards the gate. It came off in his hand, the screws pulled clean from the post. Knowing she hadn't shut the door he froze for a second, holding it.

'I'm sorry,' he said, casting around for somewhere to prop the gate. 'It's rotted.'

Liz shrugged. The screwed-up paper dropped from her hand. 'Did you tell—?' she asked quietly indicating 129 with a movement of her head, noticing her T-shirt and pulling it down. She could hear Jim crying upstairs. He had an unusual cry—people had remarked on it in the hospital—persistent but not urgent, irregular in rhythm and pitch as if he were trying to find a hidden frequency.

'Of course not,' the telephone man said. He set the gate carefully on the tangled lawn. There, Liz thought as she closed the door: a Silver Lining. Could've been worse.

Jim was lying on his side, curled tight, his face flushed and shining. As she sat heavily on the bed the crying stopped briefly and then resumed. She was beginning to get used to it.

'So!' she said, her voice shaking slightly. 'You notice me.' After a few minutes, she carried him downstairs to the bathroom, sat herself on the toilet, placed him on the changing mat on the floor between her feet and reached down. His soft skin, opal white, was covered in sticky yellow. Her bladder emptied steadily as she folded the nappy up and began to wipe him. The pair of us, she thought. Him and her, both caught short. Her legs had blotched purple, her feet on the lino tiles were bloodless.

'Phone . . .' she muttered, slipping the soiled wipes into the sink for removal later. 'If Purvis thinks I'll walk into that one, she's wrong! Because I know how to hide.' Her breasts ached. One thing, she thought, one thing at a time.

'It was Grammy,' she announced, realising that she had more or less succeeded in forgetting Grammy, hadn't thought of her, not directly, since that time in the hospital . . . 'It was Grammy, Jim, who taught me how to hide, when I was very small.'

Hiding was an art, Grammy had said. 'Always choose the unexpected place,' she had said—like the railway carriages. Also, she'd explained how to plant false clues; to imagine herself in the seeker's position, and calculate what they would see and how they would think; for instance, not going to London, where everyone would look . . . To open the cupboard door a little, but not go in. To screw herself tight and stay like that, waiting, head in lap, waiting. To hold her breath impossibly long. To hide so well that even she herself scarcely knew she was there and then leap out with a roar. But, according to Grammy, the real, the most difficult hiding was more than that. It was something you could do without, actual physical concealment. Using the exact same tactics—that was the real art. Always look them in the eye, tell them what they want to hear. Then do what you want, quietly, Grammy had said.

THE TIES THAT BIND

Grammy took her wedding ring from the ship matchbox in the kitchen drawer and held it out on the creased palm of her hand.

'Now you've got one,' she'd said, picking it up between finger and thumb of the other hand and holding it to her eye like a lens. 'You can see what they are. No protection against the worst things in life. Just a bit of gold, like a Polo mint. Suck if you want, but don't swallow it whole . . .' Then she laughed the laugh which Liz's mother said was like a fishwife's. Later, in bed, Liz slipped the thin, pale ring into her mouth. It tasted bitter, and she spat it onto the pillow. If you did swallow it, you would probably have to be cut open, she'd thought, for them to get it out. You might bleed to death in the operation; definitely there would be a scar, crawling across your stomach like a white centipede.

At that time, just before she moved into the Black Swan with Liz and her parents, Grammy was sorting through her possessions. She wanted to dispose of all but the essential. The rest—piles of magazines, shelves full of jars and interleaved plastic bags—was all packed up and collected by the council. Parcels of clothes, many unworn for decades, were washed, ironed, folded in brown paper and despatched to

charity shops. The inlaid writing bureau was sent as a surprise to an old friend who had once admired it. The next-
door neighbours, who had for twenty years kept faithful and
fruitless watch for burglars, received the silver cutlery and a
selection of tinned food—ham, chicken, mandarin orange
segments, some of it very old.

Grammy's last week in the flat was spent with only one
chair and no curtains. She was nothing if not thorough and
she made no secret of the fact that she had written a will in
which she bequeathed the proceeds of the sale of her flat to
a complete stranger—a young man she'd read about in the
local paper under the caption 'Sound Worlds'. He wanted
to write music with only the tiniest of spaces between the
notes: it was a life's work and he needed expensive computer
equipment to do it. Grammy had never before shown any
interest in music of any kind, but declared that it was a fine
idea. *'Always,'* she said, 'try to be original.' Grammy spoke
mainly in imperatives and assertions of fact. Questions were
entirely foreign to her.

'Always avoid the ties that bind,' she often said, and: 'When
I'm gone, try to forget me. You can forget anything if you try
hard enough. Forgetting, like hide-and-seek, is an *art.'*

Another of her commands was to always search for Silver
Linings. It was worth it because with a flick of the wrist a dull
garment, something like a school mac, could be transformed.
It was a kind of magic, perpetually waiting behind the every-
day, the intractable, the *boring.* Finding a Silver Lining made
Grammy laugh like a fishwife. She did it as often as possible.

'Damned if I can see one in this place,' Liz's mother would say.

The search for Silver Linings, the avoidance of ties that
bound, hiding and forgetting: these were Grammy's most
repeated, most strenuous commands. But there were many
more. Some began with *always,* others with *never,* but only the
one: 'Try to forget me,' with *try to.* In her later years Grammy

issued her commands from bed, sitting straight up, her face immobile and her hands resting on the turned-down sheet:

'*Never* sit with your legs crossed.'

'*Always* look people in the face when you're speaking to them. Especially if you're telling a lie.'

'That child,' Liz's mother said, 'will do nothing we ask, but she's putty in your mother's hands.'

Long before all this, the first thing Liz remembered anyone saying about Grammy was that she was a widow. At that time she hadn't known what it meant, but guessed it must somehow refer to the ways in which Grammy wasn't like other people of her age. She genuinely enjoyed playing hide-and-seek; she left bits of her dinner she didn't care for on her plate without even pushing them to the edge; she loved to watch television, the same things as Liz herself: vampires and rayguns, shootouts, aliens—*rubbish*. She was someone who slipped through the net that held other grown-up people fast. She had her independence, then, and couldn't be told what to do.

Against a tide of disapproval, Grammy dyed her wisps of hair jet black and this made the scalp glow even whiter beneath. As they both grew older—and it was important, too, that they both counted years—Liz helped her with this, standing behind the upright chair to paste on the foul-smelling dye, her eyes torn between the task at hand and the television screen. So although people naturally would say that it was the divorce, or pubs, which had made Liz turn out how she did, they would be mostly wrong. It was Grammy, who in her own way had predicted it all.

'Of course,' Liz's father often said, 'I don't expect anything back. She struggled to bring me up—'

'Probably had a right old time while she did it—'

'—But she might leave that money to help her own grandchild. Or something like cancer research.'

'Something like *us*. A sum like that.'

'I never asked them to bring me here,' Grammy told Liz when she had moved into the Swan. (It was an Edwardian structure and stood miraculously preserved in the middle of a modern housing estate. The inside had been done up in modern style. Just like the one before, it was going through bad times. Nightclubs, Liz's father said, were to blame . . .) 'It was a *fait accompli*,' Grammy continued. '*Always* avoid, dear, the ties that bind. Indeed, you really ought to avoid me now.' But when Grammy said that, she smiled. Ought was like try to; it didn't seem to be quite so absolute a command as the others. There was room for failure.

Grammy was awkward. Sometimes she answered the telephone and put people off. She was temperamental, she was ungrateful and selfish. Grammy was senile: her brains, Liz's mother explained, were slowly thickening and scrambling, like eggs. Liz's mother had a way with expressions like that—said them in a tone of voice somewhere between distaste and wonder so that they seemed to mean exactly what the words said. In the end, that voice suggested, Grammy's brains would stick to the bottom of the pan and a great deal of scouring would be necessary.

Her wrists were weak and she regularly left taps running, so draining the hot water tank. She would rise in the middle of the night to stand on the balcony and search for stars and unidentified flying objects, or else walk downstairs, through the deserted bar, right outside, and, because of her wrists, leave the front door open when she came back in. A tomcat once followed her back, leaving a stink which lasted for weeks. After that, she was locked in her room at night or when everyone was out. Grammy turned night into day, Liz's mother said.

But the worst of all was that Grammy was incontinent, doubly and prolifically so. It was this which made Liz's mother call Grammy 'Your Mother' when she talked with her husband, just, Liz noticed, as she herself was often called 'That Child.' It was another thing they shared, the way she and Grammy often seemed to feel less than connected to both Liz's parents. 'That Child is besotted,' 'Your mother will stop at nothing.' Her mother's tone when she spoke of Grammy was one of icy relish; her father, Liz noticed with horror, said nothing in Grammy's defence.

Grammy shrugged. 'He'll suffer for it. He just married my opposite. People are always doing things like that. It won't last.' And Liz had wanted to carry Granny off and live with her in a cottage miles from anywhere. They could watch what they wanted on the television, far into the night, and only eat when they felt like it. She would do all the chores without complaining. It would be a love without duty, a pure thing. That, Grammy said, but softly, was both a contradiction and a tie that bound.

'It's all very well,' Liz's mother said of Liz's passion for Grammy. 'But I have to change her sheets. I never expected this.'

'I'll do it,' countered Liz. 'I don't mind.'

Her mother paused long enough to look angrier still, then bundled the sheets into a plastic bag as she continued. 'She depends on us. On me, in fact. So do you, until you grow up.' *Avoid the ties that bind.* But only days later her mother pulled down the covers of the bed, stood aghast, then folded her arms and said, 'Here then. Go on, you do it. A bit of practice'll stand you in good stead, if you ever have a family of your own.' The smell of piss mingled with that of the lavender cologne which Grammy sprinkled to conceal it. Thinking of her doing this, in the dark, made Liz want to cry.

'See what I mean?' her mother said. 'It's not a bed of roses.'

'She is no longer the woman I remember . . .' declared Liz's father—he was Grammy's only son, named Richard after his father, long dead or departed, it was never clear which—shaking his head from side to side. Liz recognised her mother's words emerging through his lips, as if swallowed and regurgitated, or as if there had been some kind of infection or transfusion such as took place when vampires kissed. To stop it, she knew, you had to drive a stake hard through their hearts.

'We have to be firm,' he said. *Firm* meant: not indulging melodrama, balanced meals at set times, sleeping pills at night and then finally, for a reason never explained but which could only be some kind of punishment, rationed watching of the television set.

Liz's mother came up from the bar when trade was slack, to check, and she unplugged it if it was on. The picture shrank to a dot, leaving them both feeling somehow naked and shocked, even though it was a simple matter to get it back when she had gone. Liz's mother had always hated television.

'That child's being raised on TV,' she often used to say, years back when they first acquired one, as she served a hybrid of lunch and supper when Liz arrived home from school. Once a day the family would be together the way other people's were. Except that she herself rarely sat down to eat it, and Liz's father said that eating so early upset him.

'Would you prefer me to make our tea after closing time?' she'd ask—for such questions she often used her softest, sweetest voice—as she set the plate before him. He picked; Liz cleared hers rapidly. They talked as if she were intermittently invisible. She stared at the wall, feeling what it would be like if it were she who decided when.

Occasionally Liz's mother would take her aside and whisper that she was sorry that everything was dreadful and she was so bad tempered, but she was hounded to it. When they got out of pubs, she promised, things would be different: everything. But it didn't seem to happen. Clutched between her mother's arms and knees, the soft words tickling at her ears, was, Liz grew to feel, something like being embraced by a vampire who charmed her victim into the first deadly kiss.

'If I help you in the bar, I haven't much choice but to leave her watching TV for hours on end. The rest of the kids in her class can already read.'

'She doesn't seem to mind,' her father said, adding, 'I was a late reader. It's not the end of the world.' After this the silence ached.

I'm *glad* I'm raised on TV, Liz thought. Everything her parents said was dull and flat and had been said often before. There was no music, just the scrape of spoons in bowls, the clash of knives and forks in the sink as her mother washed up from the first course. No special effects, no real fights with blood and laser guns and flashing lights, no last-minute escapes; no one won and nothing ever changed. As soon as Liz was finished, she could leave the table. Without television, she thought she would die.

'How long?' Liz's mother said abruptly one day. 'I never expected this, you know.'

'How long what?'

'Until—'

'When we get to the new pub, we should be able to take on help,' her father would say. When that had proved itself several times wrong, he'd come up with another idea. 'My mother could come and live with us. She could help out. Not in the bar—I mean company, for the kid.'

'But she can't look after her own self!' Liz's mother said, her gloved hands steaming. 'What *help* is she going to be?' Nonetheless, Grammy had come to the Black Swan.

And because the television was kept in Grammy's bedroom, sanctions against it were obviously aimed at both of them. Watching secretly with the volume right down drew them even closer together. Mostly you could get the story, even without the words and sound.

'Means we can talk at the same time,' Grammy said, her eyes fixed straight ahead, pupils wide—that, of course, was the Silver Lining. By then it had become a habit. They found them for each other automatically and only noticed if one wasn't there. Liz sat next to Grammy on the bed in the dark watching the pictures move. Sometimes they sucked sherbet lemons as the watched. If she ever thought of the rest of her life, Liz just imagined it going on like that. In her infatuation and outrage Liz didn't at the time see the irony, nor believe, as her mother had warned, that one day *the chickens would come home to roost.*

The chickens were brochures for old people's homes. They flapped their way through the letterbox and then landed clumsily one by one in a dead heap. Liz's parents had agreed to avoid the tie that bound them to Grammy. It was impossible, they both declared, to run a pub and a nursing home at the same time. There was, for a while, peace between them. Perhaps it was the desire to avoid being seen as a hypocrite which made Grammy sign the forms without complaint. And perhaps she did purposely choose Christmas Day to die on, when she was supposed to move into the home on the first day of the New Year—meaning they'd gone through all the bureaucracy but got none of the benefit.

Liz was nearly fifteen then. Grammy had lived with them for six years. The sickbed was taken to the council dump, its odour of lavender and ammonia lost amongst less astringent smells. A desk was moved into the spare room so that Liz could use it to do her homework: she'd got very behind at school. The television also was disposed of.

'Forget!' Grammy had commanded.

Liz sat in Grammy's old room, with her textbooks and exercise book open on the desk. The dry little letters marched across the page, endlessly across and back again. She found she couldn't focus her eyes, though there was nothing wrong with them. She couldn't make much sense of the letters. But if she stared long enough without blinking they faded and went away.

'Back to normal,' Liz's mother said. 'If such a thing exists.'

They had always been in pubs. The first one Liz could properly remember was The Grapes; huge, Victorian, badly maintained and situated on the railway side of the city where everything was perpetually being demolished. The Grapes was jinxed, her father said, as a joke, though no one laughed. Three managers had left in the last year and one had committed suicide. You couldn't make the place run on lunchtimes, not unless the customers wore suits, and who would want to risk their neck getting out there and home in the dark? In the short, irritable afternoons he would talk endlessly of using some of the upstairs rooms for functions, but it was a question of persuading the brewery. *Functions* or not, Liz's mother pointed out, people would still have to risk their necks. She sounded the 'k' and the 's' very sharply.

In The Grapes they had two floors above the bars—more space than they knew what to do with. All the rooms, even the toilets, were enormous and echoed if you so much as cleared your throat. Most of them had fireplaces that had been sealed over to allow the fitting of gas fires. It all seemed to have been made for a race of giants: the fist-thick marble mantelshelves on their clumpy brackets, the dirty mirrors so high that not even grown ups could see themselves inside. None of the furniture looked right in the rooms. The place swallowed things, her mother said.

Liz slept at the back in a room with two sash windows, larger than any windows she'd ever seen before. Plaster vines twisted around the central lamp, light from which seemed to struggle to reach the floor and corners of the room. When the bulb died her father had to fetch a ladder to replace it. The milky glass shade was always full of dead flies. It was difficult to fall asleep in such a huge room; it stretched about her like an empty auditorium. Any minute, in the dark, something would happen to fill it up, or else it would swallow her along with the furniture . . . Draughts sneaked through the old sashes and puffed out the heavy curtains, dragging their hems against the carpet with an uneven sighing sound. Noise from the bar rose faintly, too distant to be of any comfort.

It wasn't a room for a child, and her mother told her father so. Leaving her high-heeled shoes downstairs she would come up halfway through the evening session to make sure Liz was all right. She sat gently on the edge of the bed. At that time, she'd be wearing her pearls and would smell of yeast, sweet-sour spirits and the heavy tang of tobacco. Her stockings rasped gently as she crossed her legs. Her hair would be up.

'It's a bit busier tonight,' she'd say as she smoothed the sheets again and again, *'compared,* that is . . .' Sometimes she would stay for almost half an hour, explaining in soft monotone why the Grapes would never succeed. 'Fifty years ago, yes, but nowadays people have expectations . . . It's not right, is it, love? It's no life, is it?' she'd conclude. 'Dreadful.' Each time her mother went away, Liz knew she would be wearing something different the next time she saw her. And sometimes it seemed to Liz that her mother was not one person but many; different ones for different times of day, put on and off just like the clothes.

After closing time, when the street outside erupted with clattering and song and her parents had climbed the creaking stairs to sleep in the bedroom next to hers, her mother would come in again, wrapped tightly in her frilled dressing gown. Lipstick off, hair down, she would sit heavily on the bed and rest her chin in her hands. At that time she smelled of soap and her voice evaporated in yawns.

'Think of nice calm things. Think of the seaside on a sunny day. Hopefully we'll go away—somewhere, even just

England—in August. Let's hope we'll be out of this dump by then. I sometimes *pray* for bankruptcy . . . Or think of eating strawberries, or learning to fly, things like that. Now, be good.' Again, she'd leave.

With effort, Liz learned to banish the shadowy room and replace it with the swimming pool. She had been there only once, with school. It had struck her as she turned the corner of the changing rooms and saw it as a most beautiful thing, shimmering and huge like another planet or universe. She had stood at the edge, gazing enthralled at the sloppy knitted patterns on the water's surface, but as she climbed in she had felt afraid of the water and been unable to obey Mrs Jay's barked orders to put her head under it and breathe out through her nose. It was optional, and she'd not gone the next time. In her mind's eye, however, she could see herself walking confidently to the deep end and standing a moment looking down the length. It was a gala; her mother and father were seated in a crowd on the ranked seats that surrounded the pool, leaning forwards and holding hands—they were no longer in pubs.

Liz saw herself dive in, emerge and breathe slowly in and out, the way you were supposed to do when you swam. She saw herself sliding through the water, alternate lengths of breaststroke and crawl, registering the crowd's appreciation as she lifted her head for air. She swam longer and longer between breaths and imagined a turquoise world, which she populated with shoals of small bright fish like those in the dentist's tank . . . One moment she was making everything develop nicely, the next everything slipped into nightmare; something caught one of her legs—an octopus arm with sucker pads was winding itself around her, pulling her under water. Circles of skin tore off, the blue water was threaded with red. For some reason it didn't hurt, but any moment it would. As her lungs grew tighter and tighter, no one came, and then she had to open her mouth and gasp the water in—

She would lie a few moments listening to her heartbeat echoing in the bedsprings. The room was dark. She feasted her eyes on its emptiness and felt her pulses slowing down.

The bedroom door was flung open. Her mother's voice was abrupt, and now she was only a shape against the landing light. 'What are you doing, calling out now? Count to twenty, and when you've got there, start again. *Bore* yourself to sleep. Think of nothing. Now, shut your eyes.' The door closed firmly; there would be no more mothers until the morning one, lipsticked but pale, wearing a housecoat and smelling of nothing at all.

The vision of the swimming pool came most nights, with variations: sharks, submarines, piranha fish, cramp. It was only when the television arrived that Liz learned how to make the swimming pool vanish—just as the channel could be changed—by thinking very hard of something else or, in drastic situations, by opening her eyes, which was like turning off the set. Sleep still eluded her, but time passed.

And then they moved to the Black Swan and Grammy came . . . And then she was gone, leaving behind her a space that seemed bigger and more yawning than that drafty old room at the Grapes. She knew something would happen, and it did.

A few months after Grammy's death Liz's mother announced another move. It wasn't one of the ordinary moves to a more promising pub; Liz and her mother were to live in one place, her father was to stay behind. On Wednesdays he was to call and take her out, and her mother discussed with her how she was to deal with him should he call on the telephone and ask about her; Liz was to tell him nothing. She was not to mention him to her mother, nor her mother to him. These were the rules.

Liz helped pack clothes and kitchen things. Her mother's eyes were red, her movements abrupt. She wore a pair of new denim jeans which looked stiff like cardboard and a sweater with embroidered flowers round the yoke. She had taken off her wedding ring.

'You know I've never liked living in pubs,' she said. 'Always hated it. We'd've been all right, if it wasn't for that.' There had been no discussion as to whether Liz should stay with her father, in pubs, and just as he had never defended Grammy so he had never asked for her. But perhaps he wouldn't be in pubs for very long, because the brewery preferred couples.

Liz's mother wrote what was in each box on the outside with a thick felt pen which Liz thought smelled of sick. Liz herself had no objection to pubs. She liked the low red glow when the lights were on in the bar, and helping for half an hour in the early evening. She liked the cellars and the smell. A house, a permanent house as her mother called it, would be odd.

'I said when you were born—it's no place to bring up a child. I said, I'm not having another one if we carry on like this. And I didn't. Well now—' her mother's voice began to break—'I don't need to set foot behind a bar ever again.'

Liz knew that pubs weren't the reason for the divorce—she saw that very clearly as Grammy's revenge, from Beyond the Grave, on her father for wanting to send her away—*It won't last*—but she put her arm briefly around her mother's narrow waist and told her that, yes, that was the Silver Lining to it all. Startled, her mother looked her full in the face.

'You're a funny thing,' she said. Her eyes filled with tears, but at the same time the corners of her mouth pulled upwards in a smile. 'Now we'll be able to get to know each other, won't we?' Liz grunted and bent over the box they were supposed to be packing. She felt frightened and then the frightened feeling separated out into layers. Just beneath fear was a kind of barbed spite, terrifying to feel.

It was confusing. She knew the stake had to be driven home hard, right through the heart when they least expected it, but at the same time it hurt them—you felt sorry and you had to screw your eyes tight shut to go through with it . . . It just wasn't possible, but she would have liked to warn her mother that she was going, too: tell her that the Silver Lining to that was having a completely clean slate, and not to worry, she would be all right. She looked older than she was: Grammy had taught her many things, and the very first of these, years back when she still lived in the flat, was hide and seek.

JUST THE TWO OF US

'**O**f course,' Liz informed Jim on the morning of the telephone man, 'we all make mistakes. I did get caught out in the end . . .' The real catching—had it been done by Henry Kay, who made her pregnant with Jim, by the police, the hospital, or by Mrs Purvis? It was Purvis whom she blamed. Purvis was a skinny woman, about thirty-five, with mousy hair cut fashionably short and her lips painted bold red. She had huge grey staring eyes that followed you around the room and rubbed up and down your face like a pair of cats that wanted feeding. Somehow Mrs Purvis seemed older than her appearance; it was, Liz thought, the way she *fussed* and the way that every remark she made included Liz's name, as if she thought there were others present who might think her words were intended for them. If it wasn't the first word of the sentence, a terrible kind of tension built up until it was uttered. It made Liz writhe like Chinese water torture, which she had seen once in a programme.

'What about the father, Liz? What about your family, Liz? Liz: why did you decide to leave home? Where did you get that ring you wear, Liz?'

'Mind your own,' Liz had muttered, tucking her hands beneath the covers the way Grammy used to.

Mrs Purvis had never grown angry. The ruder Liz was, the softer yet more insistent her voice became. She fiddled with her jewellery, then moved from her chair to the edge of Liz's bed and sat there with her legs wound tightly around each other like barley sugar twists, her hands in her lap.

'Listen, Liz, I've got to be satisfied that you and the baby'll be all right. Otherwise we'll have to take him into care. So, Liz, okay, perhaps you don't need to tell me about your family, but I do need to know your surname, otherwise how will you manage? How will we register the baby's birth, Liz? How will you get somewhere to live and all the help you'll need? Do you see my point, Liz?' And that had been the last time, before this, that Liz had thought of Grammy. For an instant she'd actually seen her, sitting up straight in bed just as she herself was at the time, bolt upright with her thin jet black hair tied in a knot on top of her head. A prisoner, but hiding. Her eyes were canny, sly. Liz could tell she didn't approve, but on the other hand, she had nothing helpful to say as to what to do in circumstances like these.

'Well, Liz?' asked Mrs Purvis, making Grammy disappear. Under the sheet Liz had clenched her hands over her huge belly. The baby that was to be Jim kicked. Could YOU escape? In the TV programmes, of course, they did.

'Elizabeth Anne Meredith,' she'd said. The truth. It couldn't be unsaid. It had been, without doubt, a mistake.

'After that,' Liz told Jim, as she sat on the toilet in Onley Street and smeared his buttocks and genitals generously with zinc cream, 'I couldn't shake her off . . . Came every bloody day. I'm surprised she didn't sit and watch while I gave birth. "Push, Liz. Harder, Liz! That's it, Liz . . ."'

There had been three low lounge chairs arranged around a circular table. The doctor leaned back in his; Mrs Purvis sat straight up as if a string were attached to the top of her head and tied to a hook in the ceiling. They both had clipboards on their laps and there was a plastic cup of machine tea in front of Liz's chair.

Liz put her feet on the table, and then took them off. They'd said their bit and then waited for her to speak.

'Well,' she'd said, examining her hands, now so peculiarly clean, then looking up. 'I never wanted one at all. So I suppose it's not so bad not having a proper one. Not so bad as it would be for someone else.'

'Proper?' said Mrs Purvis. 'Another way to look at it, Liz, is that he's different. Special.' Her voice was over-bright. Both she and the doctor were embarrassed. 'There are just lots of different kinds of babies, Liz.'

'Mmm . . .' said Liz. It seemed fair enough, but not the point. 'What I mean is, so long as I just do the necessary things, as kindly as I can, that's it, isn't it? I won't have to worry about what school, or teaching him things myself. Or about his career and stuff like that.' She looked up at them. 'This is *better*,' she said, and smiled. 'I'm not like the rest of them in that ward.'

'Just—' began Mrs Purvis, but the doctor had interrupted:

'Of course, there's always some hope . . .'

'We can certainly do without *that*,' Liz told Jim, though at the time she'd been hiding well; she had half smiled, looked the doctor straight in the eye until he looked back down at his notes . . . She set Jim to air on the mat at her feet, wiped herself, examined the tissue, and wondered idly if Jim's shit would change to the adult colour all of a sudden or gradually.

'Just the necessary things is a lot, Liz,' Mrs Purvis had said when the interruption was over. Her eyes slid away from Liz's relentless gaze, then returned, slid away, returned.

'There will be problems later. When you're thirty-five—I know that's difficult to imagine, Liz—Jim will have grown up, but he won't have left home. There are facilities, but they're always under threat. And it's harder to let go later on. You might get terribly lonely and frustrated.'

'I don't,' said Liz proudly, 'get lonely.'

The doctor cleared his throat. 'You're saying you want to keep Jim?' he'd asked.

Want wasn't quite the right word, but agreeing saved time and so Liz nodded forcefully.

'Liz, you're barely nineteen,' Mrs Purvis said. The word *barely* had made Liz want to laugh, but she kept her face still. 'You're on your own. Perhaps care is an option you should consider seriously, Liz.'

'No. I'll try it on my own,' Liz had replied, because the thought of filling in another official document made her insides melt. Years ago she and Grammy had watched a programme in which a man was spread-eagled on the ground, his arms and legs tied to pegs which were driven into the ground. Each of the forms she had completed and signed since she'd made the mistake of telling Purvis her name had made her feel just like that. She was losing her freedom— not that she'd used it for much, but that was her business. Now she lay exposed in bright midday light. Anyone could find her, if they wanted to. A broad column of ants would march in a straight line across the sand and begin to devour her bite by bite.

'You're sure?' Mrs Purvis had asked, fingering the slender chain that went around her neck and then down inside her blouse. Above the enormous grey eyes her brows were pulled together and her forehead divided into wavery squares. 'Liz, it's easier now. When you've had him for a few years, they'll think you can cope and they won't put themselves out. And, Liz—you could still go and visit him, every day, if you wanted.'

'No,' said Liz, tossing back her hair, then remembering: 'thanks.'

'If she wants to keep it, you should let her,' the doctor said. Liz could tell that he cared about her less than Purvis, but somehow she'd liked him more.

After, Purvis had walked back with her to the B & B. For a long time—and for once, Liz had thought—Purvis didn't seem to be able to think of anything to say. Then, when they were almost there, she cleared her throat and asked, 'Liz, I know there were problems at first, but do you *love* Jim now?'

Liz wiped her sleeve across her face. She thought that if she answered right they would leave her alone, and that was worth almost anything, even the loss of a limb or faculty—even having had a baby. She met Purvis's eyes and said, 'Yes.'

Purvis took her arm and she'd let her, though she felt like seizing it back. 'I'll do what I can, Liz,' Purvis said. 'I'll put your point of view as forcefully as I can. I think you and Jim need a house. With a garden. But it might be a bit further out of town. Okay?' They'd parted at the front door. Liz slipped inside and slammed it hard behind her.

So when they'd arrived at 127 Onley Street a week ago there were newly installed gas fires, bedding, a cooker—and on the floor just by the door lay a fat letter from Purvis. It had *Liz* and *By Hand* written on the envelope; inside was a wodge of leaflets stapled together and a handwritten letter. Purvis's writing was like a pile of string tipped onto the page. It explained how a cot would arrive the next day and how Liz was entitled to an allowance for paint, then went on to say that Purvis would drop by at 3:15 next Monday afternoon, but not to worry if Liz was busy—if she missed her, Mrs P would phone and fix another time. It wished her the best and was signed *Annie*. Liz had noted with satisfaction that there was no telephone for Purvis to ring her on and thrust it deep in her pocket. She should have known.

The downstairs ceilings had recently been repaired and the fine pink powder of plaster dust lay on the floor, showing tracks where various people had been in and out. A pile of rusting floorboard nails lay on the bottom stair. It was cold, the windows were blind with condensation, but there was running water, both cold and hot; you didn't even have to wait for it to heat.

She had put the cushions she'd brought in the front room, then unloaded the baby things in the kitchen. The back door was stuck, but she could see the garden well enough from the back bedroom window: a strip of land between two high fences—a thick scalp of wet green parted by the paths of other people's cats. Here and there was a bald rubbly patch, or the submerged bulge of some different growth: a yellower green, a bush half buried, a few flowers on thin light-seeking stems, purple or white. Now and then a blowing drift of dandelion fluff rose and passed across the garden, then sank again.

Liz had looked at the back garden several times since. It seemed to grow taller and thicker almost daily, and she had a feeling that it was waiting—waiting for the low siren, the almost underwater wail that precedes the slowly gathering sound of a train accelerating down the line, shuddering past the stationary carriages in the sidings, carving its swift way through the still-ness, then gone and back and gone again as the land further down the tracks shields and then releases the noise and its echo.

She missed that sound. She had lived in the carriages lon-ger than anywhere else except the Black Swan, and she had found them herself. The trains came every hour. The garden was a bit like the sidings. She could imagine a train shooting through the back of Onley Street, flattening the fences one by one, shaking out windows. But she was in a house now, with hot and cold, and when she watched the grass stir in a breath of wind she was glad of the protection glass seemed to afford.

One door was enough. It could stay stuck.

'And one good thing about you, Jim,' she'd said as she fin-ished the initial inspection of the house, 'is that there's no need for me to do that baby talk routine. If I want to speak I'll say what I want, when I want, how I want. Perhaps you'll enjoy the sound, but that's it. There's fuck all I can teach you. Nothing.'

No capacity for language, the doctor had said, while Mrs Purvis went to get more tea from the machine.

'Whatever that means,' said Liz on the morning of the telephone man, still sitting on the toilet as she reached for the tap to rinse her hands. 'It's possible of course just, *just,* that they're wrong. You could somehow be understanding, the way animals do; just different, but they don't realise, because the clever-dicks can't measure it.' The sink, plugged with nappies and wipes, filled with what looked like pond water. She turned off the tap and paused, considering her own words, as she dried her hands on her T-shirt.

'But even if you don't, makes no difference to me. Because it's just the same with talking people anyway. Purvis, for example. *Yes, yes,* she goes, *I know what you mean, Liz,* she says, *mmmm*—but I don't think she does. In the hospital there was no end to it. Not just her, though she was the worst.' Liz screwed a piece of damp tissue into a ball, stared at it a moment, then looked back at Jim, bent to wipe his nose.

'Maybe,' she continued, lowering her voice, 'that understanding crap isn't so important anyway. Not the point. I've thought of that. But even then, see, it's still better I talk to you, because you probably *can't* and so nothing I say will upset or confuse you or make you do anything and you won't make me lose the thread by reacting. Makes it easier to say what I want. Complete freedom. If I want . . .'

She bent low over Jim and stared into his eyes, examining the two tiny reflections of herself. He still wasn't blinking very much, even though they'd managed to teach him how at the hospital. As an experiment she tried not to blink herself, but it made her eyes water. His skin was cold. Liz fastened the clean nappy, fed his legs back into the pink babygrow. She set him on his back in the bath while she cleared the sink.

'All on our own,' she smiled at herself in the glass. 'Just the two of us. And let's keep it that way.'

It was a long time since she had had so much—the first time really, and it worried her. Things, she knew, could be ties that bound. People attached to them like barnacles to rocks. She remembered a girl called Suki at the carriages who talked all the time about being attached and how it fucked people up. Things involved people in getting and keeping them.

She thought of the things she had: one three-quarter-size bed with head and footboards in dark oak, plain, except for a moulded border at the top; one mattress, satisfyingly sunk in the middle; two pillows in striped ticking covers; three pillowcases; three off-white sheets; two crocheted blankets; one faded pink satin eider-down; one lime green candlewick bedspread; one wooden cot, with sides made of dowelling bars, painted yellow; one plastic covered mattress with pictures of kites (split at the side); various small sheets and blankets. All of this had been in the house when she arrived, given by Help, arranged by Annie Purvis.

Neither the cot nor its furniture had been used for Jim, though she did drape her clothes over the cot's sides: one calf-length Indian-print skirt, purplish, voluminous, with an elas-ticated waist and tassels around the hem (the only thing that wasn't thrown away by the hospital); one track suit, grey with maroon piping, saggy at the knees; one horizontally striped T-shirt; one plain white T-shirt with the sleeves cut off; two acrylic mohair jumpers, one purple, one black; one pair of Dr Martens boots; one pair of flip-flops; two nursing bras, little worn; various underpants, socks; one pair of skin-tight footless tights; one navy blue woollen coat, second- or third-hand like the rest, a little stained here and there but good quality—thick, lined, with deep pockets and a wide buckled belt, a coat to shelter in, to live in if you were stuck with no things and not even a roof over your head . . .

She'd decided to use the front bedroom as a kind of enormous closet for Jim's clothes. Those that were still slightly damp hung over the wooden frame of an unfinished airing cupboard which surrounded the hot water tank. The rest were arranged on the floor in piles: velour babygrows, small vests, felted woollen jackets, tiny socks, plastic pants—too many to count. In high-street shops, baby clothes cost a quarter of what she and Jim had to live on for a week, but second-hand they were virtually free. The world must be littered with them, she thought; so many people had been born and temporarily inhabited a series of such garments, sloughing them off like snakeskin every month or so . . . She liked looking at the piles, stripes of different colours. Like liquorice allsorts. Already some were too small.

Downstairs, there were two rooms, matching the bedrooms upstairs, plus an extension for the kitchen and bathroom. The bathroom contained two packs of disposable nappies, the powder, soap, toothbrushes, cotton wool and cream, one plastic bath that fitted inside the main bath, one bowl, one bucket, one thermometer, one mat, three towels on the rail . . . But these were things for Jim, so probably they didn't count.

In the kitchen were two pans, one non-stick; one mug, blue with white stripes; two side plates the same; one dinner plate in pale green with faint ridges around the rim; assorted cutlery—all there on her arrival. On the shelf above the counter were food supplies and the book, *Infant Care,* which Mrs Wingfield had given her at the clinic. She had overheard Mrs Wingfield talking to the receptionist last week, 'It could be avoided,' she'd said. 'Look at the poor kid. I don't think it'd be wrong.' Soon, the book warned, there would have to be other kitchen things, in particular a fridge; it talked as if there were no question of someone not having a fridge, though so far Liz had managed perfectly well without, drinking the last of the carton of milk every night so as to save waste, buying small amounts. It made sense when you had to carry everything home.

'Always store in the fridge,' *Infant Care* said of almost every-thing, and warned that there would have to be bottles, teats, brushes, a steriliser, a spouted baby mug, a bent plastic spoon, a stiff bib with a ridge and more. Perhaps, though, it could be avoided.

The room next to the kitchen—the one with the stuck door—contained only the brackets for the shelves someone took away with them and a paper lampshade left behind. The room was just something to be walked through on the way to the stairs. Apart from this path, the dust on the floorboards had been undisturbed since that first day when, halfway between kitchen and stairs, she had paused and on impulse crossed the room to open the door of the understairs cupboard. It had been—still was—full of clean jam jars, packed in softening cardboard boxes.

In the front room, where the television aerial socket was, were the four cushions Liz had brought with her. She had made the covers herself, when she was at the B & B, stuffed them with other women's discarded tights. On the ledge of the ceramic tile surround of the gas fire she kept several pine cones, a white-coated flint, the skeleton of a holly leaf brought back from one of her walks—these were not real *things*, she felt, nei-ther possessions nor possessors; they were more like visitors.

'I don't think somewhere to live is a thing,' she informed Jim. 'Food neither.' That just travelled through the body and came out the other end. Cotton wool, nappies . . . They cost money, but were just a means to an end—like all Jim's things, they were safe. 'I don't think you'll get too attached.'

Things that people had given her, unasked, were also safe; she could walk away from them any time. But what about a television set? 'The main point is the pictures,' she explained to Jim. Pictures—as clear and large and lifelike as possible, and then the sound, second—both produced by immaterial signal—these were as un-possessable, you'd think, as water or air. 'A television set, really, is part of somewhere to live.' Part of home, which wasn't a thing. That was why the aerial socket was there in the front room, waiting.

Next door had TV. She could hear it in the evenings. And probably the other side did too, though you couldn't see because of the blinds. Alice and Tom would have a long job running through their possessions in their heads. They'd be defeated by the contents of their own fitted wardrobes and bedside tables: twenty, thirty, forty garments apiece on separate hangers; drawers crammed with underwear, socks and ties, swimming costumes; soft blankets; empty suitcases on the top shelf; five or six pairs of shoes; alarm clock, radio, cold cream, tweezers, paperbacks, massage glove, anglepoise lamp . . . But the 24-inch television set glimpsed in their front room was the only thing of theirs she coveted.

'That girl, Suki, was a junkie!' she told Jim as she felt her way carefully up the stairs. She had never used to talk to herself but now she found herself liking the sound of her voice in the empty rooms. The words were heard, but at the same time left intact, like fresh snow.

Frank lingered in his shady kitchen, watching coffee sludge harden in the bottom of his cup. He had drunk far too much of it but he knew it was not caffeine but the far stronger drug, fear, that made his pulse flutter so. *Katie Rumbold,* it seemed to whisper, *Pete Magee* . . . He was frightened of the future. He knew that Katie Rumbold and Pete Magee had started a process of change—activated it, against his will. There was no telling when or where it would end, but he was certain that today was the first day of something terrible, a course of events which would work itself out step by step, dragging him along and, at the same time, back.

Once the tiled walls of this kitchen had been painted in sickly gloss, the floor covered in linoleum. There had been a

60-watt bulb, not spotlights. Once there had been a metal sink with a plastic curtain, matching the one at the window; a cream-coloured cooker that leaked gas; a counter, sticking out from the wall, covered in speckled Formica, which lifted at the edges. He used to run things underneath, seeing how far it would rise.

'Stop that—you'll only make it worse. You shouldn't have run,' his mother had said in that kitchen on the evening of his first day at school. 'You shouldn't let them see you care . . . Come, whisk these eggs up for me . . .'

Girls ran away from Frank—then John—the fastest. Their hair streamed out behind them; they gathered together around the corner, in a close bundle, like one many-limbed creature. John ran heavily after them. Everyone had a cross to bear, his mother said, separating eggs. Look at her and her life, but she wasn't complaining: 'I still have my Johnny, after all . . .' And he had her. It would always be so. She hugged him. But of course, he understood much later, only for one of them, most likely, and as it happened, her. He didn't realise then that he would sit for hours in that room where he had first met his own ugliness—the dressing table in the window, his mother in the bed, the photograph on the table by her side. In the last years she had been terrified that he would send her away.

'Frankie! Frankie Styne!' the girls had called, mistaking, he was later to discover, the maker and his monster made of corpseflesh, scraps and tatters not fitting, doomed. Always they kept their distance, just so. They would not close that gap even together, even to be cruel. Yet neither would they run right away . . . He must be brave. He must stick up for himself, she said. '*I* love you.' She did. 'To me, you're *beautiful.*' He was not the only one. There were people far worse off.

Have him different? Of course not. Or, only if it made him happier. Maybe the answer really was 'no': she wouldn't have him different, even if it were possible. Often she said how happy she felt and that she loved him. They were far closer than most mothers and sons. They ate with the best silver cutlery, walked together in the park, arm in arm, her stately as a ship. And when they grew older they still walked just the same and he always accompanied her to the doctor's and made her take her pills on time. Perhaps she had even made him how he was, on purpose.

Dear games teacher, she wrote for him, *my son has a delicate constitution and should not be forced to perform strenuous exercise, particularly out of doors. I would appreciate your co-operation in this matter . . .* Regarding the rest of education she was, however, strict: 'You need to develop your brain.' *She* needed someone special in her life: 'You, Johnny, my special little man.'

It was a pitiless world and many of its injustices would only be righted after Death, when the poor were rich, the suffering were happy, the separated were reunited. Meantime, you had to fight in any way you could, and be brave.

'Do you want to know,' John, becoming Frankie Styne, roared after the girls in the playground, 'about the hairs I've got on my back?' No one said 'yes', but they stopped and no one ran any further away. He described parts of Frankie Styne they couldn't see, making them even worse than they were. 'Do you want to know . . .?' Their jaws dropped. He took a step closer, they—almost in unison—took one further away. 'Do you want to know about the maggots that live in my armpits? I eat them.' He told them how he ate rats, dug up graves. 'The corpseflesh feels like butter,' he said, 'smells like old pilchards. Your fingers sink through it and suddenly they hit something hard and cold that's bone.'

Their eyes grew wide. Still no one wanted to sit next to Frankie Styne, but they listened to him. He had made them listen, and made them change what they did, and was excited by the power he had over them. It was his reward for being brave. They believed him and they wanted to know how the worms twisted and turned, millions of them: 'I swallow them down and I can feel them wriggling and tickling inside.' He almost believed it himself.

Behind him, even the boys listened avidly. 'Go on, Frankie!' Some tried to copy, but no one, *no one,* could do it the way he could. Things were all right for a while.

'All the time,' his mother said to her friends, who listened respectfully despite having heard it before, 'I could never believe my luck. To me, Derek looked liked a god. I could watch him for hours. Muscles like iron. Every feature perfect . . . When he touched me the hair stood up on my flesh.'

Flesh. At school it was called tissue. Frank learned about sex; how the woman and the man got married, how they had intercourse. The penis swelled and grew. It had happened to him already, in the bath. The pleasure involved was nature's way of encouraging reproduction and not the main point. The real purpose was that it could go inside the woman's vagina and put in the sperm. The real point, then, was making him, his mother's own, John, also Frankie Styne.

'I felt like I'd got the prize,' she'd say. 'I felt so ordinary myself. After that, you don't bother with second best . . .'

The girls, lipsticked and too dignified now to run, bent their heads conspiratorially over their books. He, who always got good marks, shaded, printed his labels and obediently underlined them with his ruler. He knew it would become a joke, the idea of one of them and him. Of which there could be no point at all.

The result of the procedure was fertilisation. The egg split into two and each half grew and split and so on. After nine months the baby—made somehow of half of each of the parents—was born through the vagina. Another joke: perhaps his mother had had sexual intercourse with someone else. With something not human. Occasionally the local paper would report strange lights or expanses of flattened vegetation on the common, and people walking their dogs would claim that they had encountered visitors from outer space. She would have had to slip out in a billowing nightdress, perhaps with a coat over the top, and wait shivering in the dark for whatever it was: half vegetable, half man. But why would she, when his father was like a god and anything else would be second best?

According to biology, it all happened on a scale far too small to see. There were dominant and recessive genes, chromosomes, DNA. Tiny bits of code which made you how you were, writ large and visible. One day science would understand, but in the meantime it felt like fate or chance depending on your view.

It was awesome and not something, the teacher said, to be undertaken lightly. It would happen to each of them in God's good time and there was no need to hurry. At all, Frank thought. In case. People should think. He sat without moving on the science-room bench, at the back. Even then he had preferred the present, had wanted to stretch each minute of the lesson so that they would never get to go outside.

'Blown to bits,' his mother would conclude. 'A mine.' Anything could happen. Anything. 'Nothing left. And I could still keep count of the number of times . . . Still, when you have a child, it's a blessing. You keep going. You have to.' God, Frank thought, just let me off. Give me a note. Some of the class walked home hand in hand. Another joke: that any one of them would let him get that near—nearer than near, inside their body. If he was them, he wouldn't. And in any case, the bathtime erections stopped—though he thought, to begin with at least, that sometimes they still came in the deep privacy of sleep. Awake, nothing—no picture, thought, or touch, no situation real or imagined would bring his penis to life.

And so, bewitched, desire slumbered endlessly in the fetid and crumbling castle of his body. A good thing really. Even then it had seemed that the present was tolerable, even good, compared to what had been and what might be.

But soon everything was sex. Pictures of naked bodies replaced Frank as a source of breaktime entertainment. He didn't want to look; they frightened him. He lost his power. The others might want to know if he said that he fucked corpses or raw liver, or donkeys, or old men, but it would scarcely make him popular or powerful and in any case it was a subject he needed to avoid. Perhaps there was some line—to do with telling some kind of truth, however twistedly, somewhere—and he wouldn't cross it. There was self-exaggeration, which protected, and self-fabrication, which would hurt.

He had discovered Cougar books. The first books he'd ever liked. In them were sewer-dwellers, terrible diseases, intestines, charnel houses, pits of snakes and psychic death traps. A book, he felt, was a curious and miraculous thing, just words on a page written by someone named but unknown, and safely invisible. It was not personal, like standing up and saying, 'Do you want to know?' By the time you'd bought a book, you already did want to know. He began to write his own books at break time and he illustrated them in Art. Teachers seemed to let him do what he liked. He gave himself an official pen name for signing the pictures and the books: Frank Styne. He left off the 'ie' to make it sound more mature. The third novel was accepted by Cougar when he was seventeen. Things had been quite good, again, for years.

Some odd angle, a break in the routine of dressing could still bring him down. Chance encounters were worse than mirrors, which could be sought out sober and prepared. But by and large being brave had worked.

Frank sighed. Yes, he thought, sometimes I am lonely. But mostly I'm content with the way things are . . . It is my life. Who does Katie Rumbold think she is? She makes the present hurt. She's spoiling what I've made.

He knew her words would be very hard to fight—the black on the white, laser-etched. What could you do to revenge yourself on a person of such a kind? Someone who could dictate a gush of words that would leave someone else—him—reeling? Blind her with hot irons? Remove vital organs (liver, skin, bowel) whilst conscious? Bury her alive? Saw off limbs? Suck out her brain through a small, drilled hole? Force her to eat her own flesh raw, or cooked in a barbecue?

All these dreadful fates had befallen characters in his books. And all of them had happened, somewhere, at some time, were maybe even happening, now in some other place—but none of them seemed achievable, by him . . .

The morning had gone. The coffee had worn itself away, leaving him exhausted. The gulf between the written and the lived world ached, huge. He felt so *weak*.

THE SILENT ZONE

'**D**efinite improvement, not having a gate,' Liz muttered to Jim as she set everything down and locked the front door—it must have been about two o'clock—'too much faffing.' When she heard the brisk click of heels she knew without turning that it must be Alice from next door. She picked up her bags.

'Hello,' Alice said, coming to a staccato halt. She smelled strongly of the hairdresser's. She smiled and gestured at the bags of washing. 'Yours broken?'

'Haven't got one.' Liz twisted the two black plastic bags around her wrists then let them spin. The bags, Jim in his sling at the front; it was odd to feel so many weights at once.

'Pop it in mine. I've got a drier too. Won't take half an hour.' Alice gestured at her front door with its big brass number plate, 129, and letterbox to match. Liz twisted the bags around her wrists again.

'Thanks. But I've got to go to the shops anyway,' she said slowly. All morning she had been thinking about talking. It could almost be a programme on TV: how people had got talking wrong. You needed to express things, somehow needed the words to make your thoughts come alive. But on another planet they knew that really people should only talk on their own. Humans weren't strong enough for it yet, or they'd started off on the wrong foot or got diverted. They talked to each other and lost the thread. It was a gift, but the humans had squandered it . . . Now she was very aware of her own words, as if they were something solid in her mouth.

'Jump in the car. I'll give you a lift. Come on.' Alice grasped the bags, scratching one of Liz's hands with her fingernails as she did so, but not noticing. She hurried to the red car parked askew outside number 129. Liz followed. It wasn't worth arguing. The reason she'd chosen this particular time to do her washing was in order to avoid Purvis's visit at 3:15. Alice glanced over her shoulder as if to reassure herself that Liz hadn't vanished. Then she laughed, heaving the bags onto the back seat.

Maybe, Liz thought as she climbed in silently beside them, there was one thing every person had to say to themselves, once in a lifetime, and that's what it was all for. It might be the same thing for everyone or it might be something special for every person. You couldn't know, because when it had been said the person moved over to the other planet. A higher plane. The Silent Zone, that's what it would be called.

'Oh! Of course. We don't have a car-seat,' Alice said as she got into the car.

'It's okay,' Liz told her.

'Well... It is only a two-minute drive. But maybe you should put the belt on,' she added 'between you and the sling?' Liz ignored this. 'Steering's jammed,' muttered Alice. It meant nothing to Liz, who couldn't drive. The air inside the car was heavy with Alice's hairspray and her jasmine perfume. But beneath them Liz thought she could smell something else, bitter, the faintest whiff of sweat, not hers and not Jim's.

'Do you want some gum?' Alice asked. Liz shook her head. There wasn't enough room for her legs. She could hear Alice's breathing, the rustle of her clothes as she wrestled with the wheel. She knew that if she raised her own eyes, Alice's would be waiting for them in the mirror. She wound down the window and looked determinedly out of it.

Their houses were very different. Hers, 127, was the last of the small terraces, just wide enough for a window and a door. But theirs, though it shared a party wall, marked the beginning of the older, bigger houses, almost double the width, with an extra floor, and a loft conversion as well. The windows of 129 had been replaced with hand-crafted replicas of the Georgian originals, whereas Liz's had knock-together frames with tiny lights at the top. Their brickwork had been cleaned to a mellow glow, whereas Liz's had been rendered with pebbledash which was beginning to attract algae. Both front gardens were the same mean depth, but Alice and Tom's sported a neat square of almost fluorescent green laced with smart yellow tulips and tiny cypress trees; they had a wrought-iron fence and gate painted white. Liz's garden resembled the back of a piece of embroidery: all loose ends, knots and crossed threads. The border and lawn were indistinguishable, the path nearly lost, the abandoned gate already sinking beneath the sodden grass. Liz considered it all. It's just different, she thought. *Special.*

'I've just been to the hypnotist!' Alice announced brightly, letting out the clutch. The red car's engine was whisper-quiet. It was years since Liz had been inside a normal car, unless she counted police vans and the ambulance that took her to the hospital and then moved her and her things when she came from the bed and breakfast to here. She settled herself warily, mistrusting the softness of the maroon upholstery.

'We're both going, separately,' Alice continued. 'I hope it works.' She took a left turn so fast that Liz had to put out her arm and push her hand into the seat to stop herself toppling over. She braced herself with her forearms and bent so that she could see Jim's face when he woke . . . The people from the Silent Zone, she thought, wanted to help. They had to communicate with humans, to let them know that they were on the wrong track. But, of course, it couldn't be with words. That was the problem. 'Maybe you're already there,' she thought at Jim, 'and you've come to fetch me.'

'Lovely baby. I'm very jealous. I really want one,' Alice said. 'Should be easy enough to park. Might as well come in with you. Years since I've been in a launderette.' She made it sound like some kind of treat.

Liz stood and watched as Alice loaded two washing machines with her and Jim's sheets, pants, socks and underwear, methodically dividing things into light and dark. She held a pale pink babygrow up by its arms, the flat shape of two months old.

'Did you set your mind on one or the other?' she said coyly. Liz shook her head. Basically, she hadn't wanted one at all. 'I want a boy, Tom wants a girl,' Alice said as she loaded the dispenser with coins from her own purse. 'It's okay. Can't stand having too much change,' she assured Liz. 'Expect you have to count the pennies. Be a while before you can get out to work. You look so young. Babies age some women dreadfully.

'Does she take after her father?' She sat down and gestured at Liz to do the same. 'Smoke? I know I shouldn't and I don't often, but I always buy some duty free to offer around.

'Of course, Tom and I *would* want the opposite! We're always arguing at the moment. Didn't used to be like that. You see, Tom's had an affair—lasted two years. I had no idea until the end.' She smiled brightly. 'It's over now, but I find I can't forget about it for long. What I can't do is understand. I mean, at the time, we were at it twice a day. What more can you do? I keep myself in shape—well, don't you think?'

A shape, yes, Liz thought, slipping back into the morning's observant alien; humans do vary enormously . . . The emerald-green covering seems to be made of something very soft, and the big buckled belt seems very tight but has no obvious practical function . . . The hair is very curly and bounces as she talks—investigate possibility of some kind of transmission system . . .

'Then I find out he's still been dropping in on this other cow—excuse me—on the way home from work. Well it's really all over now, but the slightest thing sets me off. Then that makes him feel guilty. A few nights ago he said to me: "Alice, I've hurt you so much and I still am. I think I should just clear out and you'd be happier on your own." He was crying. I felt dreadful. But then I thought, you just want me to make it easy . . .' Alice exhaled, staring at the blur of washing opposite. Liz didn't think she could tell her to save her breath because she already knew. Instead she made to reach for her carrier bags.

Alice grasped her wrist. Again the nails bit home. 'Look—I wanted to ask you something . . . I wanted to say—you would tell me, wouldn't you, if you saw him—saw him with someone else?' For the first time, she stopped talking and waited for a reply. It was like kidnapping. No—hijack. At wordpoint. The woman could hire herself out to terrorist groups and slip onto a plane without any suspicion at all . . . Liz had watched a programme about hijacking, ages ago. You couldn't so much as cough or move your arm without someone poking a gun in your face. One of the passengers became hysterical, just suddenly stood up and waved her arms then tried to run down the plane. They shot her in the leg. Hijackers wanted you alive until they decided different, or lost their cool.

'Would you?'

'Oh, sure,' Liz said, in much the same way as she'd answered that other talker, Purvis—because it was easiest. But at the same time it was difficult . . . She leaned back into the vinyl chair, breathing out and trying to think of snow, acres of it, undisturbed. It often calmed her down, but was hard to do in a sweltering launderette beset by a swarm of words, just when she was wondering whether they were necessary at all. Well, she calculated, I've missed Purvis. That's a Silver Lining, or almost.

Jim's nose was running badly. She shifted herself, searching for a tissue. Beaming, Alice held one out.

'Now,' she was saying, bright and very matter of fact, 'it turns out that she's pregnant! She sent a letter to his work. I found it in his lunchbox, but he said he was going to show me anyway. So maybe that's why; he's always wanted a baby but we've never had any luck. But he says not. So I said, maybe it's not yours. So he said, yes, he thought that too and he'd tell her he wouldn't have anything to do with it. Do you think he'll stick to that though? It just isn't fair. We've been trying for years, particularly the last two. We've had some tests—there's nothing wrong. So maybe it's psychological. That's why the hypnotist, you see.'

There was something in the pit of Liz's stomach trying to get out. A monster that had been living there. It bucked and heaved, stretched her skin, squashed her kidneys, stamped on her liver, twisted the intestines around and around . . . She'd seen one like it on a programme called *Alien,* bursting out with a scream. And it had been like that in the hospital too, but there she was on her back and it went on longer, and he came out between her legs. There was a strange smell, blood and pepper and strawberries all mixed, and the scream. The baby, a streaked thing that couldn't see, was placed on her chest.

'A boy,' someone said, and various masked people gathered round.

'Poor kid,' she'd heared someone say. 'Didn't go to any classes. Nothing. Doesn't know what's hit her.' I can get out now, she had thought as she closed her eyes.

'What are you having for your tea?' Alice asked. The washing went around and around, the whites and the coloureds. The water was purple in one; something had bled.

'Hypnotic,' Alice said. 'Perhaps I should just come here, instead of paying Mr Mandell forty pounds an hour . . .'

In unison, the two machines began to vibrate, drowning her laugh, sucking the water away, hurling the clothes around.

Buttons and studs clattered on the metal drum then everything stuck to the sides. Then they all fell down.

Outside it was beginning to grow dark. Hang on, Liz told herself, to the Silver Linings.

In fading light, Frank hesitated outside the shop. It had blacked-out windows. He caught a weak reflection of himself: the sloped shoulders, the folds of skin at the neck, the thin wisps of hair, the ghostly image staring back—from behind, he thought, it would make quite a dramatic shot. Because of Katie Rumbold's letter he had caught himself seeing himself like this all day, as if he were in some dreadful documentary on television. A commentary, spoken in a nasal, slightly sarcastic tone of voice was following him around as well, audible in snatches, when he paused in the day's activities.

'Despite the fantastic nature of his work,' it was saying now, 'Styne's method is one of dogged realism. Although his plots are simple and basically similar—some kind of monster intruding into some kind of real situation and wreaking havoc—he prides himself on making them believable, and this he achieves largely by means of the sheer conviction with which he describes ordinary things. It's a simple but effective tactic: belief runs over, as he puts it, into the unreal things, covering the seams. Here we see him on one of his research trips, about to . . .'

Frank had seen such programmes, and found them excruciating even when they were about other people. If he was to have fame, it would be of a different kind: one day someone would make a film of one of his books. *Dear Frank,* Katie Rumbold's letter would begin, *I have some very good news . . .* Someone would buy the rights—he had absolutely no desire to write the thing—and while he got on with his life they would make it, spending millions on special effects . . . Not that financial reward drew him to film, nor any particular positive feeling for the medium, which in fact he tended to despise. No—it was the idea of himself sitting there in the munching crowd of men, women and children, watching the picture—his picture—just like everyone else, anonymous, unnoticed; the same in the dark.

He didn't want to be the subject. He wanted to be on the other side, in the audience, watching a made-up story, with his name, Frank Styne, in red letters at the beginning or the end. A story, not his real life . . . Keep on the move, Frank thought, picking up his carrier bag of groceries and pushing through the door.

It was, he told himself bravely, a voyage of discovery. A challenge. A subject he had long neglected and avoided. Certain facts had thrust themselves upon him—the existence of contraception, how much everyone thought about sex—but beyond that his knowledge had scarcely improved since his schooldays. And now the time had come, as Pete Magee had said.

He'd expected the shop's interior to be something like the public bar of the Three Compasses or the Blue Boar, but it was in fact brightly lit and arranged systematically with racks of goods, in just the same way as other supermarkets. An ioniser winked in the corner. There were special offers marked on fluorescent cards. Some throbbing kind of rock music, which he detested, played in the background, providing, he supposed, the sort of cover that dim lighting might have done. There was a sweetish smell somewhere between popcorn and musk.

The assistant, seated close to the door in front of an enormous image of two buttocks and a closed-circuit screen, glanced up and then ignored him. Frank paused again, trapped by his own image on the screen. They were often rather flattering, the way they broadened the shoulders, dwindled the rest of the body to a pair of point-like feet and painted the complexion a stark but even white. Only his overcoat and paisley scarf were recognisable.

Afterwards the camera would cut in closer, and the commentator would joke, 'There's no end to the unlikely places a writer's vocation may lead him . . .'

The sooner this is over, Frank told himself, the sooner I can go home and cook the trout. He stuffed his gloves in his pockets and went to the nearest stand—a display of penises and breasts, ceramic, plastic, metal, functional and ornamental. There was a woman's body, legs doubled back, with a pencil sharpener between them. He examined it. He took a pencil from his breast pocket and tried it surreptitiously, sweeping the shavings carefully from the shelf. Rather childish, he thought. He went to the underwear, and then a rack of plastic chains and handcuffs, and a stand of inflatable women with usable orifices, under a handwritten sign saying,

'She never has a headache and she doesn't talk!'

Behind him a group of young people in padded jackets came in together. They were shepherded to the middle of the shop by an older man in a flowing coat and oversized glasses. He cleared his throat and said in a booming voice, 'Now, take your time and don't forget to keep noting your reactions. Don't censor . . .'

The group stood unmoving and the leader pushed one young man gently forward. Frank stared over his shoulder but no one else in the shop paid any attention.

'This is a perfectly commonplace thing to do,' the leader continued. 'If there's something that disgusts or upsets you, make a note of it so that we can discuss it in the group later on. If there's something that turns you on, make a note of that too! Or buy it,' he added, glancing in the direction of the till.

Supposing there just isn't, Frank thought, anything that turns you on; suppose there's nothing at all? I'd better just find what I want and clear out.

Magazines dominated the back of the shop; good, he thought, to see that paper is still holding its own. He slipped between two other men. The magazines were sealed in plastic, sometimes taped together in threes. The cover of the first he selected showed a woman with wet hair and skin, her hands over her crotch, her breasts exposed. The background was a bathroom. Her eyes were wide and startled, but she was smiling, as if she had been caught midway between the two emotions. He could see that she was attractive, young. But also that it was a lie: in reality, he was quite—leadenly—sure, she wouldn't want him in her bathroom, and he felt nothing except his own strangeness.

The next he selected showed a woman chained at her ankles and wrists to some kind of concrete wall. The lighting picked out her breasts and her head, which was tilted back and to one side so that she looked at the viewer through hooded eyes with an expression of fierce concentration. Her lips were picked out in a deep crimson and smudged. What am I supposed to do? Frank, exasperated, wanted to ask.

He ran his fingernail quickly down the side of the next bundle and flicked through the pages, which still smelled strongly of printing ink. Flesh, salmon pink and blue black, greeted him from every page, a good deal of it bruised or bloody. He studied it for several minutes. This kind of thing, chaining, whipping, bruising, throttling and so forth, was obviously a particular genre, and more expensive. There seemed to be—though he was obviously the worst person to judge—a complete poverty of imagination, perhaps because of it being photographic. And nowhere were the parts he wanted, just the place where they could be imagined, if, that was, you'd seen them before. For a few seconds a childish kind of despair enveloped Frank, causing an odd tightness in his throat and behind his eyes.

'Many men would envy him this part of his job!' his imaginary commentator joked.

'You'll have to pay for those,' the assistant called from the till. Frank noticed that a large ginger-haired man was standing by the door, his arms folded across his chest.

'They're not exactly what I was looking for.' His voice, he thought, sounded petulant.

'Shouldn't have opened them then. What is it you want?'

'Close ups of women's vaginas,' Frank said. The camera would be cutting delightedly between the two of them now, back and forth.

'Round there, at the side,' the assistant called, adding, 'but you're paying for what you've opened.'

The shop had filled considerably since he arrived. People called in on their way home from work. Men and women, old and young, pale under the fluorescent light, but unremarkable. A woman, examining a penis Biro, looked up, caught him staring at her, and glowered until he looked away.

'No detail is lost,' the imaginary commentator said. 'He always makes meticulous notes on the bus home.' Astounded at the clumsy style and the number of typographical errors, Frank scanned the beginning of a short story in which a woman was stripped and tied up with a washing line. The sheer repetition was stunning. He felt irritated. What to make of it, the tying up, the hitting, the way they looked like they liked it? Did they? All the pictures, he thought, looked real, but it was simply impossible to imagine. To connect, to conceive of how it came about. And they smiled . . . Even the ordinary stuff . . . Let alone how the rest . . . Perhaps it only worked if you'd already seen and done it for real? The pictures would remind you, then, of the real thing. Something to key into. Perhaps you just had to at least have seen for yourself what a real woman's vagina looked like, and felt the effect, before the pictures would work, before you could understand it at all.

Cougar books were just fantasy, he thought. Inside people's heads the world is endlessly plastic. People who read my books don't expect them to happen in real life. They just liked believing things. Perhaps this is the same?

There was a queue at the till.

'That lot from the polytechnic,' grumbled the assistant. 'He brings them in every term and they and just crowd the place out. Never spend much . . .' The customer immediately in front of Frank was buying some vinyl underwear. Frank found himself feeling rather contemptuous. He was unlikely to get home on time and would be late eating and late starting work: all this because of Pete Magee.

Perhaps he could use the shop in a book? Things could turn real when people got them out of the shop. They'd wake up in the morning with a bruised woman lying on the floor, refusing to leave or to get dressed. Or they'd open the carrier bag and inside would be a bloody penis stump, or a pair of sawn-off breasts. They'd panic and try to dispose of them. Police would be baffled . . .

He counted out thirteen pounds and ninety-nine pence.

SILLY

F rank was glad to be home, but even so he could shake off neither his feeling of exhausted irritation nor his imaginary commentator. 'Styne loves to cook,' the voice gushed. 'His kitchen would be the envy of many a chef.' There was a pause, while he unpacked his carrier bag, and the camera followed him, showing the leaf-wrapped cheese and out-of-season vegetables, the rack of knives, the herbs and spices in their special vacuum-sealed jars, the food processor, the two ovens, the water purifier. 'For him, cooking is a time for meditation. Preparing and eating a meal is a way of settling himself prior to work . . .' The word 'work' echoed with a terrible hollow reverence and Frank turned on his radio hoping to drown the commentator in a babble of real voices.

He cooked patiently, working precisely from the recipe. The pink and white trout fillets had to be cut into thin strips, braided; the tomatoes skinned, simmered with fresh basil and sieved. Meanwhile, the new potatoes were steaming, and when the timer went off he would begin the mushrooms—already, like the cherry tartlets for dessert, prepared. The recipe took longer to make than stated in the book and he made a note of that in the margin.

When his mother had taught him how to cook there had been only one kind of mushroom bought just four ounces at

a time and they weren't in a position to use things like auber-
gines, or to cook beef in vintage wine. But he had made sure
that she had had decent three-course meals right until the last.
Consommé. Duck in orange. Trifle. Even though she couldn't
taste or smell, she could see, and it was important.

'Read me what you've written, Johnny,' she'd ask as he
removed the tray. Frank never worried about it; he knew she'd
hear perhaps two or three words before she fell asleep. He'd
shuffle his papers, ask her if she was ready, clear his throat and
read as much like the BBC as he could:

'He looked down at where his foot used to be. The stump,
cauterised, ached and throbbed. How much of him could he
watch them take and still live . . .'

He smoothed a linen cloth over half the table, and savoured
his trout in silence so as to fully appreciate it. No music, no
wine. A habit. Habits, he sometimes thought, were what made
the world go round. Or him stay on it while it did. One would
be lost without them: when he washed up, he took trouble to
render each pan as new—that was something she had taught
him, an inherited habit; so, too, turning the bowl upside down
when he had finished. These things were what stayed to remind
him of her. She would not, he thought as he dried, have particularly liked the trout; on the whole she had preferred substantial meat dishes with thick, multi-flavoured sauces. He shook
the tablecloth outside and took his manuscript from the cutlery drawer built into the table's central support.

He glanced at the clock—8:40—and read the description
of his man-monster through to remind himself.

It was cold despite the radiator. Liz could see her breath. She
ran the hot water and tested it with her elbow, the way they'd
shown her. The bathroom was small, with door, bath, sink and
toilet each taking up one of its sides, then bulging out to fill the
tiny rectangle the walls contained. The floor Liz knelt on was

covered with lino patterned like oil and milk mixed together. Jim's small plastic bath was set inside the big one, the sides of which reared up like smooth cliffs marked by a strata of stains, sandy brown and copper green. Steam filled the tiny room and the handfuls of water she tipped onto Jim shrivelled to momentary lace on his skin, then vanished. He seemed to like water: he slapped at it and made noises that sounded eager and excited—sounded so like pure pleasure that Liz found herself smiling, even though it was probably just some accident, a facial coincidence—though, really, that all went back again to what exactly the doctor had meant by capacity for language. She rubbed some water over her own face and leaned back a little on her feet.

'Suppose you are from the Silent Zone I was talking about,' she began, 'sent to teach me how to get there. Main problem, as I've discovered today, is other people. Not on the same wavelength.' She rubbed a minute quantity of shampoo onto Jim's head, working the lather gently but intently as she continued. 'It's not just, like I said this morning, a matter of not getting through. Lies, too, people making things up, forgetting that what happens is what counts, not what people say.' She held a flannel over Jim's eyes, tipped a cup of water over his head to rinse off the shampoo.

'You—you really should thank your lucky stars . . .

'Talking spreads like measles. Because other people have got it, they want to pass it on, like tag. If everyone else catches it too they won't stand out. I saw a film like that once. You caught it by kissing and it made you lose your identity. It spread like wildfire and that made the whole fabric of society break down. There was a research doctor who fell in love . . .'

Frank made the monster's penis huge, barbed like a tomcat's and covered in tiny interlocking scales. The monster's wife, Sandra, was slender and small, her skin unblemished, the colour of cream, her breasts large, their nipples prominent and pink, her belly a smooth curve, her pubic hair as soft as that on her head . . . He chose his words slowly, testing them in his head before writing them in tiny longhand. He was working hard to blot out the commentary, not to see himself from odd angles as he sat there bent in a pool of anglepoise light; to stay in the present, and not to think for more than a second or two of that letter from Katie Rumbold, which said, *The shortlist (rumour has it that you are on it) will emerge this week. I'm sure you'll be as delighted as I am . . .*

He was successful, as authors go. His books had been translated: he made a reasonable living. The letters he received were always appreciative. *'I read page 123 four times,'* they'd say. *'My favourite part was the scene when his head splits open. I was almost sick . . .'* When readers bought one of his books he liked to think they could be confident that somewhere in it would be at least one passage like the one that he was just beginning: the mating of the monster and his impossibly beautiful bride. Really, a rape. *Daring and experimental work at the cutting edge of contemporary fiction . . .*

Dwelling for a full page in almost microscopic detail on the monster's penis, which he called 'organ' so as not to be too medical on the one hand, nor break his style on the other, Frank wrote steadily in fine-tip felt pen on plain white paper, rising from his chair only to switch on the extractor fan to eliminate the lingering fishy smell of his meal.

The monster was strong and cruel. He held Sandra around the neck and squeezed if she struggled. He squatted over her, his terrible penis weeping unpleasantly all the while. Her face was red and screwed tight in an agony of revulsion. With his free hand the monster parted her labia and began to rub her clitoris with his thumb. It was the only way Frank could think of getting her eventually to smile, despite herself and the situation. He had to keep referring to the magazine.

The photographs were disturbing. They were all different: flaps and folds every which way, hair all over the place. He had expected something neater, like the visible bits of women. Secondly, he couldn't begin to imagine what it would feel like, going inside, there, between the *labia minora:* but fortunately, he reminded himself, the point was not to describe that so much as the spectacle of Sandra's fear and distaste, which he felt he could do with some confidence . . . Bile rose in her throat. Her breath came in gasps—it was, he knew, procrastination. The imaginary commentator knew it too:

'Because of chronic impotence and a lack of female acquaintance,' he explained earnestly, 'Styne has not before written a scene requiring precise description of a woman's genitals . . . Here we see him struggling to convey . . .' Shut up, Frank thought at it, at himself. Shut up! He could feel his lips yearning to say it aloud: shut up, you ugly son of a bitch!

He made Sandra dribble. Her face was torn between weeping and laughter. Her genitals were crimson, plump . . . They were real things, like the living room in the Barratt estate, and so had to be correct. At least, he'd thought as he made his way from the sex shop to the public library, carrying the violent threepack plus the one he'd been looking for—which was called *Explicit!*—it's something I'll have to do only once. He'd passed half an hour correlating the pictures with diagrams in a medical textbook, labelling them and taking notes from the section on sexual arousal. I have all the information, he told himself. It is simply a question of accurate attention to detail.

He described the odour and prodigious lubrication, the glistening and the sucking noises. Despite herself Sandra arched her back and offered herself to the monster's touch. She begged for release. The monster's foul breath came in gasps . . .

Frank was glad when the figures on the digital clock in his kitchen flipped over to 10:00 pm. He went to the toilet, washed his hands, and turned on his electric blanket in preparation for sleep.

The terrible and bloody conjunction, the monster's vile orgasm, could wait until tomorrow. He glanced again at the clock— 10:06—and set himself to read through. At 10:25 he would swallow two sleeping pills. Quite possibly he would become addicted to them, but at present, he felt, it was the lesser of two evils.

He read his own words, absorbed by them yet unmoved, making minor corrections to grammar, crossing out repetitions and underlining parts that would need to be looked at again. It was good, and he felt relaxed for the first time all day. He knew there was an infinite supply of Cougar books inside him. If new things had to go in them, well, with effort he could do it. He would manage. The books welled up from a seemingly inexhaustible source, and people wanted to read them; it was—I am, he thought with some pride—a perfect machine.

'Once people know you can talk they won't take no for an answer,' Liz told Jim as she added more warm water and mixed it in, her hair falling like two curtains on either side of her face as she reached down to scoop handfuls and slosh them over him. 'That means, as if it isn't bad enough getting them through the walls every other night, you have to sit in the launderette for an hour listening to a woman who wants to get pregnant by means of hypnotism . . . Well, no one hypnotised me.

'Should she leave him, murder him, have an affair back, kill herself or get a divorce? Or should she forget all about it and get on with life, perhaps train for a proper career? Should they try and adopt the other woman's child? If so, would she be able to love it? Or just stick with the hypnotism, and see how it goes? Mind you, it's expensive . . .'

When Liz stopped talking, the bathroom was quiet enough to hear both of them breathing. She was aware of an angry tightness in her chest.

'It was like being buried alive, being told all that . . . Like I'm in a coffin, paralysed, but lucid, looking out through a crack in the lid at people standing around the grave, unaware. Thud, thud, thud go the shovels. Try to scream, but only a rasp comes out. The air grows thicker, the sound fainter. You can't move. Soon no one will be able to tell you were ever there; but you are, lying with tons of soil on top, a terrible heaviness and the air running out. That's what it felt like, sitting with her in the launderette . . . But this is different, different, for reasons I've explained. You understand, don't you?

'I only asked because I knew you couldn't answer,' she said, quietly. 'That's the beauty of it. You're lucky. I've got it, but you're immune. So I'm lucky too, in a way: no need to struggle with my conscience, like the doctor in *The Kissing Disease* . . .' A drop of water fell from the ceiling above into the bath. She glanced up. Others hung ready to fall, brownish dimples, gelatinous, like sea anemones. Between them were circular stains, where others had formed then dried to death.

'Ugh,' she said. 'Still, it's better than the B & B. And that was better—in some ways—than before. Disadvantage of the carriages was water. Carrying it up along the path in gallons. And then heating it—I can't stand to wash in cold. I only bothered once a week or so . . .' Jim, her hand supporting his head and neck, appeared to be looking at the suds, gathered in drifts around the edge of the bath.

'I got head lice,' she said.

'It's a miracle you've got nothing worse,' the staff nurse had said.

'I was there two years.' Liz's hands fell still as she remembered.

'Your baby's life expectancy is more or less normal,' the doctor had said.

'Two years isn't long, really.' One-handed, she spread a towel on her knees, then hooked Jim out of the bath. Blood rushed to her feet as she rose. 'I really like the house. That's a Silver Lining and a half. And I wouldn't have got it without you, not in a million years. Purvis took a shine. Every cloud. Even a baby with something syndrome.'

'*Spinney's is very rare,*' the doctor had said, '*it's associated with a silvery hair colour but there are no physical abnormalities, though at first we thought—*'

'Jim—it's all going to turn out fine. And I'm going to give you another name,' Liz announced, holding him in the crook of one arm as she flipped down the toilet seat to sit on. 'Silver, after the lining. Silly for short. So, thanks for the house, Silly.

'I know a lot about her. Alice,' she resumed, searching out the moisture buried in creases and lurking between fingers and toes, the way she had been told to. Jim was a lean baby, and kept pretty still, which made it easier. 'She's called Ally to her friends. She's got grey eyes and wears soft contact lenses. She has seven 'O' levels and works four mornings in the building society. She's made chicken curry tonight and she bought white wine to go with it, though she doesn't drink, especially now, because it might damage her fertility . . .'

She sprinkled Jim with the powder and rubbed it in, making him look, she thought, even more silver than before.

'As for Tom, his hobby is karate, Thursday nights and Saturday mornings; used to be rugby but he got too many injuries. He's the manager of a computer shop. He buys her underwear to apologise for rows . . .' Jim lay heavy in her arms, his eyes sealed, his mouth loose.

'Oh, Silly . . .' She shifted him to the floor, and fastened a disposable nappy around his waist.

'*Incontinence,*' the doctor had said, '*may well persist.*' Though there was another Silver Lining, because if she had a washing machine buying these'd be more difficult to justify long-term.

'Silly—no point in pretending. Manners is another thing you're spared . . . I can see this is sending you to sleep . . . Nice that we share the same attitude to life.' She wrapped him tightly in a square of blanket with *hospital property* woven into it. Then she did something for the first time. It was over and above what she had described to Mrs Purvis and the hospital doctor as 'the necessary' and doing it, despite the fact that she and Jim shared the same bed (leaving the cot Mrs Purvis sent unused in the corner of the room), made her feel a little strange. She bent and kissed him, properly, on the top of his head. It was the new name, somehow, that made it possible.

PART TWO

PURVIS

After the birth Liz had scarcely spoken. Between feeds she would sit in her room at the B & B watching television. *Bonding difficulties,* Annie Purvis had written. *Apathetic.* At first—before the tests—it had seemed that Jim's sluggishness was a reaction to Liz's indifference. The pair of them were acting as if somehow the whole thing had been a mistake they'd rather forget.

'Do you worry that you'll hurt him, Liz?' Annie Purvis remembered asking. 'Is that why you never pick him up? Do you wish you'd never had him? Is that why you don't look at him? You can tell me, Liz. It's quite understandable. It's not, Liz, as if you planned on having a baby so young.'

'If you can't cope, you really don't have to. But once you've agreed to an adoption and filled in the forms, you can't change your mind.'

'Sometimes, Liz, we have to learn to love.'

'Pick him up now, Liz, hold him, and see how it feels.' It had been a strange and sweet feeling, that combination of pity for the silver-haired baby boy and understanding of his mother, herself just a girl. Being a third person, knowing and watching as change took place. Being a childless woman, saying, 'He might like it if you talk to him while he feeds,' then noticing her own nipples harden, and a wave of warmth spread across her belly, increasing with each of the baby's sucks.

'Liz, have you made any plans? Thought what you'd like to do?'

'Go to Corsica. Or Mexico.' She had mentioned it before. It wasn't a good sign.

'With Jim?'

'I suppose so.'

When the test results came through everything had changed. For a start, there was a great deal of interest. Spinney's Syndrome was rare and not often tested for, although the procedure was simple enough and could be done early. Fortunately the paediatrician at the hospital had just been to a conference about it. And so, all of a sudden, it seemed that perhaps Liz was reacting to Jim, rather than the other way round. And it had become clear, quite clear, that she didn't want her baby taken away . . .

Annie Purvis looked around the faces at the table. Today there were more than usual, including a police inspector and a WPC, as well as an elementary school teacher and the three of them from social services. At the beginning of a meeting, there was often a silence while they waited for the late people to arrive or not. Some used it to gather their thoughts and notes together. Mrs Purvis looked at hers, but found herself still thinking about Liz Meredith instead of Clare Moat and her parents. It was at this point far more enjoyable to think about Liz. Her telephone should be connected by now. The roof over her head, the thin wires joining her up to the rest of the ordinary world were, Annie Purvis thought, very good signs.

'We'd better begin,' said Mrs Newby, who, being Area Director, was acting as Chair. She wore a business suit but her skin glowed, as if she had just returned from a beach holiday. Next to Annie sat Mandy, both younger than Annie and

senior to her, with an office, of sorts, to herself. She was sol-
idly built, and legendary for the terrible state of her clothes:
everything she wore was creased, even things that looked new
would somewhere harbour a stain: today, there were three buttons missing from her purple cardigan. Her desk always had at
least one drawer open, another stuck—yet somehow she managed to seem attractive and to be extremely competent. On her
other side was Mrs Thomas, the teacher whose concerns had,
eventually, brought them to this point.

The Chair leaned back, as if it were story time. 'I understand
that the parents have declined to attend. Annie?' she prompted.

'Jackie Moat,' Mrs Purvis began, 'is twenty-four and Clare,
aged six, is her only child. Clare's father isn't known. A year
ago Jackie moved into her boyfriend's flat. Brian is thirty; he
used to be in the army but now works mainly on building
sites. Jackie cleans early mornings at the local supermarket. I
first visited Jackie and her family six months ago when Mrs
Thomas, Clare's class teacher at primary school, alerted the
department . . .'

Mrs Purvis wore a fine gold chain around her neck, slipped
invisibly beneath her blouse, and her fingers reached between
the buttons to feel for it as she spoke. It bore a plain gold cruci-
fix, so thin that it could be bent between finger and thumb. Yet
if someone had asked her whether or not she believed in God
she would have looked up in surprise and said no.

She had taken a minor in philosophy at university: it seemed,
at the beginning, necessary to get things straight, though by the
end of it she had not and was sick of the attempt. In her entire
life she had been to church perhaps five times, and those long
ago and best forgotten; she didn't pray. She had bought the
cross long after all of that, chosen it instantly from an assortment of charms and pendants spread on a blue velvet pad. For
days or weeks on end she'd forget it, and then suddenly she'd
feel it slip on her skin, a faint snagging somewhere private near

the heart. When the chain chafed, when the crossed slipped, or its corners dug in, it made her conscious of herself. It reminded her to ask herself questions, to consider her actions and evaluate their purpose; it reminded her of her own frailty, as a stab of pain, a fall, or sudden dizziness might.

'When Clare first came to school,' Mrs Thomas said, 'she was the kind that attracts a following. Very lively.' Mrs Thomas herself was about forty and stolid, her face heavily coated in a tinted cream which gave it a mask-like finish and made her eyes, by contrast, seem frighteningly unprotected: the wetness and shine of them, the tiny veins, the pupil shrinking as she looked to the light. Sitting next to her, Annie Purvis had to twist her neck to see Mrs Thomas, and noticed, as she spoke, that her breath smelled as sour as it had the first time they had met in her office.

'But then she got mopey, cold-seeming. Withdrawn. Still perfectly behaved, but she wanted to do everything on her own. And she was beginning to read quite well, but now she does it without seeming to enjoy it at all and she won't learn new words.' Mrs Thomas's voice was fluttering very slightly. It was as if something fragile and living were imprisoned in her throat, dashing its wings against its damp and heavy sides, and Annie found herself wanting somehow to stop it, not necessarily kindly.

'She won't join in any more. As if she was there in body but not in mind . . .' Annie looked away at the walls, which didn't help; they were painted with huge leaves and flowers of all nations sheltering a muddled assortment of animals, the domestic looking wild, the wild domestic. The mural had just been finished. Some parts, done by the art students, were very neat and professional; others, painted by the children, ran over their sketched outlines, dribbled their way down the wall: a tiger melted beside a *trompe l'oeil* bush, a large bird hovered over a heat haze of green and red that threatened to consume it. The overall effect, she thought, though well intended, was alarming.

'Children do go through phases. But then she got this thing about being touched: no adult can touch her. If they do, she'll scream. And it isn't acting . . .' The tremor in Mrs Thomas's voice seemed to magnify. Annie Purvis imagined she could feel it through her hand on the table and so slipped the hand to her lap, but then the voice seemed to be shaking at the legs of her chair, climbing from the seat to the top of her spine—she fought the impulse to stand, and glared at the paper before her.

'The first time that happened, I asked her at break time if there was anything wrong, and she just said "no" very politely, and waited for me to let her go.' Annie Purvis could see it: the small girl with her china-pale face, her fine hair fastened in a ponytail with a silvered band, the big woman bending or sitting down, the smell of cosmetics and stale breath, the tiny hairs on the upper lip clogged with powder, the voice fretting and over-sweetened with sympathy. *Who would tell you anything?* she thought, then reproached herself for thinking it and reached for her pen to doodle with.

'I didn't know what to do . . .'

'So Clare has become withdrawn and disturbed,' said Mrs Newby firmly, putting an end to it. 'Thank you, Mrs Thomas.'

Annie Purvis smiled at her and thanked Mrs Thomas. 'I made three visits to the flat,' she said smoothly. 'The first time, I saw Jackie and Clare. Clare looked well, but she is a very quiet child. I took her to the park. She said little unless asked a direct question that she could answer with a yes or no. Did she like their new home? She was more forthcoming here; she said yes, because the other flat had been cold. Did she like Brian? Yes, because Brian bought her presents. Sometimes she called him Brian and sometimes Daddy. She liked having a daddy. She wouldn't talk about being touched, but Jackie said she hadn't noticed anything at home.

'On the two other visits, Clare was at a friend's house, returning towards the end rather tired. Jackie strikes me as an immature but well-meaning mother. I felt she was very open with me. She manages money well and she's learning Spanish at an evening class. The flat is poorly furnished but she keeps it very clean. Clare has her own bedroom. Jackie couldn't think of any reason for Clare's behaviour, but said she'd noticed her being more "serious." She said she herself is very happy in her relationship with Brian, and feels he's dragged her out of a dead end; she could hardly believe her luck. But he has on two occasions hit her. She said he was good with Clare, bringing her presents and playing with her if he got home on time. She thought Clare was fond of him. She said that he would be angry if he knew I had visited because he hated busybodies. My feeling was that the family was quite a caring one, despite Clare's being perhaps in some way unhappy. I asked Mrs Thomas if there could be anything at school, perhaps bullying—'

'But there isn't, you see,' Mrs Thomas interrupted. There was a brief silence around the table, which formed a low hexagon composed of smaller, triangular tables: different colours, all primary bright. Each of these triangular tables had three legs. Underneath the multicoloured octagon was a neat plantation of aluminium. Around the edges of the room were plastic hods, packed with toys. Cushions and small chairs stacked in teetering columns insisted cheerfully on the presence of another world, albeit set within and dwarfed by the jungle. A large drawing of a thermometer was pinned to the back of one of the doors, marked off in degrees of a thousand pounds. Six of these had been filled in, each a different colour. In fact, though, the room was rather cold.

Mrs Thomas continued, her voice louder. 'You hear these things—I thought about it for a long time. But in the end I contacted the social services again, because I'd never forgive myself, but then again, I'd hate to cause a lot of upset for no good reason—it's really very hard—' and she began to cry, the tears ploughing very slowly through the powder on her cheeks. She looked defiantly at Mandy.

Mrs Purvis brought her bag onto the table and searched for the tissues she knew were there. Her movements were economical. She realised she was not alone in her anger; for a moment everyone hated Mrs Thomas, the insistent bringer of bad news, the one to open the box and let the world's nightmares come screaming out. Not fair, of course. She extracted the tissue and handed it over.

'All the same,' she addressed the meeting, 'I felt that the fact that Brian has been violent and that Jackie was so adamant that asking to see him would cause trouble could mean there was cause for some concern. I told Jackie that I was still worried about Clare and it'd be a good idea to take Clare in for a hospital check-up in case anything was wrong. She had no objections.'

The others nodded; it was good that Jackie had nothing to hide. But also it was possible, Annie Purvis knew, that Jackie had everything to find out. She saw Jackie for an instant, her startled eyes, rimmed with bright blue eyeshadow, the way they looked out at the world and then hid themselves in slow blinks.

'Good,' said Mandy. Sitting between her and Mrs Thomas, thought Annie Purvis, was unsettling: on the left, what she sometimes feared becoming—or was already, somewhere deep inside; on the right, the woman who, bar the crumpled clothes, she would like, perhaps impossibly, to be.

'What about visitors?' Inspector Hunt interrupted.

'Jackie occasionally brings her women friends back after collecting Clare from school. Sometimes Brian drinks with friends, but he doesn't bring them home. They rarely go out together, and Jackie has her Spanish evening class, but she doesn't make it every week because she can only go if he's home in time to look after Clare.'

'Clare was admitted on Saturday,' said Dr Susan Spark, without being invited to speak. Her small round face was calm, but it was easy to imagine it laughing. Annie Purvis envied her both her clear voice and the limits of her task. 'She was found to be in fair general health, if slightly underweight. She was very distressed at the idea of examination but eventually allowed it. There were signs indicative of abuse: ecchymosis and edema on the *mons pubis,* ecchymosis on the upper thighs, erythema, fissures around the anal canal—' In the fractional pause that followed, Annie Purvis found herself willing the doctor not to translate. She was not normally like this. It was because of having a layperson, Mrs Thomas, in their midst. 'That's bruising, swelling and redness, cracking,' the doctor said.

'I have to say that we feel strongly that this kind of medical finding can't be considered in isolation. It may well be caused innocently . . . Its status as evidence is questionable, as we all know,' said Inspector David Hunt.

'Yes, but it does call for an explanation,' said Mandy.

'Of course,' Dr Spark said. She sat very straight. 'However, that's my assessment, based on my own findings.'

'He has no record,' said Inspector Hunt.

'There are these drawings.' Mrs Purvis didn't want to look at the pictures again as she handed them around: the waxy crayon, the stick people, the twisted furniture, smudged and preserved inside an acetate folder. The orange curtains she'd recognised instantly as those in Clare's bedroom. Next to her the sour breath, the sniffing and fumbling: Mrs Thomas made it so difficult. More difficult.

'In the interviews?' asked the Chair.

'Nothing. Clare doesn't talk at all at the moment. She still tries to please, by smiling and doing what she's told. But she won't speak at all.'

'Not a happy child,' confirmed the WPC who'd sat through the interviews and recorded them.

'Does she seem happy to see her parents—both?' Mrs Purvis willed the hiss of breath next to her to come to nothing.

'Yes.'

'So the silence is ambiguous?'

'Like the drawing,' said Inspector David Hunt.

Mrs Purvis pointed to one of the pictures. 'That is an erect penis,' she said. Someone had to.

'Could be anything,' said Inspector Hunt, passing the picture along. 'With the greatest respect, and—'

'How could he!' Mrs Thomas's voice rang out and she searched the faces around the table, pleading with each by turn. Yet, thought Mrs Purvis, it was you who thought of it first.

'Mrs Thomas,' the Chair said smoothly, 'it is very distressing to contemplate. We all feel the same. What we have to do now is to determine the best course of action.'

Mrs Thomas looked at the police inspector, who stared back at her with eyes like stones. The Chair continued, 'There are two points: one is that it is not clear whether abuse has taken place, nor who has done it if it has. The second is that even if it has there will be choices to be made. It's not always best, Mrs Thomas, to remove a child from her home.'

'With that monster living there?'

The Chair managed to smile and look grave at the same time.

'No one is a monster,' she said. 'If he is abusive, and Jackie accepts that, it might be possible to move him instead of Clare. That would save her from having to lose her entire family through no fault of her own. It is even possible, sometimes, to work with the entire family without anyone having to leave . . .'

'Perhaps the reason you're feeling like this,' Mandy had said to Mrs Purvis yesterday, 'is that you don't have enough

information to feel sure. At this stage, you must see him.'
Using the word *perhaps* was one of the skills that had earned
her seniority. She had meant, as well, that Annie should have
insisted before, which Annie knew.

'I spoke to Jackie on the telephone last night,' she said now,
trying not to look at Mandy like a child seeking approval. 'The
first thing she told me was that she and Brian are engaged to
be married.' Her voice was neutral, but several people smiled
and the atmosphere lifted perceptibly. It was what Jackie
wanted. It was a good sign. Irrationally, she too felt happier.
'Brian wouldn't come to the phone. But he agreed, in the end,
via Jackie, to visit me with her at the office later in the week.'
Then, Mrs Purvis knew, she would have to tell him in so many
words why he was there. She had done it before. But everything
seemed even more difficult these days.

She'd seen Brian's striped and checked shirts, hanging on
the balcony to dry. She could imagine the way he might sit,
and the small signs of his anger. She could imagine the woman
and the girl creeping around him, trying to keep him calm.
She could imagine Jackie after a blow to her face, eyes shut,
hands over ears, partly from the hurt and insult, partly from
the fear that he would—if not then, sometime—tell them to
go. Replace them. He had once threatened to do this, Jackie
had said. Where could they go? She imagined Jackie watching
what he wanted and working out how to please him; Jackie
telling Clare to be good, please, so Daddy didn't make them go.
Jackie wanted a family, a man.

Unless Brian told her, or Clare did, how would she know
for sure? Only in the guts, and on the balance of probability.
And inside she hated and feared him, unprofessionally, the as
yet unseen Brian, for all the choices he was forcing on her, this
versus that, all the uncertainty, the terrible responsibility, the
nightmare of it; she hated him for not being obviously impossible to suspect, for being, she already guessed, the type who

would not be straight; for being her job, both a monster and a man.

'Has anyone got any other observations?' asked the Chair. No one looked at Mrs Thomas. The hands on the big blue clock with its cloud and sun had moved almost to the hour and the silence around the multicoloured table had twisted itself tight, pluckable because the nine people around the table— six women and three men—and even those among them who hadn't said a word, had now to decide what best to do with the nightmare raised, as in a seance: concentrating, setting up currents between their fingers, turning the issue over without touch so that it slowly spelled out a message that spoke itself through Mandy's lips.

'There does seem to be cause for concern . . .' Mrs Thomas was the medium, enthralled. And other bad dreams, as yet unraised, lurked behind each chair back, waiting to be taken home.

'But I think we're all agreed that this must be handled with sensitivity, and without confrontation if possible . . . Do you think,' the Chair asked, 'that Jackie and Brian will agree to extending the stay in hospital? We prefer,' she explained to Mrs Thomas, 'to do that in preference to anything more drastic. At this stage.'

'Yes,' Mrs Purvis said, 'I'm pretty sure.' Mrs Thomas looked blank, spent. She had passed it on, now she could go home and forget. Make herself a cup of tea.

'I take it we are agreed that Clare should go in the register. As keyworker, Annie, you'll inform Jackie of that?' No one disagreed.

The chairs scraped back; the meeting finished exactly to time.

Annie Purvis's husband Simon, the name often shortened to Sim, taught Geography at Cambrook Secondary School. He was going bald, a thick fringe of grey hair clinging around the central pate; the hair on his chest had thickened, his stomach grown soft—she quite liked the feel of that, though not so much the look. They had known each other nine years, been married eight, but she hadn't changed. Something had fortified her against time. She was thirty-two, he only forty, but they were growing to look like a father and his eldest daughter.

He was always losing things, and often she'd find them for him. 'Please,' he'd say. 'I've been looking for my scarf for days.' She'd find the lost thing without asking any irritating questions, by simply using her memory and imagination. On the whole the marriage worked well, though it could scarcely be called lust, she thought, the way they made love nowadays. They were both often tired. They would lie on their sides, her back curled against his stomach and chest, his hand on her abdomen, her legs bent and his fitting into them; joined at the genitals they'd rock gently back and forth. If one of them heard a noise, or had a sudden thought, they'd pause:

'What's that?' one would ask. 'Don't know,' the other would reply. If it was a loud noise, they stopped, and Sim went to look. Occasionally, if it was a trivial noise, or one that could be explained, they'd resume, but most often by the time he returned, goose-pimpled, soft, she would have almost fallen asleep.

Once someone had tried to break in. A gloved hand had slipped through the glass panel on the door, reaching for the catch. Now the panels were plywood. The streets around their flat, the stairs and passageway that led to it, were often loud with the sound of breaking glass, laughter and screams.

Sim hated it and wanted to emigrate. He dreamed of shedding his belly in the clean wastes of a new country. Of buying several acres of virgin land, converting his own trees to timber and building a wooden house. Of catching fish through holes in the ice, chopping wood and shooting occasional bears;

trudging through snow to bring back what he had caught to Annie and the kids they might have by then, out there . . . He taught Geography, but had only ever been to Germany and France. Kids in his classes had travelled halfway around the world, taking time off school to do it. He was jealous of them, the way they took things for granted, ranked what they'd seen lower than last night's television, didn't think. It was possible, he believed, to start another life. He had heard of people no different from himself who had managed to do it.

Although it was pleasant making love their way, Annie thought, it was also odd, as if their minds and bodies were disconnected; as if they were going out for a drive on a sunny day in a well-kept vintage car. It looked good, but driving was not the point any more. Sometimes a foot slipped unnoticed off the accelerator and they forgot about arriving anywhere.

'What are you thinking about?' she had asked last night as he stroked her stomach in forgetful circles. She'd twisted her head a little, but couldn't see him and abandoned the effort. But she knew. He wanted children, and was saying so more and more frequently.

'You have got the flying saucer in?' he'd joked hopefully when they began. 'Only I'm pretty sure I'd have to get permission to breed from the DOE.' He'd squeezed her to him. 'Well?' he said, falling completely still.

'So much can happen to them,' she said, squeezing her eyes shut. She had seen far too many children in trouble—had at present almost twenty on her list. You could fill a book with the terrible things that happened to children, and anyone reading it would weep and want to make it better. Almost anyone. There were, after all, perpetrators, and she knew a fair bit about them, too. There was abuse in her background, too, though she'd never told Sim. Even so, that was not why she didn't want children, or not all of it.

'Not the best time to discuss it,' she had said. He kissed her
on the neck.

'Shall we go to sleep?' he had said, and she was there almost
before he'd finished saying it.

SEX WITH OTHER PEOPLE

F rank told them, at the lunch, that he wouldn't do any publicity—none, not even an interview with a nice lady journalist, and certainly not TV.

'What exactly is your problem with it?' Katie Rumbold asked, smiling hard. She was wearing a skirt and jacket in brown linen, nothing discernible underneath, and her lipstick left faint prints on her glass.

'It's never been necessary before,' Frank answered, evasively. His shirt was sticking to his back. He felt himself colouring and wiped his face with a napkin. The place they ate in was expensive—'Give the man a good feed,' Pete Magee had said, as if he were a pet dog. 'Deserves it,'—but it was all show. The tables were marble, the air was cool, the lights small and bright, the food tasted dead. Fortunately the portions were small. There was champagne, and he took a glass to wash the taste away.

'It won't stop people saying things about you, you know. You might as well try and steer them in the right direction at least.' She'd rested her hand briefly on his wrist. It was blindingly obvious, he thought. Their desire to make him articulate it, could only be malice.

'Maybe it won't do so much harm,' said Pete Magee, good-naturedly, his mouth full, his lips glistening. 'Not to start with. Call you a recluse, can't we? Add a bit of mystery.' He spluttered into his napkin.

'You're going to be on that shortlist tonight, John,' Katie Rumbold rejoined. Frank supposed people would call her beautiful with her soft dark curls, her stern green eyes and creamy skin. He felt himself hating her. That hate was a steel cable and everything she said or did twisted it tighter. She had such power, and seemed so unaware of it.

Suppose, he'd thought, the necessary thing was money? Compensation. You paid for it, formally and informally. No doubt money in quantity blurred her vision a great deal, could give the beast the benefit of the doubt. But even so—what would Katie Rumbold do if he so much as put his hand on her thigh? 'Don't be silly, John,' she'd titter as she removed it. Or suppose he were to ask her, for instance, to kiss him (the word vanishing and screaming itself out at the same time) just once—on the lips, or even the cheek, but just for once not in the air next to his face? Even if he were to win the Hanslett prize. Even if he were stinking rich, she'd say no.

Helplessly drunk, she might, once—given that he could get it up—given the impossible—even sleep with him. But she'd regret it in the morning; she would never listen to his secrets, rub her cheek against his. She would wake up and look at him and something would rise in her throat and stick. The worst part of it was that he wouldn't really blame her.

And suppose, as people said, that it was not your face they—women—were interested in; not your brain or your conversation, not the muscles on your chest and legs, nor even the streamlining and size of your cock: it was simply what you did to them? Suppose, then, even a monster could please? Or suppose that the woman kept her eyes shut (but that would remind him) and imagined it was someone else anyway? Reasonable, even sensible from their point of view, but it would hurt—and what, anyway, did you do to—

'You *will* be on that list. I can feel it in my bones,' Katie said as if she meant it literally and it was nice—a warm feeling, like whisky as it went down—and she looked around the table, smiling at everyone, who all smiled back. 'And of course, you'll win. *When* you win, you'll talk to them then, won't you John?'

'Of course he will,' said Pete Magee. 'It's in his contract as a matter of fact . . .'

'Do you know how to find your way back to the station, John?' Kate asked solicitously as they left. 'Or shall I get you a taxi?'

The neighbours' car wasn't there. It was no guarantee, though, of Alice being out. So Liz stood quietly in the front room, her back to the party wall, listening. Sometimes, Alice had explained, Tom drove to work, and sometimes she took him so that she could use the car during the day.

There was never any noise from the other side, where the blotch-man lived, but she could hear every single thing that happened in 129. The soft moan of the vacuum cleaner, the slow scrape and bump of it on the skirting boards as it made its daily journey from top to bottom of the house, or out on an extra excursion if Tom had made a mess with his DIY; the careful clink of stacked plates, the gurgling of water in the drain, the churn of the washing machine; Alice, briskly climbing the stairs, sliding open her wardrobe doors—sometimes three or four times a day—and riffling through the hangers and drawers inside; the soft splatter of the shower, then the whirr of the hairdrier; the whoosh of the cistern emptying; the insistent ringing of the telephone; the sudden roar of the coffee grinder, the slam of the oven door and the rattling of the trays inside.

It was uncanny how clearly the inside of their house could appear to Liz. Against her will, pictures would grow in her head: Alice blowing her nose, or mixing the hot and cold in the bath; smoothing her tights up her legs after she'd used the toilet. She wished she could switch it off. She hoped that when the television came it would bring with it the added bonus of blotting Alice and Tom right out.

She'd selected the biggest screen Bettahire could offer, with remote control and a wheeled stand, signed her name and sealed the envelope, which didn't require a stamp. She was going to post it now, on her way to the park. It would get there tomorrow, and in a week or two, she and Silly would watch together. She hoped he'd enjoy it, somehow or another. All his senses did work. He could feel when she touched him; dressing him she would stroke his arms, hold his feet in her hands a moment before sliding them into his socks. She'd slip her finger in his mouth and let him suck it, smooth his hair, silvery white like the dried pods called honesty. He could hear. And there was no doubt either that he could *see*. When his eyes focused she could tell, not just from the way the pupils shrank, but also from the set of his face.

'What do you do with what you see, Silly?' she asked in her customary whisper. Did it just vanish, each new piece of information taking the place of the one before? (If only that was what happened to the things Alice told her when she caught her on the step.) If not, where did it go and did it just stay there forever? What, exactly, was missing . . .? The pictures would go wherever they went in Jim's head, and stay or not, as the case might be. She unstrapped him from the bouncer and stood, checking again.

There were noises in the street: the measured tread of elderly feet, the whirr of a bicycle, the sudden cough of a car reluctant to start, a distant siren—but the silence inside both houses was absolute. Even when it was quiet like this, she wondered what Alice was doing; thought perhaps she was doing exactly what she herself was: listening. To see if *she*—Liz—was in. Perhaps Alice had an armchair positioned by the wall in her front room, and sat in it with her coat on and her keys in her hand, ready to emerge at the exact same time Liz did, as if by coincidence. Perhaps Tom had drilled a spy-hole for her in the party wall . . .

She gathered Jim up and arranged the sling, ran her hand over the top of his head. She pulled the latch across and eased open the door. It stuck at the bottom, shuddering painfully so that she had to still its vibration with her hand. She strode down the path, turned smartly left—so as not to pass in front of 129— and almost bumped into the blotch-man coming the other way.

'Sorry,' Frank said, grasping her quickly by the shoulders then letting go and bending over to pick up the bag he dropped, and her letter to Bettahire which he'd knocked out of her grip. 'My fault.' He held out his hand; hers stayed deep in her pockets.

'Nice to meet you,' Frank said, 'both. Here.' Liz watched as the clear part of his face flushed to the roots of his scanty hair. I hope he's not going to be like Alice, she thought. He looked the quiet type, but he smelled of drink. She watched stonily as he reached into a carrier bag and removed a paperback book.

'Have one on me,' he said. 'Out today.' Fumbling, he slipped her letter to Bettahire inside the book and handed it over. The jacket illustration showed a narrow eye sunk in folds of skin. It was called *To the Slaughter*. She glanced at it before slipping it into her pocket and walking straight off.

'On this other planet,' she began—she was glad to be able, outside, to talk at proper volume—'there are people who have different ideas about what's beautiful. For instance, they'd find you hideous, with your skin all smooth and white like this.' She walked briskly, enjoying their successful escape. The letter to Bettahire was posted. It would arrive there tomorrow. Now and then passersby stared at them, but they didn't say or do anything, so she didn't mind.

'They'd be sorry for you, and maybe try and get you surgery, in case the way you were made you neurotic when you grew up.

'What they like is scars, spots, scabs, wrinkles, hairy patches and birthmarks like the blotch-man's got. They sell creams that we'd think were *bad* for the skin. They have salons where you can have scars made, or your nose broken, or injections that give you diseases. Kids are encouraged to catch chicken pox and scratch . . .

'Best of all they like people with bits missing, or very short legs, things like that . . . And that's the same with everything they make or build—they model it on what they find beautiful in each other, so that if you or I went there, we'd be horrified by the ugliness of it all, the people, the buildings, the land-scape, and if they came here, the same for them . . .' It was almost dusk by the time they reached the park. The air in the surrounding streets smelled of cooking. There were still a few other mothers and babies about. She watched them; how they walked very slowly, stopped to talk, bent over their own prams and each other's, continued together for a while.

'Those babies cry more than you,' she observed. She was going so much faster than the other mothers were. She was different, too, could walk for miles, twenty, thirty in a day. Not that there was much scope for it any more.

'One of the ugly people and one of us ends up stranded, just the two of them, on a small planet somewhere in between . . .' She strode the circumference of the park, past the churned football fields and the abandoned tennis courts; she skirted the large rectangular pond, then took the path to the circular gar-den at the centre.

'Perhaps they'd grow more like each other—neither of them being able to get to their beauty salons . . . There'd be no mir-rors, but they'd each know something had changed, because of the way the other one behaved . . .' The garden was designed like a wheel, with a mound of daffodils and tulips at the hub and roses between the spokes, though none of them were out. The rim of the circular garden was a huge mixed border of hollyhocks, giant daisies, lupins, foxgloves and marigolds, mostly just the dry sticks of last year's growth with new green spears and here and there a sudden blaze of forget-me-not blue. She walked around it more slowly, several times, then stopped at a bench. She sat Jim on her lap, facing outwards, and slipped her hand around his belly to keep him there. He was warm.

'Most likely one of them would kill the other,' she concluded, bored. What she wanted to say next was private, so she lowered her voice. 'I've been thinking,' she began. 'We two could get on very well, now we're properly on our own. We've got a lot in common, despite the difference in size, which'll pass in any case . . .' There was a marked difference in size between Alice and Tom . . . Even when she wasn't calculating how to escape the house unaccosted, even when she wasn't creeping barefoot over the floorboards or washing up her knife and fork separately so that they didn't clink against each other; even when she wasn't whispering and making sure to anticipate Jim's every wish so that he didn't cry, they'd slip into her thoughts like this and she'd find it hard to get rid of them. It's possible, she thought, that they'd infiltrated her brain, just like the tiny aliens she once saw swimming in a man's bloodstream in a film.

'There's a lot I have to do for you, but it's simple stuff. I don't mind. And, on the other hand, in lots of ways you've got the edge on me. I could learn from you, Silly, I think so. How to get to the Zone and so on. Yes. Even just how to cope with being here and now . . . About talking: I'm going to cut it right down, except for to you—that's safe. And other things too . . .' She jogged her knees gently up and down as she spoke. Something jabbed her in the thigh. She extracted the man's book from her pocket. 'Reading can go,' she said, tossing it into the wire bin next to the bench. 'Never did it much anyway. See—perhaps the way for you and me to get on best is for me to be as like you as I can?' She wrapped her other hand around him and lowered her head so that her nose just brushed the top of his head. She stayed like that, feeling the light fade.

There, at the dead centre of the park, the air smelled fresh. Everyone else had gone home to their dinners. A whistle blew, announcing the closure of the park. Liz wanted to stay there, sitting on the bench. She felt very calm and warm. 'I might have to do it in stages. But I think we'll go far,' she said.

Jim made a noise, like someone much older clearing their throat.

'Don't try,' she said. 'I want to be like you.' The whistle blew again, louder this time.

At dusk, when the men came home from work, Onley Street's curtains were drawn again. Everyone was watching television, except of course, Alice, who had to be unloading her shopping. She left the bags on the pavement and hurried over, holding a frozen chicken and calling as she approached, 'Want one of these?' Her voice and the beat of her heels on the pavement seemed very loud. 'On offer! Got five, there's not room in the freezer. Only £1.99—take it! I'm still in profit . . . Come with me next time. I keep seeing you walking back with shopping bag and the baby: much simpler in the car. Or you make up a list for me to get for you. . . Here!'

Liz held out her hand. If she took the chicken she wouldn't have to speak, other than to say thanks. It was easier. Alice smiled and settled herself against Liz's gatepost.

'You haven't seen anything?' she asked. 'No? I know it's a cheek to ask, but what can I do? The worst thing,' she continued, 'is that it's spoiling our sex life. You can imagine. If *he* doesn't want to, I just flip. And even when he does want to, half the time *I'm* putting on an act. I know I shouldn't, but supposing he thought, well, I've stayed with her and she doesn't even fancy me! See what I mean? I have to take my temperature every morning—the sperms live for three days, you see, and the eggs for forty-eight hours—well, how am I supposed to forget about it all, doing that? Down today, three tenths of a degree. So we've got to do it tonight or the month's wasted . . . You must think I'm a real misery, but that's not my nature, not before this happened—you wouldn't recognise me!'

Jim was asleep. He really did, Liz thought, have a knack for cutting out of conversations like this. Perhaps, eventually, she'd learn to do it too; not only not to speak but also not to hear. One day she would go into a trance. Just fall asleep on her feet and wake up in the Zone . . . I could buy wax earplugs, she thought suddenly, for the meantime. But maybe it would be cheating.

'. . . *She's* managed it. So it's me that's the problem. Unless hers isn't his of course . . .'

When they send babies like you from the Zone, Liz thought at Jim, like ambassadors, like Jesus—Henry Kay was just a vehicle—it must often be a waste. If a person is lucky enough and knows what they've been given, they can learn. But most people screw it up, do everything they can to make the baby like all the others, and failing that they send it away to a home like Purvis suggested. But I won't, she thought at him. I know a Silver Lining when I see one.

'In this day and age these things aren't accidents, are they? And it wasn't just him that made this happen. He wanted to get out of it but he couldn't, he says. Like being in a swamp . . .'

The chicken was cold and slippery. Liz transferred it carefully to her other hand and flexed the freed fingers to warm them up. Every word avoided, she told herself, is a tiny step towards the Zone.

'Haven't you got any gloves? I'll look you out a pair . . .' I wasn't expecting, Liz thought, to have to hold a frozen chicken for half an hour . . . Did it count, though, thinking replies? Probably—

'I'd like to ring her up, tell her exactly what I think of her. But I don't know her number. The note I found about the baby wasn't signed. In his sandwich box! Said she'd like him to be at the birth, whatever he decides to do about it all in the end! I ask you! Just signed "A." No address, and I can't find one in his things. Maybe he never wrote it down. You know how you go somewhere once and just recognise the house by what's in the garden . . .'

If the world were in some way warmer, Liz thought at Jim, perhaps your brain would quicken into life, the way goldfish do when ice melts on the pond. If the earth heated up perhaps you'd be one of the few to survive. Perhaps—

'. . . Or maybe she lives in a big house you couldn't mistake from any other, like that one with the round window on Kimberlake Avenue. Last night he had the nerve to tell me I ought to feel sorry for her, left on her own with a baby. I said, do *you* then? He said, no, she was a bitch. So I said, why the hell should *I*? I could murder her.' Alice closed her eyes for a moment, opened them again.

'A baby would be something solid,' she said.

True, thought Liz, feeling the sling pulling her shoulders forward. When Silly was born, she remembered, he was only about the size of this damn chicken. She gazed steadfastly at the top of his head, knowing that Alice's eyes were seeking hers out.

'Not just to match hers, but a real thing between us. And something separate, for me . . .'

You are growing, Silly boy, Liz thought, all the time, every minute of the day, so many grammes a week. One day you'll be a Silver Man. That was almost frightening. But at the same time he was staying the same, frozen in time—again like the chicken—and somehow that was comforting.

'I hope she has a miscarriage.' Alice's words skipped from her lips, light as table-tennis balls. 'I'm telling you because I can't tell Tom things like this. Doesn't put me in a good light! Sometimes the phone rings and I think it might be her calling from the hospital in floods of tears and I *rush* to answer it. Born dead, or with something wrong with it—webbed feet, a great blotch on its face, no brain—terrible, but look what she's done to me. I get an acid feeling just here, all day. That doesn't help with the sex life either!'

Liz tried to ease the straps of Jim's sling and the chicken slipped from her other hand. It hit the ground with a crunch. Automatically Alice bent to pick it up, wiping grit from the plastic with her sleeve. It seemed to jolt her into another groove. 'Have you got a baking tray big enough? I've an old one you could keep.' She peered at Jim. 'Solids soon, I suppose—you could always pop around and do a batch in my liquidiser, then keep it in our freezer.' She passed the chicken back. 'Such a *good* baby, isn't she? Has she smiled yet? That's supposed to be quite something, their first smile . . .

'I can't see how we are going to get pregnant if we hardly ever *do* it. Did you know, some women are allergic to their husbands' sperm?' She laughed, but at the same time her eyes scanned Liz's face for reaction, making it impossible to think about frozen chickens or the Zone or anything at all except wanting to escape.

'Sometimes I do feel a bit sore the next day, but that's probably just not being into it. I'm having a test, though, just in case. Spend half my time in the doctor's these days. Sometimes I think the high point of my life was passing my driving test, but ever since all it's led to is going to the shops and the bloody doctors! You know, I almost wish I *was*. Allergic. That'd settle it once and for all, wouldn't it?' The stare continued. There was only one way to end it.

'Yes,' Liz mumbled, tucking the chicken under her arm. We don't need a baking tray. We don't need a liquidiser or smiles, she thought. We've got quite enough things and we know where we are.

'See you soon,' said Alice.

Hope not, thought Liz.

Frank peered into the bathroom mirror—another shot set up by the documentary crew. They'd carefully avoided showing

his face close-up so far, but now they were going in for the
kill . . . The mirror was the only one in the house, small and
round. Normally he avoided it. It magnified, just right for arty
bastards like them. It magnified his ugliness. It showed the
pores, the stretches and slackness, the lines and hairs. A single
improvement would have no discernible effect. Even if you got
rid of the red birthmark and covered the whole thing in new
skin, removed the pouch-like cheeks, smoothed over the dim-
ple, bang in the middle of the chin, unshavable, dark, huge.
Even if you grew a beard, which he'd tried. Puberty had added
insult to the original injury, and age had confirmed it.

Skin should be smooth and evenly coloured, like Katie
Rumbold's silk. This was scarcely a face at all—it was a wax-
work, warmed and then dropped on a dirty floor. He leaned
closer and soaped it. He began to shave. The razor hissed. His
breath came and went in time to the strokes. Anyone could see.
And those bastards would be quite happy to say it as well . . .

The documentary would be followed by a panel discussion:
'One can only admire the man for making a fortune of such a
raw deal . . .'

'It's obvious that he can never have—'

Drying himself, Frank noticed a speck of blood on the
towel. A disproportionate wave of misery rose up inside him,
turning halfway between his chest and eyes into fury. It bore
him to the kitchen where he sharpened a knife and began to
slice mushrooms, very fine and very fast.

He was late, because of the lunch. He was not actually
hungry, again because of the lunch. He skinned an onion and
began to slice that. He imagined a television studio built as a
combination of boxing ring and cockpit. The imaginary audience tittered, then roared and stamped their feet, threw things.

'Mr Styne—' no—they'd call him *John*—'John, surely it's
the case that you write about your own ugliness? How does
it make you—?' The camera was a kind of gun. It homed in

on him, then moved closer and closer, point-blank. It magnified, just like the shaving mirror. It would be hard not to show he was hurt, with the lights on his face as it wrinkled and twisted, shining with mucus, his mouth opening in a roar. Very, very hard. He would be unable to speak. They would film his speechlessness.

Really controversial, Katie Rumbold would say with a gleam in her eye, as she egged them on. Good for sales. He sliced and sliced. He threw the vegetables in the pan and the oil frothed. The kitchen filled with the rich smell of onions and the subtle aroma of fungi, the sweat of fat. He turned on the fan. If only it could extract thoughts, suck them away and leave peace behind . . . Suppose what was inside did count more, as his mother had so often said, in this very house, this very room, before everything changed? In the last years her voice had grown thin and querulous. He had cooked for her, but she disappeared inch by inch . . .

'What's inside counts' assumed, for no reason at all, that the inside was always better. But suppose it was worse? It could well be worse. He crushed mustard seeds. Inside even beautiful people was likely to include a lot of shit . . . literally. As for metaphorically—he smelled the faintest touch of burning, lowered the heat—he did at least eat well. Maybe his shit was better than most, but it was not a lot of consolation, because it was still shit and anyway insides took longer to discover than outsides.

How did the insides get there anyway? People, thought Frank Styne, cutting fresh ginger root into tiny cubes, are not like this; not a rich flavour and firm texture inside a shabby carapace that can simply be peeled away. He slipped a sliver of the fibrous yellow flesh into his mouth. People are more complex. The outside affects what the inside becomes. People are marinated and cooked, over time. The flavours blend. The recipes are accidental. Circumstantial. Sometimes the results are appetising, sometimes not.

He pared the pork thin, cutting across the fibres, patted it carefully dry and soaked it on a plate in the juice of a lime. He set miniature saucers of spices alongside the hob in order of their use. He tested the rice. He adjusted the flame, threw in the meat. He turned on the radio.

'The issue here,' a nasal voice said, 'is one of genre. It's a case of treading a knife-edge between cliché and its transgression or transmogrification. What's so exciting about his work is the way in which—'

'Surely much of it's just a rather infantile kind of comic strip, better written, arguably, than other such, but not, none-theless, something that should be commended?'

'But look at this passage for instance on page 145—the scene where Annie Smith is blinded with a hot iron in the bathroom. The whole point is: it could be, but it isn't. Styne has always pushed the form to its outer limits and then beyond—completely transformed it—and I think he does that because—'

It was for real. With the end of the spatula, Frank, short-listed for the Hanslett prize, cut them off. Almost immediately the phone rang. Like a fool, he answered it.

'Joel Freeman here. Congratulations, Mr Styne. Long over-due, if I may say so! Always been a fan. I'm dreadfully sorry to ring at this hour, but you've been unavailable all afternoon. You must be horrendously busy, but I would love to do a feature . . .' Frank hung up.

It was possible, he thought a little later as he began to work, that Katie Rumbold had already known about the shortlist at lunchtime. It was more than possible. More than probable. Perhaps she'd fixed the whole thing. The words of her letter and of Pete Magee's statement about contractual obligations mingled with the real discussion on the radio, the imaginary documentary, the hard-pressed words on the page, and multi-plied even as the monster pumped his vile juices into his wife; as, after, he lay heavily over her insensate body.

'Slowly,' he wrote, 'I felt my scaly lids draw together over my eyes. My muscles relaxed and my terrible sex organ began to shrink; and, as it did so, I could feel myself change with each heavy breath back into the man I had been. My breath grew sweeter, my odour salty and fresh. Later we woke, man and wife, convinced that we had suffered a nightmare . . .' But neither of them, particularly the wife, would be able to explain or to forget the blood on the hearth rug.

The phone rang again: Katie Rumbold. Frank wrote on and let it play unanswered through the machine; her voice, loud with triumph, echoed through the house. 'I knew it, John! I expect you're celebrating. Ring me in the morning . . .'

Together the husband and wife would perform and wait for the home pregnancy test, and later visit Dr Villarossa to put her in charge of antenatal care. They'd hold hands and visit their nursery, fingering the mobile and smoothing the diminutive sheets. There was peace between them, of sorts. Now and then, separately, each would remember the monstrous coupling, and see it as a dream.

The next big scene was the attempted abortion, after which the husband would lock Sandra into one room, doing with her what Pete Magee wanted, until her time came. There were pictures of pregnant women in one of the magazines . . . He leafed through. Many of the images looked physically impossible, for one or both parties. He considered for some time one of a woman crouched, her wrists thrust through her legs and tied to her ankles with washing line, making a banana-like bundle of hands and feet. You can't see her face at all, he thought.

'IMPOTENT?' asked a small advertisement on the page opposite.

A few days ago, Frank thought, I was perfectly happy. The present was tolerable, even good, the past was more or less in its place, the future was easy to ignore. Why are they doing this to me? Why am I letting them? The girl next door, he noted, had a visitor, knocking very loud. 'For God's sake, answer it!' he shouted, flinging the magazine across the table.

It was Alice.

'Sorry to bother you . . . Tom's late. Here.' She thrust a baking tray into Liz's hands. 'Whenever that happens, I think the worst. I'm afraid of being left. I'm so afraid of it all coming to nothing. I put such an effort in. I really try—look at me dressed up like this. We're supposed to be trying again tonight. I admire you, I really do, but I never could manage on my own. I can remember, clear as day, how it all started out so perfect. How could he spoil it, expect me to put up with this? And then I think maybe he did it on purpose, so that I'd leave him and he wouldn't need to make his mind up . . . But I never will.

'And I hate the thought of her being better than me. What's she got? I used to ask. Now she's got the pregnancy, hasn't she? One day she'll go to hospital to have Tom's baby. I don't even know when! I can't beat her to it, however hard I try. And he's probably there right now, whispering sweet nothings. Feeling it kick, making promises. Slipping inside her extra gently, one more fuck for luck, and then another one and another one and another one and another bloody one—might as well, mightn't he? We're supposed to be doing it tonight . . . Please, would you just come round and sit with me?'

Liz swallowed. Without Jim strapped to her it was more difficult. She couldn't look down at him, adjust the straps, wipe his face. She was going to have to look Alice in the eyes and say very clearly, *Sorry, no,* but she was saved when headlights streaked across them and the soft purr of an engine cut dead. Alice reached out and touched Liz on the arm. 'Must go. Thanks. I expect everything's okay.'

Tom emerged from the car, carrying his jacket over his arm. His shirt looked yellow in the street-lamp. He waved at the two women, then hesitated. Liz closed her door, scooped Jim up from the mat on the floor and carried him upstairs. She lay on the bed beside him.

'Wake and sleep at the same times,' she murmured. 'Even eat the same things, more or less: porridge, milkshakes, soup. Only do things you can't do when absolutely necessary for self-preservation.' She practised matching her breath to his. Even so, while his mind might not be as blank as it seemed, hers was crammed with half thoughts and longings . . . How the television would come on a stand that could be wheeled about; how it would fill the room with pictures, playing their shadows over the walls and touching their faces as they watched. With the gas fire on full they'd sprawl naked on the cushions, for days on end, feasting like the emperors of Rome while they were entertained, seeing and hearing the same things at once. Perhaps one day they would get a satellite dish.

'Tonight,' she announced an hour or so later when the light switch next door clicked on, 'little do they know they are in a time warp and that whatever they do in the next few hours they will have to go on doing for the next three thousand years . . . She is wearing a negligee made out of the Other Woman's skin. He's been making it for her secretly these past weeks—that's why he's been late home—in order to prove his love.'

But more likely Alice was wearing the set of slate silk underwear trimmed with cream lace—'Must have cost at least fifty pounds'—which she'd told Liz that Tom had given her to make up for a row. She groaned as he eased the garments off. To do this, she had to undo a huge knot inside her by imagining, hard, that it was the first time they'd ever done such a thing, and that she had a body more magnificent than her own, such as no man could resist, much less consider deserting. And so did Tom, for he too had knots inside—not thick and ropy like hers, but a fine network of small ones pulled very tight. So they both closed their eyes and made their heads into cinemas, running, despite it all, more or less the same film from almost the same point of view.

'I love you,' Tom muttered.

'But,' Liz, listening hard, whispered to Jim, 'that's just *words.*'

Alice had once read in a magazine that it was common for people to have fantasies while making love. Women, it said, imagined themselves naked on the top of pillars or in the middle of restaurants or being raped or with several people at once or with total strangers or in ancient Egypt—there was nothing wrong with it, the article said, at all—in fact it was a jolly good thing, and perhaps people who didn't, it said, should be worried, because they were boring and inhibited. So Alice thrust her imaginary body towards Tom's; she decided to make him so desperate for her that he'd lock her in the house—she thrust faster and faster until suddenly she thought: perhaps he is pretending too. Perhaps he is pretending that I am *her.* She froze and opened her eyes. Tom's face was furrowed. His tongue poked between his lips as it always did at this point. He grunted, thrust deep—and coldly, utterly herself, Alice squeezed him tight, fitting with his rhythm. She judged the moment, tensed, threw back her head and groaned.

Jim twitched and turned his head slightly in the direction of the sound.

'Don't worry,' said Liz, moving onto her side to whisper into his ear. 'It's very easy to avoid sexual intercourse . . .

'Which is another Lining really,' she reassured him. 'You'll never get all tangled up about it. You'll avoid being in a state like they are. She doesn't enjoy it, but she doesn't want him to do it with anyone else. Sexual intercourse can be almost as bad as talking. . .

'Do they have it in the Zone?' she wondered. 'I bet not. Not as such. Maybe it's the same as talking? Something in it somewhere, but lost?'

Suddenly she laughed, forgetting completely to be quiet. And in 125 Frank Styne, snatched from the edge of sleep by the ghost of the sound, buried his face in his pillow, fully awake. The place where he'd cut himself shaving burned and seeped into the linen. He clenched his fists in rage. He had never in his whole life felt so angry. And then, suddenly, the way a cat appears in a room, the idea was there.

Downstairs, he equipped himself with a glass of water and the magazine. He returned to bed and found the page he had been looking at before. 'This common problem,' the advertisement said, 'can be solved by simple surgical techniques at our modern and luxurious clinic in London's Harley Street. Why suffer when there is a solution? Top consultants, well-trained and sensitive staff, reasonable fees.' And next to it was the picture. Frank reached for his notepad.

Washing Line, he wrote. Washing line was purchasable at any hardware store, and with it he would truss Katie Rumbold naked, faceless, like a chicken. Then he would find out if a monster could really make a woman say please—though that was incidental.

Clinic, he wrote. Frank Styne would have sexual intercourse. It would involve surgery, and money, but why not, if it worked? And afterwards, when he'd ejaculated inside her—maybe made her, even temporarily, pregnant—he would be in control of what happened to him and he would avoid the shame of having had to use such extraordinary means.

Pills, he wrote. After the sexual intercourse he would take them, and leave her there, conscious, tied up, as he slowly became his own corpse. He would make sure that she knew exactly what she had done to him and why he had done what he'd done to her. Afterwards, someone might find her in time. Or they might not.

The plan was conditional. It hinged on the verdict of the Hanslett judges. The effort of preparing for it might be wasted should he not win, but the project would in any case occupy the non-writing time between now and the judgement, so enabling him to continue unaffected. The element of chance was no bad thing. It would give him a personal interest in the whole business. He had made himself into a character and it was a plot worthy of a Cougar book, to be lived out instead of written. Or, at least, not written by him.

'Sex with other people,' Liz whispered to Jim, whom she could tell was awake even though his eyes were shut. 'It's what Grammy used to call a tie that binds.' There was silence on Alice and Tom's side of the wall, though that didn't mean that someone wasn't awake, staring at the darkness. Outside, in the distance, a siren wailed. Jim coughed. She touched his face, brushing it clear of the fine hair that she was reluctant to cut, wiped his upper lip with the sheet; there was a small blister on it, in the middle. She turned on her side.

'You can do it yourself,' she whispered, slipping her hand inside the briefs she had made a point of wearing in bed since the phone-man called. 'You can do it anytime you want, in a minute or so, there's no need to make such a fuss. See,' she said, feeling herself open. 'Easy—very easy—nothing to it.' She hadn't done it for a while, and the sensation was absorbing. She fingered her breast with the other hand: Henry Kay used to do that, but she didn't think of him, or of anything at all. She grew wetter. The sound of it was like Jim's sucking. Sweat broke out on her back and legs.

Where was the harm, in the case of a child that won't think or speak or understand? One who quite possibly erased one impression with the next, beginning always afresh? It was different. She and Jim could do exactly as they pleased, so long as they hid well enough. Perhaps, she thought sleepily, being endowed with little in the way of brain, Jim's true vocation would be as a lover. Every cell sensitised, every nerve a taut thread singing like the strings of silver violins; people would envy him if only they knew.

True, you could do it on your own, but it did feel better to have someone else in there at the end. She pushed her finger inside.

'Sleeping through it, are you?' she whispered. The necessary, she thought, is what I make it. When he's grown, why not? I could. It's possible. There would be no complications. Something shared without language, without a trolleyfull of *emotional equipment*. On his part, nothing learned. 'It'd be different from the way it is between ordinary people. Perhaps it'd be a way to the Zone, if I haven't already made it by then . . . You have to do it with a Zone-being, but of course they hide often in the bodies of people you wouldn't think to do it with . . . like relatives. That's part of it, see, to take the risk.' Of course, she thought, Purvis would disapprove.

GETTING TV

'We have thousands of satisfied customers every year,' said the receptionist at the Davidson Clinic. He had a very even voice with just a trace of cockney in it. 'It really is a very simple and safe procedure. It causes less disturbance than having a tooth out. Dr Davidson is known internationally for his work in the field. He was on television a couple of months ago . . .' Frank would have to wait a little for the initial consultation, but after that it would be very quick. 'Please let us know if you wish to cancel, because we receive many enquiries every day.'

Frank wrote the appointment and the clinic's address in his diary. Then he cut the photograph of the trussed woman from the magazine. He considered it: the *labia majora* parted, the cushion of crimson flesh folding in on itself, there. He fixed it with Blu Tack to the wall next to the telephone, which rang again as he did so: 'Zelda here from Cougar publicity. Please get in touch urgently.'

There was only one call he intended to make. It was only fair to give Katie Rumbold a chance, and a warning, even though now he more than half wanted her to ignore it.

'Hi!' He sat quite calmly in his grey leather sofa and looked at the picture as she spoke. It was as impossible to imagine her walking around with one of those between her legs as it was to imagine himself growing hard and slipping inside one, but then, the whole point of the exercise was in the end to make the unimaginable real, or the other way round. The procedure, as the clinic receptionist had reassured him, was very simple.

'Lovely to hear from you, John,' she said. 'And, of course, congratulations on the shortlist! Actually, I've been trying to get you—more good news: they're going to cover the judging ceremony on BBC, and . . .'

'I want to clear something up,' Frank interrupted. His voice was controlled, almost a monotone. 'I think I should've been asked whether I wanted to be entered for this prize or not,' there was a tinkle of laughter at the other end, 'because if I had been asked, I'd've most definitely said no.'

'John—I thought I made it clear. You weren't entered. Frankly, no one would'd've thought you stood a chance. Your book was *requested*—'

'I still should've been asked. I want it withdrawn.'

'Please calm down, John.'

'I am calm.'

'The point is, there's no other writer on *earth*—'

'I don't care about that.'

'And as far as Cougar are concerned, I think they'd be perfectly within their rights, in any case, to override—'

'Listen. I'm telling you this: if I win that thing, I'll never write another book. And you will be sorry. Very sorry.'

'What on earth do you mean?' Frank reached for the remote control of his sound system where a silver disc spun silently, nudged it until the music became audible. Brandenburg, not that she'd know.

Then he said, 'Exactly what I say.' The 'c' and the 't' snipped precisely at the air. It made the hairs stand up on the back of his neck.

'I'm sure you'll feel differently when it actually happens. I know you will.'

'I thought I should *warn* you, Katie.' He hung up.

The answering machine whirred into action again. 'John—what has got into you—' He turned the volume of the music up.

It had gone well. Very well. It could easily have gone wrong. It could have backfired completely. 'Katie, I—' he could have begun, his voice thin, his hands sticky with sweat, and then a flap of skin in his throat could have turned an audible somersault. 'I—ah—'

'John?' His face twisting like burning plastic, nothing but a terrible clicking sound from his mouth, however hard he formed the proper shapes with his lips. Gripping the handset . . . And all he could do would be to nod and gasp . . . It could have gone like that, but it hadn't. Already his plan was giving him strength.

He moved to the window and drew the blind, which was the same silver-grey as the upholstery. It was raining, and people passing the window were hunched, their faces screwed tight. He was glad to be inside.

He stretched himself along the sofa with his ankles crossed. His belly rose up in front of him, heaving with the effort. He sighed, closed his eyes and gave himself to the music. At first his hand beat time gently beside his thigh, but it soon fell still. This is how it'll be, he thought; afterwards, when I've done it, *if* . . . It felt as if the music were stripping him bare. It was a gentle caustic, that had dissolved his oatmeal crew-necked sweater, the jeans that cut him around the middle, his yellow T-shirt, blue-and-white striped underpants, the oatmeal socks that matched his sweater . . . Now it began very softly to devour his skin; it ached, but it didn't hurt—far from it. The music just wanted to get close. It had no eyes, no squeamishness. It revealed him and covered him with a kind of benign indifference. He lay very still so that it could touch him and enter him how it wanted. He felt very vulnerable and very safe. He had not known a lover's touch, but he was quite sure, now, that nothing could ever be as tender as this. See how I shine, he thought, how I glisten, how my pulses throb in time and in tune—he uncrossed his ankles—this perfect rawness, as the music washes me all away . . .

He heaved himself upright and rubbed his hands over his face. He examined his front room, where it would all take place: the judgement on television, the sexual intercourse, the death—adding up to revenge, and also the exact fitting completion of all that had gone before, the proper end to a story such as his. *If.*

Here, she would be seated on the sofa, and he could reach down from behind, the washing line already cut into short and convenient lengths . . .

'Hello, John, this is Katie again. I am trying to set up a meeting with Azure Books to discuss a new edition of *To the Slaughter.* And money, of course! Wednesday or Friday? Call me back please.'

Perhaps it would be easier to acquire a weapon of some kind and threaten her so that she allowed him to do it without a struggle?

'Hello, Mr Styne. Susan Gilcrest from the *New Review.* I'd love to interview you about your work. Please call me back.'

He enjoyed the thought of it happening there, in this room, with its pale grey walls, the darker grey chairs, and the muted red of the woodwork. He was proud of the room—the way the rug picked the colours up and played with them; the way light fell in pools and the way the rubber plant by the window thrived. He liked the way it was clean, but soft; that the things in it were beautiful without being antique. He felt calm. The telephone was doing overtime, but the documentary crew had gone away.

'I sent the form,' said Liz to the Bettahire man, 'but I haven't heard.' He wrote her name in a random mixture of capital and lower-case letters, mouthing them as he did so: Mrs M-e-r-e-d-i-t-h. He bent awkwardly to reach the counter, being very tall as well as thin. There was a finger-wide gap between his collar and his neck. A badge with ANDREW MYERS printed on it—the letters large and raised, as if it were to be read by touch—was pinned to his lapel.

Perhaps, Liz thought good-humouredly at Jim, he has a huge brain and understands all the printed circuits and things inside televisions. Perhaps he's come from a planet where this stuff's Stone Age compared to other things they've invented. (Like perhaps they've got mental television where the station transmits some way, but the receiving equipment's the mind, its natural capacities refined and trained. You just go on a course and then it's yours forever—but then, how would you turn it off?) And once upon a time these aliens made far too many ordinary television sets, and they've come here to flog them all off on Earth. Perhaps Andrew Myers was an alien . . . But more likely he was on some kind of stupid back-to-work scheme.

'I'll see if I can find the application,' he said. Liz grinned. It was possible that Jim understood what she thought at him. It was possible, in that it could never be disproved.

'Come on then,' she said aloud. 'Let's have a look at it.'

Andrew Myers' smile seemed too big for his face as he nodded in Jim's direction—and that's because he's *learned* how to do it, see? So as to get on with the people on Earth and establish a good business relationship. But where he comes from, of course, they don't smile to be friendly; they stick their tongues out (which are white), or fart, or something like that . . .

'Lost to the world,' Andrew Myers said and blushed.

The carpet in the shop was very soft; the air tingled with static and sung in a high-pitched hum. 'Like the sound bats make,' Liz whispered, 'so they can avoid things. Or find them. Where's ours?' All around, colour screens large and small showed people mouthing words, their flesh tints varying from sepia to salmon according to the set, their backgrounds water-logged green, lemony yellow, studio red. There were cowboys, lovers, a cookery demonstration, a man walking around a cathedral, a busload of children on a school trip. Liz wandered from screen to screen, testing the controls. There was no doubt that the one she'd picked was the best: the colours looked just a little brighter than life, and its enormous screen was a huge window to another world. On top, a cardboard sign announced that one year's TV licence came free with the set. She turned up the sound and crouched down in front of it.

'Look,' she said to Jim, her lips brushing his ear. She wished the lights in the shop were dimmer, but still . . . The cowboy film was reaching a climax. At such low volume the whine of the shootout sounded strangely benign. She noticed suddenly that she was feeling a warm, melting kind of happiness.

It seemed to her that the most intimate thing that could be was to sit together with someone while the same pictures and words poured through four eyes and four ears into two previously separate minds; like sharing blood from the same heart, like being Siamese twins. She'd done it with Grammy, and a little with Henry Kay, and now she and Jim would share the biggest set available. It would stand in the front room, and they'd set the cushions in a heap before it; hour after hour, year after year, they'd watch together. There was talking but it didn't matter because they weren't talking to you. And if it broke down Bettahire would exchange or fix it, guaranteed . . . She stroked Jim's head, glanced at his face: he *was* watching too, as a troupe of riders swooped triumphant down the side of a hill, dust flying in the desert air, their horses snickering and rolling their eyes.

'Mrs Meredith?' She looked up at the alien and smiled. 'Please come to the desk.' He smoothed a form flat. 'This is a bit awkward. I'm afraid we can't hire you a set,' he said.

'Why?'

'I can't really say: it's not in my hands.' He raised them briefly, puppet-like, as if to prove what he'd said, and the cuffs of his shirt slipped down his wrists. 'But if you look at the application . . .' He turned it the right way up for her to read. 'You've chosen our most expensive model. At the same time— you see—' He pointed at the boxes with his pen, one by one, leaving a red dot by the side of each. Bank account: no. Credit card: no. Employment: none. House owner: no. Income: less than five thousand per annum. Previous address: none. Method of payment: cash, weekly. 'From our point of view . . . For instance, if you'd remained at your previous address for over a year—'

'I can afford it. I don't spend much on anything else. And I did,' said Liz. 'I did live at the same place for two years.' The shop seemed suddenly very hot. The whine of the television sets grew louder; it was a microscopic drill, boring slow but sure through the membranes that made ears into drums.

'Well, that might make a difference, and it might help if you applied for a *smaller* set.' He gestured at a row of them. 'They're less than half the rental and less than half the risk for us. Write a personal letter to the manager, explaining the circumstances.'

'Can't I see the manager now?'

Someone waiting behind Liz sighed irritably. Andrew Myers shrugged, indicating with the movement of his eyes that the gesture was supposed to appease both of them.

'Writing would be best.'

'Come on,' Liz said. The words were intended for Jim, but she was still looking at Andrew Myers. 'Risk? What do they think I'm going to do with it? Leave the country? Piss on it?' Her voice, habitually a mumble, grew loud and hard, shocked her. She had no control over it. The words forced themselves out like bullets. And a slow whimper rose from Jim, whose face was turned inwards and down so that she could see only the top of his head. He held his pitch for a while, then let it tail slowly and erratically down the scale. It had a hopeless persistence about it that seemed almost inhuman.

With a new breath he began again—seeking the lost sound, overshooting it, finding it briefly, then running out of breath again. Like a siren going wrong; as if the batteries powering it were dying spasmodically, cutting out, flaring up. It was her fault for losing control of her words.

Halfway to the door Liz stopped. She rocked Jim and pushed the damp hair from his face. His eyes glittered. He was still crying, but fainter now. 'There's no reason why we shouldn't stay a bit,' she thought, 'if you want.' She turned back.

The programmes had changed. There was a general knowledge quiz for schoolchildren. All six of them, Liz noted through the distraction of her misery, were wearing glasses and ties.

'Stupid parrots,' she said, still too loudly. A man was digging a hole in the middle of a lawn. Other men were playing rugby. The pictures seemed suddenly grainy and unrealistic. 'These are crap,' she muttered, striding past them. 'People are crap. I hate everyone. Except for you.'

On their set a couple were kissing in a kitchen with a pot of soup boiling over behind them on the stove. 'Did I tell you about *The Kissing Disease?*' she said, trying to settle down. 'A good film.' The pan was smouldering. Soon it would burst into flames. Jim was quiet, though he smelled sour.

The image froze. It was an advertisement for smoke detectors. Liz snorted. Then at last a film began, an old one in black and white. A turreted castle was perched on top of a sheer cliff. The title appeared in Gothic script: *Crusade*. The credits began. Point of view switched to inside the castle. Someone was looking out from an arrow slit. In the distance a thin line of cavalry inched across the plain. The column was headed by two heavily built men in chain mail. Between them, roped to his horse, was a bedraggled dark-skinned man in a loincloth with tears streaming down his face. His eyes were fixed on the exact window from which the previous long shot had been taken. Liz nudged the volume up.

'I don't trust him,' one of the two leaders said to the other. The picture, she thought, could do with a bit more contrast.

'Can I help you?' said Andrew Myers.

'Just looking,' said Liz, her eyes fixed on the screen.

'Please don't fiddle with the controls.' In the castle the watcher stepped back from the window: a woman, olive-skinned with oval eyes. The light caught her face.

'I think it's him!' she whispered.

'Look.' Andrew Myers crouched down, took the remote from Liz's hand and grasped her elbow. 'Please get up. This isn't your lounge at home.'

'Thank God,' said Liz, but very quietly. She folded her other arm protectively around Jim.

'You're going to have to leave the premises.'

Premises? Liz thought. Don't let it get out of hand, she warned herself. Her heart raced. She wanted to shout: Call these premises? I call them an arsehole!

'Don't give me trouble, please. I've been here since seven this morning,' Andrew Myers said suddenly. 'The cleaner's sick. I've got to stay until six-thirty because it's Thursday.'

'Traitor!' the woman in the castle sobbed huskily. There was a fanfare of trumpets, abruptly curtailed as Andrew Myers switched off the set. Liz wanted to cry. Then she wanted to hit Andrew Myers, to shoot her fist straight into the soft triangle of flesh beneath the lower ribs, the bit that went in and out so horribly with each breath he took. He'd fold up. They were all brain and no brawn, these beings from elsewhere . . . It was getting out of hand all right.

Stop me! she thought at Jim, as hard as she could. Stop me! And it worked. She stood very slowly, and adjusted Jim's position.

She noticed that Andrew Myers was wearing a string vest under his shirt. He was not any kind of alien, not in that. Just a boy. Liz turned her back, kept her eyes only on Jim as she wove through the gibbering television sets to the door. She'd walked the length of the High Street before she realised where her legs were taking her.

'It's quite a way,' she muttered to Jim. 'You're getting so heavy.' She turned right, up Kimberlake Avenue. The pavement was wide, and bordered on the roadside with grass, the houses set back, detached and imposing. Each one was different, though all were well maintained. Some had brick walls five feet high and big gates in front, some had banks of earth planted now with daffodils, others savagely cropped hedges of box or cotoneaster. One even had broken glass on top of a brick wall. One had a circular window in the eaves, behind it a curtain half drawn; it looked like an eye. At the very top of the avenue stood an ornately gabled house that had been rendered and painted in a muddy red that reminded Liz of drying blood. There, Station Road forked to the left, descending sharply. At the end of it was the wooden structure of the station, brighter than Liz remembered it. The window frames had been painted white and there were brand new roof tiles that didn't look quite real. A car park was being built in what used to be a piece of wasteground demarcated by a half-collapsed chestnut paling fence. But on the other side of the building site the path was still there, just. She picked up a discarded length of timber to deal with the brambles, and hurried towards it.

The sky, clear all day, was gathering pinkish clouds. Perhaps an hour and half's light remained. To their right was a cutting for the first half mile or so, the railway some twelve feet off below. On the other side the undergrowth sloped gently up to a row of fences that separated railway property from people's back gardens. There were sheds, compost heaps and greenhouses, here and there a short row of trees, their first leaves small and fresh, planted as a screen. Gradually the slope grew gentler, and the path tended closer to the line. The brambles, sprouting new growth, were higher than before, making it impossible to see very far ahead. Liz's feet remembered the way. 'Not far,' she told Jim.

'Thanks for not making a fuss. It's downhill now.' She quickened her pace as she drew closer to the sidings, where suddenly everything flattened, opened up. She stopped.

There was no trace of the carriages. The ground on which they had stood was indistinguishable from the rest: a scattering of pinkish chippings over earth, spring weeds thrusting vigorously through.

'Oh,' Liz said dully, to herself, forgetting for a moment that Jim was even there. Something in her sagged. 'Wouldn't cut much ice with Bettahire as a previous address.'

Did they have to clear it all away? She was sure the carriages hadn't been put back into service; they were far too old. Had they been taken apart, the useful bits saved? Or had they just been smashed and burned? Or maybe even just moved somewhere else? She walked slowly on, head lowered, examining the ground. There must be something left.

'You can see where we had the fire,' she said quietly. Not for long though. The black patches would, by summer, be greener than the rest, the surrounding ring of breeze blocks a mystery. How things burned! she thought, seeing for a moment brilliant orange flames, head-high, against the night sky, hearing them snap at the air. She walked on. There were other signs as well, things that had escaped the clean-up: a pair of blue oil drums that someone had thought could be used to collect rain water from the carriage roofs, a wizened scarf she remembered seeing around a woman's neck, a scattering of plastic bread crates, some of them charred. And where her carriage used to be were the two sleepers it had used to rest on: almost a foot in section, the timber dark in its oily coating of preservative. She sat down on one of them, facing the lines. She untied the sling, unbuttoned her coat and cardigan, and slipped Jim inside so he could feed.

The carriages were the best place she had ever found herself to live. There were six of them. She had slipped through the fence for no particular reason, and made her way about a mile along the embankment on the thin path bordered with leafless brambles. Winter was drawing in. At that time the line was under threat of closure, and the trains very rare. It was dusk. Nobody else was about, just a few foxes scampering across the track. The carriages were set out in a row like houses. She'd walked through them one by one. It was strange to be in a train without hearing the noise it made: her footsteps sounded unnaturally loud.

Five of them were first-class carriages, divided into little rooms. Inside, there were spotted mirrors and wrinkled oblong pictures in frames. The sixth, set slightly apart from the rest, was different: part of it had been a kitchen galley, though none of the equipment was left, and the rest was divided between an area with plastic benches and tables and another with padded seats, tables and luggage racks. She liked it best, sat down and rolled herself a thin cigarette before she decided to stay.

The carriages, resting on their massive wooden sleepers, travelled slowly through the seasons: the dried undergrowth around the sidings grew wet, then rotten, then disappeared beneath thick snow that banked up into deep drifts on the windward side, making those doors unusable. The path on the embankment became icy and Liz's shoes were worn smooth, but she knew it by heart and rarely slipped. In the streets beyond, cars were freezing overnight and lonely people died in front of meagre fires, their veins freezing like unlagged water-pipes. The high road was packed with couples and families and school children in uniform, clouded with their many breaths. If she'd stayed at home, Liz would have been one of these.

She begged. Money seemed to last longer now that she was settled. The winter after Grammy's death was the first winter in which Liz didn't feel the cold—or rather, she felt it but liked it, because beneath a skin tightened with cold she felt her own warmth more clearly. She imagined herself as a solid shape, drawn with a firm line against white; often she sat on the steps with the carriage door open and just watched the snow fall. Overnight it buried the line, so that she might almost have been looking out on fields.

It reminded her of a film she had once seen, where there was a vast kingdom of ice and snow. There were packs of wolves and pine trees and a pale princess who rode through her empty kingdom in a sleigh drawn by albino wolves. She wore white furs and sped by, then disappeared, blending with the snow which covered her tracks as soon as they were made. She couldn't remember the story, just that. That winter was beautiful. Liz spent the whole of it alone. Her hair grew long. It was good to be somewhere safe.

In spring, just as she was getting bored with it, others started to come. Most of them were around her age, though one or two of the men were older. Some of them brought dogs and motorbikes. She showed them how to remove the carriage seats and extract the foam for use as a mattress. At night they built big fires, scouring the embankment for fuel. Liz slipped into their circle, and took the bottle as it was passed around. No questions were asked. People sang and cooked. Sometimes there were fights, but they never lasted long and she could always walk away. There was talk of a network of places like the carriages, which spread all over Europe or even further afield. A beach in Mexico where you could sleep in hammocks in the open air, and a single pound would last for weeks: though of course you needed the fare to get there. Sometime soon they'd all up sticks and go to Greece perhaps, or Corsica.

Liz invited Henry Kay up into her carriage. He was quiet, only talking when he was high, and then he didn't mind if she listened or not. She reckoned she would have to share anyway, so she might as well choose the person. Also, he had a television with a tiny screen not six inches square. It ran on batteries. Often they sat together and watched it late at night. At first she'd thought they liked the same things, but really it was just that he didn't much care what they watched.

Henry Kay grew cold when the second winter came, and somehow no one had got to Greece or Mexico. He'd lost weight and began to take risks without knowing it. His teeth chattered and he said none of him was ever warm, however many covers he had. He cried when he asked Liz to let him sleep next to her. There in the pile of covers and foam on the carriage floor, they grew warm. Henry Kay felt under her clothes. His hands were rough from the cold and chopping wood but his more intimate flesh was smooth and slid easily inside her.

That first time it was nice; afterwards sometimes not, but she never complained. She didn't want him to try and please her; she didn't try and please him back. In this way, she thought, she could keep faith with Grammy's command, without being absolutely lonely. But deep down she knew she was cheating. Now and then he offered her powders and liquids which brought her a distant kind of happiness, a sense of omnipotence—like being the princess on the sleigh herself, instead of the one watching. But, for the same reasons, she never asked for it. The ties that bound lay all around, just waiting to tighten up the first time she made a mistake.

Henry Kay left suddenly, taking his miniature television with him. Some people called him a bastard for leaving Liz, her belly filling slowly out. She didn't see it that way. She thought how she had been a fool, and decided, quickly and without fuss, that none of it should ever happen again. Instead, as the baby grew week by week inside her, she practised her skill in forgetting. She forgot each separate day as it passed into night; buried it in snow and began again in the morning. She formulated a new command for herself: *take each day as it comes.* It was just the kind of thing Grammy might have said.

It was an angry, hot summer. The rubbish began to smell. Someone tried to ride a motorbike along the path and slipped down onto the track. His leg was trapped under the bike and no one saw him until it was too late. Residents complained about stolen milk, the flies, the bonfires and the noise. With autumn, a health inspector came, and an overalled workman nailed a notice to quit on each one of the carriages. Some people left, but Liz just tore hers down. It was only a piece of paper, she remembered saying.

Finally the carriages were cleared in an early-morning police raid that was shown on local TV. There were three arrests. Most people got away by crossing the lines, but Liz, at the end of her eighth month by then, slept soundly through the whole thing on her pile of second-hand eiderdowns, woke only when torches shone on her face. When they saw, they grew suddenly gentle and drove her to the hospital handcuffed to a WPC.

'It'll be warmer there, love, and you can wash that hair,' the WPC had said. 'Look at it that way.' And there it was: a Silver Lining, rustling in the dark.

And another: she'd reached eighteen and no one could send her anywhere, nor tell her what to do. They could ask things but they couldn't make her stay. As soon as the baby was born she could walk straight out of the hospital and go to Greece. She could leave the baby behind, or she could take it with her. She wasn't sure . . .

'So,' Liz said to Jim with her back to where all this had happened, looking down the line, 'here you began. Perhaps there are *still* people here,' she continued lightly. 'People who are better at hiding than I was. People who manage not to be seen by the rest of us . . . I saw some of them once in a film—people who lived in old tunnels underground—but there might be all kinds, everywhere. At night, if you cover your hands and face and sit somewhere quiet and still for several hours, you might spot them. Figures creeping by, close to a wall. You might hear voices and not be able to tell where they're coming from, however hard you look. You might see the flare of a match, then think you were mistaken. A group of tramps that have a van, and you might see that sometimes, driving slowly without lights on one of the minor roads, the engine muffled and quiet like a sewing machine. Or you might see one of the signs they leave for each other chalked on the ground, or bits of skin and fur, the remains of one of their meals, or the dryness left after a secret fire has been cleared away. But mostly they'd eat raw things, to save the risk. And you might see a bit of earth that looked somehow new, even though the stones are on the top, same as elsewhere, and the weeds are beginning to grow. And that's one of their graves. Ssh, now. Ssh.'

It was moving from dusk to real dark now, all the contrast changed, so that the dome of Jim's head seemed more silver than pale. The ground was beginning to vibrate with the insistent rhythm of a train. It transmitted itself up to Liz's knees, was muffled in the thicker flesh of her thighs, found again in the wood she sat on. 'The down-train,' she said. 'Every forty-five minutes.' At first the hiss and rattle of its coming was something which she imagined, deduced from the feeling, and then came an instant when she could be absolutely sure that she was hearing and not remembering it. At that moment the past seemed so very real. She moved Jim to the other side. He sucked hard on the new nipple, causing a sudden twist of feeling at the neck of her womb, and although it wasn't pain a lump grew in her throat and a soft pressure behind her eyes. The carriages and their inhabitants seemed to breathe gently about her—she could hear them even through the raucous panting of the train as it passed—and although she couldn't see them, she sensed that when the rattling chain of yellow lights had streaked past their shapes would gradually emerge, the still, solid rectangles and the moving figures picked out in the firelight. But when even the last faint tremor of the train had gone the thing she felt inside remained, invisible. She sat in an absence, the after-image of something gone. Without realising, she had begun to cry.

'Silly—' she whispered, then broke off. The sound of footsteps was very clear. 'Who's there?' she called, pulling her cardigan together and twisting round.

'*Who's asking?*' a voice answered quickly. The footsteps stopped. There was a sound halfway between a snort and a laugh. Liz's eyes picked over the darkness, finding the man's shape at last, half hidden against the higher ground behind him. He was standing about twenty feet away, between her and the path. She could feel him looking at her as hard as she was at him; she could hear a slight grinding sound as he shifted his weight on the cindery ground. The fact that he hadn't moved on could mean only danger. It was wrong, she knew suddenly, to ask who was there; it was possible he hadn't even seen her when she spoke.

But somehow she knew he had. Perhaps he hadn't realised she was a woman. He'd only seen her back, in the dark. But there again, she somehow knew that even if he wasn't sure, he wanted her to be one. Should she have said something casual, mumbled, 'Evening,' the way two people walking dogs do when they pass in the street, pulling a quick smile then looking back at the ground or saying, 'Here!' In any case, it was best, she calculated, not to say anything more. She stood, then paused, relaxing her grip on Jim just a little. Thank God, she thought, amazed: he's *asleep!*

At what she calculated to be a normal pace, she made for the path, keeping as far away from the man as she could. Stones on the ground seemed to press right through to the soles of her feet, inciting her, against her judgement, to run. As the sound of one step ended and the next began she veered between feeling utterly disembodied and being nothing but insides—neither more nor less than her own heartbeat. The man was large and quite tall, and as she progressed he shifted slightly on the spot so as to keep her in view. She was drawing a circle, with him at its centre: or he was drawing it, sending her around on a string . . . And any minute, she must strike out.

'Stop!' he called. She obeyed. 'Come here!' She stayed where she was, waiting to run, but desperate not to, yet. A few seconds dragged, one to the next. 'What's *your* name then?' The man's voice was scornful. It had been wrong to ask 'Who's there?' All speaking was wrong, mistaken; look where it led, to traps and bindings, even something as simple as that. But should she answer now, though, to keep him at bay? Once you start you've got to go on? Perhaps so long as she answered he'd stay where he was? Perhaps talking they'd stand here forever, caught in the moment before whatever was to be happened, happening now slowly, in words—

'What's that you're carrying?' he said, and took a single step forwards.

'It's my baby.' Her voice sounded calm, though also as if it belonged to someone much older. 'Goodbye.' She stepped out of the circle as she spoke, and turned her back on him. After three or four paces the man began walking too, his steps falling between hers. Together they were like a large animal, something fierce and wounded with a limp.

'I bet it's not,' he said quietly. 'Babies cry.' Liz reached the path, the point where running became feasible, as he was unlikely to know it so well as she did. She drew breath sharply.

'Don't,' he warned. Liz shifted her grip on Jim, holding him tight with her right arm across his back, her hand tucked between his legs—and flung the other arm out for balance as she propelled herself forward. Jim's legs began almost immediately to slip down. If she fell she'd crush him. He woke—crying, not his usual cry, but for the first time full-throated and vigorously like other babies; suddenly, as if he'd just encountered the world for the first time and wanted to blast it away. His sobs and his breath came, shaken out of him in gasps like hers and in time to her steps. Her feet glanced off the path. Brambles brushed across her but there was no pain—she could tell from the small dragging sound they made as they let go of her coat, the very faint tearing on the skin of her face and hands. She ran by feel, her eyes fixed on the darkness ahead, her ears alert to what was behind. She could tell the exact moment the man gave up, but she ran all the way to Kimberlake Avenue.

The Three Compasses lurked just behind the gasworks. The lower panes of the windows had been painted, as in a betting shop; cheaper than curtains, Frank supposed. People scratched them with keys. It was his weekly night off and he always spent it here. The public bar was huge and dwarfed the people in it.

Hanging from the void of a towering ceiling, untouched—unseen—for generations was a sixties light-fitting consisting of eight chunky wooden arms which curved ever so slightly downwards. Some were capped with red cube-like shades, some were bare bulbs, some nothing. Only the bar, with its own lights, and the colour television propped high above the door to the gents, were clearly visible. Below the dado rail was a zone of embossed wallpaper painted in cream gloss, hastily wiped at here and there, which only made it look dirtier.

Frank would rather it hadn't been so bad. In the old days some kind of gentleman's club might have served the purpose, but so far as Frank knew there were none of these in town. Besides, he had a horror of joining things, and the lack of curiosity suited him well; people were more or less content just to know his name: 'Frank,' without the Styne—he didn't want that known. Though their letters were an encouragement, he had never actually met one of his fans and didn't want to run the risk.

'Another one, Frank?' He drank Scotch, which set him a little apart: 'Don't get much of it, do you?'

'It's stronger stuff,' he replied. The other man—eldest of a pair of brothers and known as number one—grinned. At least I'm clean, Frank thought. Number one smelled of sour sweat, his face glistened as if every pore were working overtime. A rag of greying hair had been flattened across his scalp, stuck there, flat and damp. He smoked a thin roll-up and all the features of his face seemed to be gathered about it, drawn towards the mouth and crammed into a narrow horizontal zone between the expanse of forehead and scalp above and the encroaching beard below.

'Like it strong, do you, Frank?' His teeth were so yellow that they were almost brown. Frank drank whisky because he liked the feel of it, spreading slowly to his stomach, and even more subtly across the membranes that separated nose from mouth. Also, it didn't necessitate going to the urinals.

'What are you doing with that beard?' he said to number one as the drink arrived.

'Comes off on a Monday,' said number one, rubbing it with relish.

'Looks like an old pro's cunt,' said number two, sitting heavily between them, turning to Frank. He was the younger, clean shaven and he had a full head of hair, longish, combed straight back over the crown of his head.

'Doesn't it?'

'How would I know?' Frank smiled, sipped a little of his whisky as he watched the two brothers laugh at his joke. Without the sound, he thought, you'd think they were afflicted by some awful pain, such as someone applying electric shocks to the soles of their feet. When it was over their faces subsided into heavy vacancy. Only the eyes moved as they and Frank watched the barman, because they could think of nothing else to say. The barman's complexion was extraordinarily pale, mottled with soft, fawn-coloured freckles; it would have been beautiful on a shy and slender boy out of doors, blinking in a patch of light under a canopy of trees, but there, on a fat folded face caught in the yellow glare of electric light, which made the pale lashes and brows all but vanish, it was grotesque. The barman moved sedately, as if his protruding belly contained something precious, and when he reached for a packet of tobacco, he supported himself on the counter with the other hand.

'What sort of day was it out?' he asked as he turned, catching their stares and looking at them with watery pale blue eyes.

'Horrible,' said number two. 'Hot as hell.'

'The Greenhouse business is to blame.' The barman jerked his head at a newspaper lying at the back of the bar. 'Be like the Costa Del here in a few years' time.'

'Good thing,' said number two. 'We can all retire.'

Frank felt he had just a little in common with the barman, in that both of them worked indoors and had smoothish hands. Most of the men who used this pub worked outside, on the railway, in construction. No one had ever asked him, straight out, what he did. Perhaps they thought of him as someone technically unemployed, but who arranged or kept an eye on things just outside the law.

'You shouldn't use spray cans and everyone'll have to get their cars converted.'

'No harm in beer though, is there?' said number two, and Frank nodded at the barman to fill them up.

'They say it's what causes these famines,' the barman persisted, eyes on the filling glasses before him. Often he tried like this to begin some kind of conversation. Time and time again Frank had watched him give up. He himself feared the complications of joining in more than he anticipated the benefits. Besides, it was not a subject he knew much about—what he had on his mind right now he had to keep to himself. Either they'd think he was mad or they'd try to stop him.

'Desert's spreading, you see,' the barman elaborated as he reached up to the optic.

'Well that's cobblers,' said number one, 'isn't it. Over-breed, don't they.'

'Ah well . . .' the barman sighed, and set the glasses down. He slotted a tape into the cassette player. As if on cue, the rush began. A tight knot of customers formed around Frank and the two others at the bar.

In the avenue there were people and cars about. Liz sat under a streetlamp on a bench which bore a tarnished plaque in memory of someone's departed wife. Both of them swam in sweat; Jim had been sick, and the streetlamp illuminated a scratch across the top of his head. She shivered, took his hat from her pocket and slipped it on. He whimpered as she refastened the sling and wrapped him tightly inside her coat, sopping wet, acrid. Headlights streaked across them. Behind them, the blood-red house had lost its colour, become just a shape, light seeping around the edges of curtains and blazing out from the porch.

It was the time when wives collected their commuting husbands. From inside the cars they peered out, their eyes fastening briefly on Liz and Jim, then torn away by the movement home. It would be nice, she thought, if one of them stopped and offered a lift; just that, no fuss. She would say yes. But no one did.

'Okay,' she whispered after a while, easing herself up.

Every muscle in her body ached. When she began walking, something hurt in her back every time her right foot touched the ground. 'At least it's downhill. We'll get to the junction, then we can have a rest.'

By the time they reached Annerly Road the ache, the drag of Jim's weight in her shoulders and the heaviness of her legs had been joined by a fierce pressure in her bowels and bladder. There was no part of her that didn't insist on being noticed, again and again. She considered standing in the road, stopping a car, and asking for a lift. But Annerly Road was grander even than Kimberlake Avenue, the houses old and all but hidden behind mature trees, the road humped and subject to a 20 mph speed limit as if out of respect. Very few cars passed through and those that did, lumbering carefully over the humps in the road then turning into gravelled drives and crunching slowly into silence, seemed ghostly and unapproachable. It was as if they were walking through a time before proper traffic existed. The people in the screened and shadowy houses, 'Deepdene,' 'Tadhurst,' 'Sandymere,' were marooned here, between the SLOW signs at either end of the road. They couldn't go beyond, for then they would suddenly turn to dust and their houses would crumble down behind them in silence and slow motion.

'We'll get to the next entrance,' Liz said. There were no street-lights to go by. 'Loughton,' it said. She leaned for a while on one of the posts that marked it, thick as a railway sleeper but planed smooth, then slipped behind the fence and the hedge which spilled outwards over it. No lights showed through the trees. A thick layer of dead leaves collapsed softly beneath her feet and new living ones whispered faintly above. The trees were densely planted, their lower branches tangled. There was no point in wandering about. She loosened Jim's sling and squatted, empty-ing herself violently on the ground. After, it took some time to recover. Her legs shook, as if the train were running again.

'We stink,' she told Jim, 'the pair of us. Let's get to the next corner.' Draymuir Road was lit, narrower, its houses more uni-form though still large. Soon they'd be back among the ter-races, home.

'We'll get up to there.' A hundred yards or so ahead was the solid shape of a builder's skip. Perhaps someone had died. It seemed to be full of furniture and household debris: sev-eral ripped suitcases, wads of damp papers and books, a tangle of sodden curtains, carpet sweepers, a bicycle, rusting cans of paint, broken chairs, cupboard doors, washing line, an electric fire, an ironing board. And right on top, towards the middle of the pile, was perched a 24-inch television set. She couldn't quite believe it. She stood, stock still, staring. Then she wrapped Jim in her coat, set him on the verge, hoisted herself into the skip.

'What a Lining! Nearly new!' she called back, pulling it bit by bit towards the edge. The plug was still attached. 'Even if there is something wrong, it can probably be fixed! Getting it down is the problem . . .' She lowered herself carefully, reached up. She slid her arms around its base, braced herself and took the weight gradually onto her chest. Only then it occurred to her how difficult it would be to get home.

'Could hide it in one of these gardens—get you home first—come back later—' she twisted her neck to see Jim—'or even tomorrow.' The balanced TV careened suddenly forwards then and slammed into her chest, knocking her to the ground. A second after impact the screen shattered, the sound of it muffled by the bulk of the set and the grass verge beneath, and Jim began to cry. His foot was caught beneath her shoulder.

By nine o'clock the Three Compasses had lost its transitory trade and settled down at about half full. Frank had drunk two singles and two doubles and was playing darts with Brian Farrar, whom the others were avoiding. Brian, Frank thought, as he watched him eyeing up the board, was very much an instance of the grown ugly. Examining his features carefully and using some imagination it was possible to see that once he could have been a good-looking child. The proportions were large, like the rest of him, but near perfect, the nose straight and sculpted. But whereas many of the drinkers in the Three Compasses suffered from excrescences of flesh, Brian suffered from spareness. The planes of his face were flat and blank, the lips were thin, the eyes blood rimmed. He looked, Frank thought, as if he might be a copy of a human being: technically perfect, but in some deadly way inanimate. Everything about him spelled spite. Two lines crossed his forehead, deepening.

'Christ!' he spat as his first dart clattered down the face of the board. 'Fuck!' as the second fastened itself outside the circle. When the last dropped as well, he turned to Frank and said, 'Drink?'

'Scotch. Thanks.' Frank thought how he could all too easily win the contest and that wouldn't be a good idea with Brian the way he was. He moved to follow him to the bar, but Brian barked, 'Stay here, man. Here.' He thrust a pint-mug of beer in Frank's direction. 'Better for you.'

Frank squared up to the board. The mug was uncomfortably heavy, and there was nowhere close by to put it except the floor. He felt Brian's gaze, huge and malevolent, as a thin stream of beer ran over the mug's rim onto the Three Compasses' well-trodden carpet.

'You're spilling it,' Brian said, as Frank put his lips to the rim of the glass. It was foul; Frank marvelled at the quantity of it drunk, every night, in the Three Compasses and all the pubs in town. He noticed a tremor in his hands. It should, he hoped, help him to miss. But all the same the first dart landed respectably in the doubles.

'Seen the paper?' he found himself saying, turning to Brian, swallowing another mouthful of beer as he forced his eyes to look into those of the other man.

Brian tipped his head back and drained his mug before replying. 'No. Drink up. I want to get pissed.'

Frank drank as much as he could bear, flung the other two darts at the board, managed to drain the rest. 'My round,' he said, without daring to look at the score.

'No,' said Brian, taking the glass. 'You haven't marked up the score,' he said when he returned.

Frank pulled his darts from the board and secretly glanced at his watch as he chalked the figures up: almost three quarters of an hour to go. He gulped some beer.

'Shit!' said Brian. Veins stood out on his neck. 'Fucking shit!' he glanced sidelong at Frank, who hated him and also hated himself.

Any moment, the situation could explode. There was nothing to do but drink the beer, even before Brian made him. He swallowed and swallowed. It was, he sensed, some way of identifying with Brian, mollifying him by doing the same. And drinking seemed to slow down time, to postpone the inevitable. He knew that the third dart would miss too; he knew that Brian knew it, and that no expletive would be big enough. But drinking also prolonged each moment into a sort of agony, and suddenly the Three Compasses' stinking urinals seemed an attractive proposition.

'Going for a piss,' he said, turning his back on Brian and walking across the bar, under the television and into the gents, still holding the empty mug.

No one else was there. The dribble of water seemed inordinately peaceful, almost pastoral. Frank sighed and placed the mug on the ledge of the small window, which was glazed in wired glass. A tiny sliver at the top formed an opening light, which was propped wide for ventilation—not enough, however, to cope with the stench of the blocked toilet in the only cubicle. Never mind, thought Frank, as he unzipped himself. At least he'd escaped and it was a real relief . . . The door banged, and Brian was beside him.

Frank stared fixedly at his own urine, willing it to flow for ever.

Brian said, 'You married, Frank?'

'No,' he replied.

'Don't.'

Frank noticed that Brian's piss was a different colour from his. Paler, but also slightly cloudy. It stopped and then started again.

Brian said, 'I'm in real trouble, mate. Real trouble. Social Services, bitch. And the thing is, will she stand behind me? That's the nub of it.'

'Wh—' Frank began tentatively. He registered that this was a different Brian; that he was now at least temporarily safe. But what hit him with greater force was that Brian would appear to have been able to get a woman: get *married*. Always he'd assumed that the men who came here were like him in that respect. Brian was an ugly man—grown ugly, rather than born, but ugly nonetheless. And there seemed little doubt that his inside was at least as bad as his outside. Both of them had finished, but stood there, staring at the wall.

'Don't ask,' said Brian. 'Just don't ask. I'm just telling you. That's why I can't hit the board. I'm going home.'

Frank zipped himself up and waited a few minutes after Brian's departure before stepping back into the bar. Numbers one and two turned to face him as he emerged.

'Here,' said number one. 'What happened?'

'Nothing,' Frank said. The pair of them looked at him with a mixture of disbelief and respect.

'Probably go home and slap up the wife,' said number one.

Number two's head was in his hands. His elbow slipped. His breath rattled. All the lights went suddenly on. The barman slipped from behind the counter and moved from table to table collecting glasses, and Frank set out for Onley Street.

'Last time I go there,' he muttered to himself. He had been very scared of Brian. Not just for himself, but for his plan as well. The plan protected him, but he in turn had to protect it . . . It felt almost beyond him. A mission.

As he turned into the street he saw the girl from next door, hurrying from the other end. It was an odd time of night to be out with a baby.

'Hello!' he called. 'Okay?' She said nothing. Was his speech slurred? Maybe there was something wrong with her. Maybe she was deaf and dumb. Or plain rude. She slipped straight into her house; she must have had the keys ready in her hand.

'Bitch,' he muttered. You should watch out, he thought, with people like me about! It tickled him.

A corner of the picture of what would happen to Katie Rumbold had come loose and folded over. He stuck it back. He took a pill—just one, because of the drink—and went straight to bed. He was reading *No Forgiveness,* one of his best, according to fans.

> Dear Mr Styne,
>
> I've written to you before. Every one of your books is better than the last. I got my girl Laura to read *No Forgiveness,* that bit on page 233, well she wouldn't and so I read it aloud and she was SICK. Right there and then. I can't describe things the way you do, but I thought she was going to choke. Her face went bright red and her eyes watered and then out it came. Strong stuff! Keep it up, Mr Styne.

Indeed he would. Dr Villarossa would be present at the birth, and at the death as well. She would wear an oyster-coloured linen suit by Chanel and fine red leather gloves, when she came to claim her own.

Liz took Jim's foot gently in her hands and tried to feel through the softness for the bones. The minute toes with their soft crescent nails poked from a bag of flesh which obscured everything from the ankle down. At every touch the cry came again. With it, his face burst into angry life, and Liz felt as if she were grasping an electric fence; again and again the expectation of its shock, worse each time until she could no longer bear the nausea it produced. After each wail his face closed down again. It was as if pain has summoned him from somewhere very far away, and when it was over he went back.

'Is that the way we could talk?' she said, scared. There was no answer. There never would be. Very gently she stroked the foot. Again, he cried. She held Jim still and stared out of the uncurtained bedroom window, fixing her eyes on the smallest star she could see, until it stopped.

'Oh, what do you want me to do . . .' She could hear nothing except his breathing. She set him to feed. He sucked hungrily, but the damaged foot, poking out of the bundle she'd wrapped him in, haunted the edges of her sight. Her voice, low before, rose: 'Do you want me to take you to the hospital?' If she touched the foot he would cry, signalling no. But that would be cheating.

'They'd ask all kinds of questions,' she said. 'They would say it was my fault.' That, too, was cheating. 'It was my fault,' she admitted, 'but they might separate us.' His lips were folded around her nipple. The foot stuck out. His eyes were closing. 'I'll take you if it gets any worse,' she whispered. She removed him carefully, pulled back the covers, set him on the bed and switched out the light. It was so good to lie down. Her ears strained in the silence. It seemed as enormous as the sky. She was relieved to hear Alice's voice.

'Don't—please—tonight I just can't.' There were creaks and shiftings, but the reply was inaudible.

'Did *she* ever not want to?' said Alice. The light went on. Tom didn't answer. Liz saw him lying clenched, foetal, with his eyes shut.

'Please. I need to know what she's like.' Alice began to cry.

'I can't say,' said Tom. 'I've forgotten.'

There were no curtains in Liz's room. Out of doors looked lighter by far than in the room where everything was black and double black in the corners.

'Okay,' said Tom. 'Her name is Andrea. Does that make you feel better?'

'Where does she live?' An answer came, but couldn't be heard.

'What's her phone number?'

The voices grew quieter and quieter. Liz didn't want them to stop. While she waited for the next bit, she searched the sky for the star she had looked at before. Come on, she urged, there must be something more. But everything was quiet, terribly quiet, next door. She wanted to squeeze Jim to her, but she was worried about hurting the foot.

'At least the skin isn't broken,' she whispered. Skin, she dimly remembered from school, was an organ. It died and grew, replacing itself and filling the air with sloughed-off cells. It healed. It was what separated a person off from the air, the world, the universe, but only just. Once she'd cut herself and had spray-on skin from a can. Suppose skin was see-through, like cling-film, or glass. Or that people were born with one skin and that was it. Like clothes, or brains, it had to last you. From day one it was shedding itself, gradually becoming even thinner.

Knowing this, everyone would go about their business very carefully, avoiding washing, wind, sun, chemicals and so on. The parks would be full of mothers yelling at their kids: 'Don't do that! You're wasting your skin! They don't grow on trees, you know!' Some places would wear out first: the tops of your legs, the palms of your hands. Not even men would wear trousers. Eventually, it wouldn't be so much a skin as a net. Like nylon stockings with ladders. It wouldn't last anything like as long as you lived. Once it was gone, you had to go on without, all red and wet. You started another phase, with nothing between you and the world. Some people were impatient to begin, picked the last scraps away. But most were afraid and hung out as long as they possibly could.

'I'm really sorry, Silly-boy,' she whispered as she turned on her side to sleep.

NOT MUCH TO ASK

'You might get jealous,' Annie Purvis said to her husband, Sim. Sim always made himself clear: what he wanted, and what he felt. He was persistent without being unduly aggressive. He was rarely unreasonable: the easiest thing, often, was to agree. But having a baby was not something which she could do just to keep the peace.

'I don't expect so,' he said icily. 'It's not as if I see much of you anyway . . .'

They started and failed to make love. She knew right from the beginning that without the spermicide she'd be as dry as paper. She couldn't find any enthusiasm. It was almost midnight.

'You'll have to make your mind up soon. Time passes.' He made a sound, half grunt half laugh.

I feel so exhausted, now, she thought; how would I be able to manage? Of course, he thinks—

'Listen,' he said. 'Do something for me, will you? This is scarcely the best time to talk about it, is it? Will you please try to get home early tomorrow, just for once? We can eat together, talk before we're tired. Doesn't seem much to ask. After all, if I wanted to spend all my time on my own, I wouldn't have got married.

'It's an instinct,' he said, loudly because he was breathing out a sigh, 'to breed. I work with the evidence of that every day . . .'

'It's not so simple for me—'

He grunted again, this time dismissive. 'Will you?' he said. 'What?'

'Get home early?'

'Yes,' she said. 'I promise.'

Often I forget, she thought, but I do love him. She was more in the other world, the complex nightmare of work, than in the simpler one of home. Sometimes they were hard to separate. Sometimes it seemed that one was mixed into the other, suspended like mud in water. You would need a filter, or a great deal of time, for it to settle out. Which she didn't have.

Brian Farrar had come to see her that morning. Close shaven, his jeans and sweatshirt freshly ironed and exuding a withering smell of soap, he stood in the doorway and glared at her.

'Hello, Brian, where's Jackie?' she'd said.

'Busy.' He sat in one of the two low chairs, leaning right back into it, but keeping his legs close, the way women often do.

'That's a shame, Brian, because really I need to discuss things with you both together. Have you been to see—?'

'No. I went once. But I don't want to go there with everyone thinking I've done it.'

That's not a point in your favour, she thought. Nor is the way you won't look at me. Be fair, she'd told herself; how would I feel? *I wouldn't be in this position,* she thought.

'Well, Brian. You seem a bit nervous. I am too, you know.'

She sat down opposite him.

'You're being paid for it,' said Brian.

'Tea?' He nodded. She hadn't wanted to get it for him. 'Just help yourself.' He didn't move.

'Jackie seems very happy with you, Brian,' she began. 'Have you lived together with someone before?'

'Why?' he said, jerking forwards, elbows on knees. 'Don't beat about the fucking bush.'

'All right. Brian, we're still worried about Clare. There are signs that strongly indicate—'

'Has she said anything happened?' asked Brian.

'Not in so many words.'

'That's because it hasn't,' Brian said, settling back in the chair again. His knees moved fractionally further apart. 'You busybodies, you should leave us alone.'

'Brian, our responsibility is to protect Clare. I would like you to help us with it.'

'Maybe it's someone at the school,' he said carelessly. 'But most likely it's no one at all. You lot are obsessed.'

'One way you could help is by understanding why we want to keep an eye on Clare.'

'So you can brainwash her?'

'So that she can feel safe to say anything she wants to.' *You did it,* Annie Purvis's guts began to scream.

'If I say no, you'll think it's me.'

You can't actually say no, she thought; not yet, not to this. But you can make Jackie—'Why would you want to say no, Brian?'

'Because I know what happens. It'd break Jackie's heart. Have you thought of that?'

'What do you think happens, Brian?' she asked.

'You take the kid into a home.'

'Actually, Brian, we really try not to—'

'And the bloke that's suspected gets arrested and locked up, and probably knifed by the cons.' I wish someone else would do this, she thought. I hate him: his threats, his big hands around a little arm, his fist in Jackie's face—he won't speak now, but *then* he shouts. He doesn't deserve me being fair. Why is he my responsibility? I don't mind caring for Jackie and Clare, but can't someone else deal with *him? No one's a monster*, she had reminded herself, and continued, 'We do try to help everyone concerned, including the—'

'Even if he didn't do it.'

'Did you do it, Brian?'

'Do you think I did?' She waited a moment before speaking. Took in his freshly shaved jaw and pink cheeks, the red-rimmed eyes that would not quite meet hers.

'I have to say I think it's possible. The only way I'd be sure would be if you told me, or if Clare did. And then we could get down to the business of carefully deciding what to do for the best. We'll have to do that anyway, but of course it's best to do it knowing the full facts.'

'She won't.' Brian was very sure of this. Without her noticing it, his legs had slipped and splayed apart; they were completely relaxed now, held in position only by the limits of the fabric that covered them.

'Will you, Brian?'

'What?'

'Tell me.'

'You've made your mind up in any case,' he said, and she had. But what they had wouldn't stand up well in court; she knew he knew.

'Do what you like,' he said. 'I can tell you one thing: Jackie'll stand by me.'

I hope she doesn't, Mrs Purvis thought as the door slammed, ineffectually because of the heavy closing mechanism fitted at the top. She fished inside her blouse to scratch at her chest. The skin there felt greasy and bumped, adolescent. She saw herself and Brian, competing for Jackie's assent to their version of events. Brian offered marriage and a flat. She offered grief.

She ate a chicken mayonnaise sandwich at her desk, and sucked a carton of orange juice. Her diary was open in front of her, each day divided vertically into two sections: on the left hand side in red appointments and things to do; on the right, in blue, things that should have been done by other people to be checked on if she got the time. At the end of her day she would cross off what had been achieved and carry over the rest. Meanwhile she ate with total absorption, ignoring the ringing of her phone and those at other empty desks, oblivious to colleagues rushing in and out. When she was finished, she brushed the crumbs from her diary and tried Liz's number, but the low tone indicated that there was nothing there, still. She made a note to deal with it on Friday and went to see Mandy.

'Something I think about all this,' Mandy said, leaning back in her chair. Her tights were laddered right up the front. 'Here, before it gets to the courts and all that, a man has to prove his innocence to the women. It's a very unusual situation, perhaps the only one of its kind. A tiny loophole. Because most of the time it's the other way round. Look at rape. Look at what they call crimes of passion. Frankly, I wish we had wider powers.' Being not married made it easier, Annie suspected, for Mandy to think and say things like that.

'You don't look well. You want to be careful,' Mandy said, just as she was leaving. 'Strikes me you should cut out anything you can. What are you doing with Jim Meredith and his Mum?'

'I think—'

'She's a sensible young woman. It's tough, but they'll be all right. Wouldn't the clinic be good enough, just to keep an eye? Just a thought,' Mandy said. It was difficult to tell when she was making a suggestion and when she was pulling rank.

That afternoon, Annie Purvis visited the George Meridel Centre. It had only been open a few months, and she had it in mind for Jim. One of the mothers had told her how it had transformed her life. She had thought there was nothing that could be done for her little girl, Sue, who cried constantly, stared at the light and then banged her head if it was turned out. But now she brought her to the Centre three times a week and there was clear progress. There was no such thing as a non-communicating child, the head mistress said. It was just a question of patiently working out *how* to communicate. At home, the family had a rota of twenty-eight people, friends and friends of friends and kids from the grammar school. Someone came every morning and every afternoon for a couple of hours to play with the child. A newsletter was posted to all of them once a week, so that everyone knew everything that had happened and they all worked together. They were going to have a party on Sue's birthday.

'We might have a child with some kind of special needs,' Annie Purvis muttered at Sim, moving to free the chain which was biting into her neck. 'I know it's hypocritical, but I don't think I could take that.' She heaved over to face him, looked briefly at him in the dark before closing her own eyes. She could guess at his expression from the overall shapes: cautious, rather stern. He was her first love and there had been no others and when they first met they sometimes made love three times a day. What had happened to them? The bulk of him was comforting. Right now, the bulk of him, touching her here and there, was also frightening. He so clearly knew what he wanted. She closed her eyes.

'You know that's really not a thing worth worrying about,' he said softly. The cross skated lightly down the curve of her breast. 'The chance is very small. There are tests.' Outside, a gust of wind dragged cans along the street.

'One of my clients,' she said after a while, 'Only a girl, still. Supposed to be at risk, but I don't think so. Her baby looks fine, ever so pretty in fact, but he's quiet, and slow; he's never going to grow up, or not much, mentally. It's one of those things they don't really understand but give a name to all the same.'

'You shouldn't be doing that job,' Sim said, sleepily and automatically.

Yet she did know some things that she wanted. For instance, she wanted Liz and Jim not merely to survive, to pass muster as most do; she wanted them to have everything imaginable. She wanted Liz to be happier than other people, even than herself. Liz and Jim made her think of a painting. Something from another age, done carefully in oils. It grew in the velour of dark behind her eyes, slowly, the way a photograph does in the developing tray. The faces were luminous. The tones of flesh pulled themselves out of the surrounding darkness, a background thick with the dirt of time which stole colour yet bestowed depth. The woman sat, the baby lay across her lap. The baby was naked, male, the small genitals painted as carefully as the features of the face. Both faces were empty of conflict: the child gazed in blank fulfilment at the woman, the woman looked out, her eyes seeing and blind at the same time. She seemed to have no need of the viewer.

Liz and Jim glistened from the dark velvet. Two lucky charms to set against the world—Annie had been watching them for months, and now she plucked them up to hang around her neck. She didn't wake Sim and tell him but she made a conditional kind of decision: if they're all right, she thought, we can go ahead.

I WANT YOU TO SEE

Alice's face was flushed. 'You're out early. Taking her for a walk? Look—would you do me a favour? You might as well walk the way I'm going as anywhere. It's not that far, but I don't want to go on my own. Please. You're *always* going for walks on your own . . . Left at the end, and down the ringroad a bit.' Her voice changed gear: 'By the way, we're getting our gutters redone in the summer and we thought we'd pay for yours, too. It won't make much difference to the cost. Most of it's the scaffolding, would you believe . . . It'll look better if they're both the same.' Just before the corner, she touched Liz's shoulder, stopped and peered down at Jim. 'Such a darling—I'd love to carry her for a bit. Take the weight off you. Please? I'll give her back if she cries.'

She held her arms out. Liz continued, slower, for a couple more paces, then, despite herself, glanced back. What she wanted to do was just walk on and leave the other woman there, her arms out as if pushing an invisible trolley, statue of a shopper turned to stone. But it was impossible. She despaired of herself sometimes. Silly must get sick of her, shilly-shallying around.

'Oh go on,' said Alice. 'Look, she's smiling at me.'

'He's a boy,' blurted Liz, regretting it instantly because she had blown away something that hid them. Speaking was lethal. A tiny chink existed now; prying fingers could widen it.

'Why didn't you say?' Alice closed the gap with two quick steps, and waited while Liz undid the fastenings of the sling. The sudden lightness felt wrong, not quite believable, as if she'd lost a limb. 'I'll just hold him in my arms, like this,' Alice said, a little breathless, bending over.

'Careful of his foot!' Liz snapped. Although the swelling was subsiding and she was sure it was going to be all right, the way he'd cried was something she would never forget.

'What's your name then?' Alice said to Jim. Both women studied the pale face, very delicate and lean for a child, the hair silver, the skin opal, the eyebrows a mere suggestion; if he were a photograph, Jim would seem overexposed.

'Come on then, pretty boy.' Alice rested his head in the crook of her arm and walked on, slower than before, her head held high. 'Sometimes,' she said, 'I think I should call it a day. Lots of people do, after all, don't they? They look around them and know they deserve better. Up sticks. I think sometimes: Alice, you're not happy. But I'm going to do every last thing possible to make this work. Tom's my second husband, you know. The first only lasted a year. We were kids really—a complete disaster. I walked out. I promised myself this would be different. I said to myself, there's a good basis here. He makes me laugh, or used to. He works hard. In bed, he . . . We'd better cross here. We've got to go down Albemarle Road.'

The two women stood on the curb, heads craned to the right. The traffic advanced relentlessly. Without the weight of Jim pulling at her shoulders and back, Liz felt all wrong, almost weightless and somehow exposed, being out of doors. 'Terrible road,' Alice said, starting forwards then thinking better of it. Panic scalded Liz: a feeling almost sound, a finger pressed hard and high on the thin metal string of a violin. Silly-boy, she thought; he's scared—

'I'll take him back,' she said, reaching.

'Come on!' Alice called, stepping out. 'It's fine,' she insisted when they reached the other side. She set out down Albemarle Road. The beat of her heels on the pavement and the words that poured from her seemed connected, as if something from inside her had got caught around her ankles and each step pulled more of it out—and walking hard to keep up, she felt as if her steps too were pulling Alice's insides out, but she had to go on because if she stopped Alice wouldn't: it'd all get tangled up, stretch between them, break—

'Right from the start I thought—the way he could make me laugh, so sure—it was a hint, it made me feel safe *and* scared, you know? Like he knew me. Like he could pick me up and change me, make me feel different. Happy. So I thought: I'll make something of this. A very serious kind of feeling. Important . . . Whatever's happened since, I still feel kind of solemn when I think about it. And scared. But I'm always scared of something . . .' Alice's voice sank lower than usual, and grew steadier, which made it easier to listen to.

She says things to me the way I say them to Silly, Liz thought. Perhaps she thinks I'll get her to the Zone . . . But she's wrong. Because to do that she mustn't talk to anyone else, certainly not to Tom, not to anyone at all.

'I feel cold when I think that it might come to nothing. Might—sometimes I think it *will*, or even *has*—sometimes I think, oh, dear, this is the end of us—but I've got to stay and watch. Sometimes it seems like there's a clock-work thing, not big, but full of tiny springs and wheels—you know those watches they make now, that you can see inside?—moving little by little; there it is on the carpet in some corner of the house, some kind of meter, and one day all those moving parts inside will come to a certain point and that'll be the end. Like the lights going out. But putting more money in this meter doesn't work, not once it's run out. There you are in the dark. Oh, listen to me . . . Straight on here, down Livingstone . . .

'Then I think: shape up, Alice—there's always something you can do. You *can* put some more money in. So I really try, but all the time it's there, tick tick tick . . . Maybe you *both* have to feed the meter. Two slots in the damn thing, his and hers, like towels. I said to him, it feels like only I'm trying. *Paying.* I'm trying to cope with this and still, you know, love him and forgive him, believe him and so on. Well, he says, I've stayed haven't I? I've given *her* up. So I say, is that an *effort* then. And he says, no, I want to, she was all a mistake. So where's the *trying* then? How's it *fair?* Buys me things, I suppose. And he puts up with me being like this from time to time. But even so I feel I can't do it too often or he'll get fed up. Meters everywhere. He says he won't have anything to do with her baby above what's a legal requirement on the financial side, provided she has a genetic test. *That* must be an effort, mustn't it? But he says no. I think he's doing that for me, but it's a rotten thing to do, isn't it?'

They turned into Summerhill Rise, where the houses were detached, post-war, large and on the whole similar, screened from view by mature trees. Alice walked more slowly, looking about rather than straight ahead.

'I hate our house now, even though I know it's nice. If I had lots of money, this is the sort of place I'd live . . . You see,' she said, her tone suddenly light again, 'I know this can't go on. Look at me. I've got to do something. I've let myself go . . . Inside first . . . I can feel my pulse racing at night. It echoes in the pillow. And now it's beginning to show on the outside. Look at my nails.'

Liz looked at her, smiling faintly. There *was* something different: Alice's face had the flat, grainy look of something once carefully polished but now giving way to the scouring of weather and time.

'What number's that, on the other side? The one with the cherry tree.'

'Ninety-six,' said Liz.

Alice stared at it as they passed. 'My mum, I spoke to her on the phone last night, she said, "You'd be better off on your own." Talk about helpful! And this man we've been to see. Not the hypnotist, someone else. We go together. Talks about decisions and doesn't understand how I'm dangling on the end of a so-fine string. Sometimes it feels like it's attached to my spine, just between the shoulder blades. Sometimes I think it's where my heart is. It can even feel like it's joined to my hand, when my hand stops halfway through doing something and feels like it isn't mine, dropping things. Sometimes it feels like it's joined to my brain. Sometimes it feels like it isn't joined anywhere, but runs straight through me like thread through a needle's eye. It's a gristly thing, like the tendons you find in chicken legs, close to the bone. Everywhere I go it tugs, sometimes faintly, sometimes hard, but it's always there. If it was cut, I'd fall. Or I'd walk on forever the way I happened to be going at the time, with nothing to pull me back home.

'At the end of the string is Tom. To meet each other, one or the other of us has to haul it in. You know how people feel after amputations? They can still feel the bit that was cut off, even though it's gone. It's called a phantom. Well sometimes I think my string might even be that. That the feeling of being pulled is a memory. He's not at the other end any more, and the string's just trailing behind me like a tail.'

'A tie that binds,' Liz said.

Alice paused briefly to consider this paraphrase of what she'd said, but made no comment. 'If I think carefully,' she glanced over her shoulder and continued, 'I sometimes think I wasn't even happy before all this happened. And all this is common enough too, isn't it? Some people get over things like this and live happily ever after. Tom tells me we'll laugh about this one day. But others don't. Laugh? Whole days when I felt, well, disappointed. It always seemed to be raining; horrible dark streaky mornings before I had to get to work—didn't start till ten, but sometimes I got there early, just to get away from myself. I used to feel relieved when I pushed open the door and saw the permanent staff sitting there already, in those stupid blouses and cravats we all had to wear. It was dead boring, working there, but I miss it.

'You can always think of a reason, can't you? It's the time of the month, I often think. Women go loopy, don't they? You hear they get off for shoplifting, even murder—but suppose those four days are the only time, you see? Suppose they're more real than the other twenty-four? Suppose they're the time when truth bursts through, like a sudden break in fog. Rest of the time you're just hugging the wheel, blind . . . So suppose I wasn't happy anyway? If I could look at it that way for long enough, what Tom's done could be a blessing in disguise.'

'A Silver Lining,' Liz said. They'd reached the end of Summerhill Rise, and both of them stopped together.

'Yes,' Alice replied. Her eyes were shining and her cheeks wet but she smiled. 'You know, you don't say much, but I always feel you understand. Thank you.' She handed Jim carefully back. His eyes were very wide and seemed to struggle to distinguish the two women from each other from a muddle of faces and arms. His mouth, too, was a small, startled circle of surprise.

'Weighs an absolute ton,' Alice said. 'But I'm sure carrying him like that's the best thing. Read it in a magazine somewhere—must have been in the doctor's, where else do I ever go?—that it makes them grow up secure and well adjusted. Got a feeling it didn't happen to me! Well . . .' She thrust her hands in her pockets and looked back. They'd been walking downhill for the last few minutes; the road rose in a steep hump, most of its length invisible.

'Listen. I know you'll think this is funny, but you carry on down there and you'll get to the ring-road. I'm going back, another way, on my own. I'll explain another time...'

At just after five, Annie Purvis was alone in the office. She should have been at a meeting, but Mandy had said they could manage without her. She had reports to write. She was trying to keep her promise to Sim and when the telephone rang she thought it might be him, checking or reminding her. But it was Brian Farrar. She made her voice welcoming, though she could have done without the interruption.

'Hello. How can I help, Brian?' She looked around the office—it had the look of a bus station, the other desks empty, the corners shadowy, litterbins brimming because of the strike—and prodded at the small spider plant on her desk with her pen. It grew in a discarded cup from the drinks dispenser.

'How's the kid?' he said. *She's got a name*, Annie thought irritably, *use it*.

'Clare is fine. Brian, you know you can ring or visit the hospital whenever you want, don't you? And by the end of the week—'

'I don't want to.'

'Are you all right, Brian?'

'I want you to come round.'

'To talk?'

'To see.'

'See what, Brian?' She heard him catch his breath.

'What I've done. I want *you* to see.'

'I'll come, Brian, but what have you done?' Her voice was soft and even but she began to feel sick. He said nothing more for a while, and the nausea grew.

'Brian?'

'She started to think I'd done it,' Brian said. 'She said she *didn't know*. Come around,' he repeated. 'Come around!'

'I'll be around, Brian. Just wait for me there.' Mrs Purvis's mouth was paper-dry. She hung up and immediately called the police. She put on her coat, turned out the lights, locked up, and waited for them outside.

He wants me to see, she thought as she emerged from the police car. The ambulance was flashing blue behind them, but they had no sirens, just the light and panic on the radio. Now, he wants me to *see*.

'You'd better wait down here,' the officer said and she obeyed. Let the men, she thought, the men in uniforms take over. Look after their own . . . She didn't want to see. Seeing had been to tell her it was her fault. Whatever it was, don't dare think. It was not her fault. Not even her responsibility. Or anyone's but his. *He* did it, whatever exactly it was. Because Clare was taken away: she did that. Mrs Thomas made her. Poor cow. *He* made her because he did it in the first place. Protect: well, the child's all right, tucked up safe. She'd done that—her duty. But when did people stop being children? Jackie was twenty-four. *He* was thirty. Protect Jackie, *him?* How? It is too much, she thought, too much to expect.

Uneven footsteps echoed on the stairs. It was a block in which the lift never worked and the flat was on the fourth floor. He wanted her to see. She wouldn't. She didn't look. A car door slammed. Sirens whipped the air, then pulled into the distance. And then a stretcher was coming down, four feet in heavy unison. She wouldn't look.

'Wasn't armed. In tears,' the police officer said. 'Lost his temper. She's dead.' Brian did it. 'Not,' the officer added, 'a thing to see.' But Brian had wanted her to. There were more sirens, and lights everywhere. 'You'll have to come I'm afraid.'

'I know. I'll need to telephone my boss.'

'Did you have any idea that this might happen?' they asked her. They were mad. 'After all,' they said when they saw the expression on her face, 'you're the social worker.' If she'd thought it would happen she would have done something! If he'd rung her before instead of after. But he hadn't! Things you wouldn't think of happened all the time. Things no normal person would think of. Some of them were her job: bruising, tearing, soreness. Some of them, surely, were not.

Brian had abused Clare. Then he had killed Jackie for not believing that he hadn't. He'd killed her in the kitchen where Mrs Purvis herself had sat. Beneath the polystyrene tiles and the strip light that Jackie always said made you look as if you'd just got up whatever time of day it was; but she mustn't complain—far, far better than the kitchen she had had before, in her own bedsit. The wood effect, and the blind with poppies on . . . Jackie putting away the dishes, and Brian following her from sink to cupboard then back again.

'Why did you talk to that woman? Why did you let them?' he says. 'Let them keep her in?' Jackie slips the knives and forks soundlessly into their compartments and doesn't answer, pushes the drawer to with her hip. Her eyes search the room for another task to take her away from him. She holds on to the tea towel even though there's nothing left to dry.

'They can make you anyway,' she says.

'Just because she's been *quiet at school!* They're supposed to be fucking quiet at school! And some woman doctor with one thing on her mind—'

Jackie, trapped with her back to the sink, lowers her eyes. 'It's only till the end of the week,' she says folding the cloth and setting it down on the draining board. 'Everything'll be all right.'

'Look at me!' He grabs her arm. She looks at his hand which circles her narrow forearm without effort. His skin is dry from handling plaster and cement, the fingers both muscular and swollen. On the back of his wrist, just before the hairs begin, her name is tattooed inside a heart.

'Do you think I did it?'

Jackie looks at the heart and the veins now rising across it, making her name illegible. She realises she doesn't really know the ends and edges of what Brian could have done or could do, but says, 'No, Brian.' The voice loses itself as she swallows hard. She clears her throat, still looking at her arm and his wrist. The two limbs might come from different creatures, so different . . . 'Of course not. We've got to put up with it a bit, that's all. Go on, love, let go of my arm.' The kitchen's full of breathing. Even the plastic, the glass, the vinyl floor, they all heave. In out in out—

'Say: Brian, I know you didn't do it.'

'Brian, I know—'

'And look me in the face while you're saying it.' Something in Jackie can't do what she knows is best. The breathing in the kitchen stops. She raises her eyes and looks him in the face. 'Brian, it's just—' she says, 'just—there's moments, just moments mind! When I'm not sure, Brian, and she's my kid, I've got to do the best—' That's when he starts with his fist.

And afterwards he'd rung so that she, Annie Purvis, could see. She'd rung the police. It was their job now, to make sense of it; she must answer their questions so that they could.

'I know he had hit her before,' she answered. 'She said so. But of course I didn't think that—' One thing led to another. It was obvious, that being why she could imagine it so well. He was under pressure (because of her). He lost control. Lost control?

Eventually they drove her home, where Sim sat at the table in the lounge, wearing his tortoiseshell glasses. He didn't look up from his marking. 'You're just a tiny bit late,' he said. 'Been out caring for someone?' Because of the way he hunched over the work his belly was exaggerated. He looked old. It was just after midnight and normally they'd be in bed. He must have been waiting for her.

'Not exactly, Sim,' Annie said, calm, as she had struggled to be for the last four hours. 'Sorry. I've been at the police station. I asked Mandy to ring you—'

'I think,' he underlined something in red, 'that some day very soon you're going to have to choose.' This was the kind of tone that saved him in the classroom; its cool menace, giving nothing away, stemmed the tide.

It already felt impossible to tell him. She prised her shoes off. I will not, she thought, let Brian ruin my life. But stopping him would be pretty hard.

'I should say there's at least a hundred people that could do with a bit of care between here and the second lamppost you can see,' Sim said.

'It's always been like this, Sim. It's my job.'

'Stop Simming me,' he replied. 'You live in such a morbid world. I'm sick of it. Personally I think we should take a stand against it. I want a family. I want to emigrate.'

'Can we please talk about it later, Sim?' She could tell how her voice sounded, how it would irritate, but she could not stop it.

'When would suit you?'

'When this case—'

'As you want.' He looked at her, and she felt in his gaze like a stranger appraised. Or a small girl suspected of lying. He shrugged before turning back to his work. The tortoiseshell glasses—not his proper pair—were very old and one of the arms was fastened with sticking plaster. They made him frown, because the lenses were now too weak. The proper glasses were probably in the bedroom, somewhere near the bed, but she didn't mention it, because she knew they were fighting. Not blows, not even a raised voice between them, but taking things away one by one and then losing them.

'I'm going up,' Sim said. Though it wasn't up, but across.

Jackie. Dead. None of anything is real, Annie Purvis thought. Sim was her grey-haired father; he was a little boy who lost things; he had used to be her lover, now, she hardly noticed him go. Jackie. She pressed her face against the glass.

It was cool. If she pressed hard enough it would break.

Someone would have to tell Clare. Someone would have to explain that her mother was *dead*. That suddenly there was no one left at all, not even Brian . . . I can't do it, Annie thought. *He* should have to do it, not me. They should *make* him. She couldn't keep still, strode into the kitchen for water, back into the sitting room, around it, across to the window again.

How often Sim had described her work—or was it her?—as pathological and unhealthy. Care should not be professional, he said. Once people were paid to do things like that, everyone else abrogated their responsibility: look how everyone blames you lot if something goes wrong. You're just there to carry the can. Suckers, that's what he said, same as me; but at least I know it and I want out. I know what I want, I know what I want . . .

She didn't. Not all of it. She could see that there was no need to be what she was. She could retrain, even now, as a computer programmer, an electrician; she had administrative skills. She could have children. No need even to be so practical, so obvious. She could be an artist, an engineer. She could go on television, or bum around the world, crewing on yachts and writing travel guides . . . There were other lives possible, millions of them. She longed for them. Any of them but this.

Opposite, in the block of maisonettes, open passageways ran along the side of the building, lit by lamps set into the underside of the balcony above. Each bulb cast a weak pool of light. On the third floor a bulb had failed or been removed, spoiling the pattern. The dark patch drew Annie Purvis's eye in under the jutting balcony to the windows beneath, and suddenly, as she watched, a light came on. In the room it revealed two figures, women, amongst white units and a forest of potted plants. One woman stood by the window looking out, the other bent over the fridge, removing things rapidly and throwing them onto the table. This finished, she came over to the window too, and slipped her arm around the other's waist.

Annie Purvis stayed where she was, squarely placed, and looked back at them. She knew that they and she must be invisible to each other but she felt that if the sun was suddenly switched on, like a huge lamp, they'd all three know in the moment before they blinked and turned away that they'd been staring straight into each others' eyes. Other lives. It was frightening to think of. Because anything was possible. Really anything.

Jackie lived with Brian because he provided a flat and she didn't have an alternative. But in her case that was not true. There was choice. Yet she'd ended up here. *Here.*

At those moments, in the past, when she'd used her choices, she'd done so quickly without wanting to know what she was doing. She'd moved as smoothly as possible down preset tracks, a passenger on a long train, scarcely noticing the click of points at junctions. So hard to step down, she thought, when what is seems so familiar; and meantime the train rolled on with her sleeping through sudden night-time stops when she could have stepped off, and now she was here in a very particular and very terrible place. And Jackie was dead, Clare going into care, and she mustn't let Brian ruin her life as well as these others. He would be locked up because there was nothing better to do with him. And Sim would tell her it was time to get out, to go to Canada, have babies and start a new story there.

Tomorrow, an emergency meeting. A briefing. A postmortem. Eventually a trial on two counts; she would have to give evidence. Very likely a scandal. Accusations of negligence. Eventually, possibly, resignation. Annie Purvis clenched her fists until the nails bit home, and remembered how she'd made exactly the same gesture as a girl. It had been in a church, a place full of whispers and dappled light, and then, as now, everything had seemed to be all her fault. Don't, she told herself, let the bastards get you twice over. But she felt weak.

Sim always left the bedroom curtains open. Sodium light from the streetlamp below gilded the window frame without seeming to touch the inside of the room at all. She closed them, felt her way carefully over to the bed; the room was untidy and treacherous in the dark. In the quiet, the gasp of her skirt's zip, the drag of her tights, the crackle of static from her blouse, sounded like stifled human exclamations.

'Sim?' she said, quite loud, as she fitted herself into the bed. 'Sim—please . . .' Even if words were impossible, she would have liked to be touched, but Sim had locked himself away in the garage of sleep. He would not touch her. There would not— never, she felt, never again—be even the briefest and most desultory of rides, stopping somewhere, nowhere, aimlessly on the way, forgetting to start again. For heaven's sake! she told herself, at a time like this. Jackie's dead! Dead! She began to sob. Still he slept. Pushing the covers away she searched on the floor for her dressing gown. Something brittle collapsed beneath her foot. She knew instantly that it was his glasses. It was 3:00 am. She felt very cold and wide awake.

PEACE AT LAST

For what seemed like hours, a tangle of gasps and grunted commands had been pushing their way through Liz's wall. It sounded like a couple of steam trains, boilers full-on but unable to move. Liz, lying down, imagined Tom's face, befuddled, idiotic, shocked, and Alice straddling him, her hands on his shoulders, squeezing him hard with the muscles inside as she worked herself up and down, breathing out between her teeth, which Liz could hear.

'Oh God, Alice, oh God,' Tom burbled.

'Come on!' Alice spat. When everything had finally died down she said, so very clearly that Liz could almost imagine that she was meant to hear, 'I've been around there, to Summerhill Rise where your Andrea lives, and I punched her right in the face. I pulled her hair and split her lip and I spat on her and I called her a *cunt.*'

'Christ!' whispered Liz.

Tom, his penis sealed between his groin and Alice's thighs, knew to believe her. They were motionless, looking at each other in the dark, until with a creak of bedsprings Alice straightened her back, pulled away and sat next to his prone shape, looking down. She jerked the covers around her legs and prompted, 'Well? Aren't you angry with me? Do you want to go around there and see if she's all right?'

'No,' Tom had said eventually, his voice a monotone. 'I've felt like doing it myself, to tell you the truth.' They both tried to laugh. Perhaps she moved closer, dragging the sheets with her.

'So you don't mind?'

'No.'

'Suppose she did it to me then?'

'She wouldn't,' said Tom.

'You mean she's somehow a better class of person than me? Or because she doesn't have to?'

'She's *pregnant,* for God's sake!' Liz had never heard Tom quite like that; he'd sounded on the verge of tears.

'She said she'd report it to the police . . .' Alice's voice was uncertain. Then, very softly, she laughed.

That weekend Alice and Tom were home together all the time. The weather was improving, and Liz observed them busying themselves with outdoor tasks: edging their patch of grass, cleaning the windows and the brass door furniture. She waited as long as she could, but had to go out for milk early on Sunday morning, even though Tom was already there, repainting the external woodwork. There wasn't anything she could have done to avoid her reflection appearing in the gleaming glass and in any case the pair of them probably had eyes in the backs of their heads: small ones, black and shiny, hidden beneath the well-groomed hair. Those were the seeing eyes; the others, at the front, were just for putting on a show.

Tom twisted his head around, paintbrush poised above the can of white gloss. 'Hi!' he beamed at her, even-teethed.

'Settling in? My wife said she'd had some chats with you . . .' He set his paintbrush on a piece of newspaper and came to the fence. 'Hmm—I expect you've heard all about me . . .' he said sheepishly. 'I'm not all bad really, you know. Difficult times, but I think it's all over now . . . Didn't disturb you the other night, did we?' He winked. Liz kept her face blank.

'I'm afraid it's been the creak of bedsprings one night and breaking china the next!' Tom said cheerfully. He was very tall, and Liz felt the vertebrae in her neck beginning to protest. She bent and picked a potato chip packet up from her path.

'I think things will settle now.' He stared at her earnestly, the way Liz imagined a hypnotist might—then looked abruptly away and lightened his voice. 'You need to fix that gate, really, or dogs'll start coming in . . .

'In fact, I'm seeing a specialist next Monday, because I think a knock on the head I got years ago at rugby might have something to do with all that's been going on.'

It was not, Liz realised, a question of deliberately avoiding speech any more. Quite the reverse. Even the simplest of phrases had to be searched for, as if from among a whole beach of pebbles; one or two must be selected. Why this one and not that? The task seemed absurd, her lips slack and reluctant. It was not a loss, as such, and it was different with Silly, of course.

'Do you see what I mean?' Tom prompted. 'Mmm?'

Liz felt her face jerk into a conciliatory smile, something she couldn't yet completely control.

'People lose their memories, don't they? Why not other faculties? Well, mustn't be seen talking to you for too long or Ali will be on my back!'

Instantly, Liz was soaked in rage. It pushed itself through the pores of her skin and drenched her, smelling heady, volatile, like gasoline. She had no desire to answer back, as she had had in Bettahire, nor even to punch him in the stomach. She'd grown at least a little stronger since then. She wanted simply to obliterate him by the power of thought.

If you hadn't been special, she thought at Jim, examining Tom coolly—his heavy brow, his tense jawline, his mottled green front eyes—you might grow up to be something like this particular human being. Grow those shiny black, spying eyes in the back of your head, a fat wet tongue for pushing out stupid, stupid words . . .

Tom's face was creased with laughter, but through it the front eyes still stared straight at her, waiting to get something back. She met them steadily. Staring out, she thought, is something Grammy taught me how to do; I can beat *you* hands down. She stared harder as he ran his tongue nervously over his lips, then glanced away, back at number 129.

Alice was watching them from an upstairs window, an orange duster in her hand. She waved it in the air and beckoned with the other hand. 'Have to be careful!' Tom added, waving back. 'Jealousy. I mean, you're *her* friend. Come for a cup of tea with us both? Bring the baby. She would like that,' he pleaded, adding, 'now that everything's settled down to normal, and peace at last.'

'Sorry,' Liz mumbled as she opened her door, 'no,' and she closed it. The house was quiet but for the sound of her shoes on the boards. Still standing, she prised them off, then climbed the stairs.

'I love you, Silly-boy,' she told him. 'I really do.' His legs twitched. The swelling on the foot had almost completely gone, though the bruise was multicoloured and spectacular, and the angle of the joint was a little different to the other one. He didn't seem to notice when she touched it. He was growing, and soon would be too big to carry around. One day he might even be bigger than her. One day she might be as silent as him, and not even want a television anymore.

She picked him up and hugged him as hard as she dared. Purvis seemed to have left them alone. Perhaps the neighbours would do the same, in time.

PART THREE

PART THREE

HYDRAULICS

That April, spring and summer merged into one. Overnight, colours brightened, and seemed wet-looking, as if recently applied. Trees and plants grew almost visibly exuding the scents of pollen and sap. On Onley Street, builders' skips and scaffolding appeared. Alice and Tom had the guttering done. Old windows were replaced, roofs were retiled. Window cleaners followed the builders, and women crouched in the gardens, pulling out couch grass, clover and dandelions, and shearing away last year's dead growth.

Jim grew, too. He was too heavy to carry in the sling for long walks, but cried when he was put in the stroller. If Liz thought about the whole of her life like this, lived one season following the other in a street like this—suppose she never got away—she felt almost as scared as she had when the man followed her, that night down by the carriages. She felt sick, her heart raced. Yes, she knew they were lucky to have the place, and what else could she do? She took to using the bus more often: to the city centre, or to different parks. She needed to be out and about, she explained to Jim. If you were on the move, it somehow felt as if things might change.

Frank worked on. He did not feel the urge to tidy or renovate. He sometimes liked to sit in the back garden, and he liked to look out on it, but the maintenance was dealt with by Green Fingers, who visited bi-weekly during the growing season. Towards the end of the month, he dressed in his suit and took the train to London to visit Dr Davidson's Harley St. clinic in connection with his real-life plot.

The clinic was situated in a four-storey Georgian terrace. Stone mullions graced the ground level, and above them arched windows were guarded by wrought iron balconies. Frank mounted five steps to a brass plaque and bell and a wide pan-elled door. Inside, Vivaldi seeped into the waiting area where he filled out the medical history form. He was then taken down a corridor to a small room where an elderly doctor, not Davidson, but a colleague, tested his reflexes, blood pressure and so on and took a blood sample. He was given coffee and sandwiches while he waited for the results of his tests. Finally, he was ushered into Dr. Davidson's consulting room, which was more like a formal lounge in someone's very expensive home than a medical office; there were abstract paintings on the walls and the tops of a blos-soming cherry trees showed above the blinds covering the lower part of the windows, in front of which three Italian leather arm-chairs arranged to face each other.

'Well, Mr Styne,' Dr Davidson said—he was young and lean, tieless, but wearing a cream shirt which looked like silk—'you seem to have passed all our tests with flying colours! Sit down, please, sit down… I'm glad to say that I'm sure we can help you. But the first thing to say, really, is that I see forty new patients a week. This is a very common issue and there's abso-lutely no need to be embarrassed.'

Frank nodded, and indeed, perhaps unexpectedly, he did not feel self-conscious at all. The leather chair supported his back perfectly and the whole thing seemed so smoothly and professionally done, interesting, too.

Nothing physical was wrong, Davidson explained. Losing some weight and taking more exercise might help, but it could well be that the problem was psychological. In which case, such things took an age to unravel, talking about the past and so on twice a week for years... It was likely to be upsetting, the outcome was always uncertain, and meanwhile the problem persisted, possibly worsened, definitely cost a fair amount, since psychotherapy could be expected to last for years, whereas an implant could be purchased, installed, and only a week or so later, discretely pumped up at will, in seconds, in any situation one chose. Admittedly the pump was something some men felt to be a drawback. The doctor was sure that in a decade or so there would be a drug, a simple pill to be popped at will, but meanwhile, there were also self-administered injections, if the idea of surgery was alarming or prohibitively expensive . . .

'Many normal men,' he continued, 'would envy the range and sheer reliability that either solution provides. I do feel countless joyless marriages could probably be saved by these techniques. It's not a matter of deception, simply one of breaking a vicious cycle. Of *re-education*. One associates pleasure with the object involved: Pavlov. For instance, it does sometimes happen that what gives the wife greatest pleasure may be something of a letdown as far as the husband is concerned. This can upset both parties, especially over a number of years. Or it may be that with the passing of time the wife, though much loved (or perhaps there are children involved), has changed physically in some other way such as to make her seem unattractive to her spouse. We can solve these problems and save both partners a great deal of anguish.'

'The fact is,' Frank began, 'in fact, I'm not—' They were seated opposite each other with only a low coffee table between them. Dr. Davidson leaned in closer.

'As for the single man, it can make a relationship possible. More than that, it's also a ticket to adventure. Situations that might perhaps intimidate can be taken on—and thoroughly enjoyed—without fear. One can return to the polymorphous perversity of one's youth. The world's your oyster, if you'll excuse the stock phrasing! We are,' he said, leaning back, smiling, 'talking about a pretty simple mechanism here.'

It has not, Frank thought, been simple for me. He shifted in the chair. 'I worry that it won't feel real,' he said. But then again, how would he know?

'I think it feels real enough to most men! I know this can seem almost too good to be true, but don't put the cart before the horse,' Davidson said, increasingly falling back on the stock phrases he had earlier apologised for. 'Above all, studies have shown, the impotent man's problem is confidence. And once you're A-OK in that department, all kinds of other problems will just disappear in a puff of smoke. And what I am proposing is pretty much bound to give you confidence, though of course I can't give a one hundred percent guarantee.'

Given the capacity, Dr Davidson pointed out, Frank could do whatever he decided to do, and enjoyment would be guaranteed... He could, therefore, Frank supposed, tie Katie Rumbold up with washing line and have sexual intercourse with her even if she was vomiting and even if she hated him, and enjoy it thoroughly. One thing led to another: an effect could be battened on to the cause of one's choosing. Any cause at all. The plan was completely viable.

'You're saying that I can make myself enjoy anything at all?' he asked.

'Absolutely. Nothing is out of bounds. This is a physical response. Bodily events in response to stimulus, feedback. Put your hand in fire and it burns; real as that, though pleasanter, of course! Just, as I said, you need a kick start, to break that vicious circle. It's a question of taking the plunge.'

Dr Davidson took an implant and attached hand-pump from the drawer of his desk and demonstrated it. It reminded Frank of the thing they'd just used to measure his blood pressure. Not very elegant, he thought.

'I would need it by the ninth of May,' Frank said.

'Well,' the consultant smiled, leaning back in his chair and counting on his fingers, 'yes, I should think we could just about be up and running by then . . .' He squeezed the rubbery bladder and up it went. It was simple. Perhaps arousal was not a thing to be properly remembered without re-experiencing it, all there was being knowledge of the facts?

'Hydraulics,' the consultant said, ignoring such philosophical niceties. Hydraulics came first, the feeling came after. 'Of course, allowing your partner to operate the pump could well become an erotic experience for her—or him. Or even them! And surgically, it's child's play. There are a range of models, all effective and durable, though those at the higher end of the price range are perhaps a little more convenient.'

The cost was not unreasonable and far cheaper than facial reconstruction about which Frank had also enquired. Extensive facial reconstruction—frog to prince—grafts, tucks, shaved bones, such as he'd require, was not something he could afford even though he was comfortably off, and in any case could not be done in time.

'Besides,' Dr Davidson said, 'that's a long and uncertain route. Suppose you went through all that and still the problem persisted . . . But I sense you're uncertain, Mr Styne. Is the idea of surgery putting you off? We men can feel rather vulnerable down there.'

I don't feel anything down there, Frank thought. But surgery certainly wasn't something he welcomed and he grasped at the idea. Surgery introduced an element of risk he would rather be without. He had often used operations in his books, though not one exactly like this. Things went wrong. People died under anaesthetic, knives slipped, infections flourished. And the fact was, though of course he couldn't say this, he didn't need something permanent. It was only to be used the once.

'Maybe,' he said. 'You mentioned alternatives.'

'Perhaps you'd be happier with the injections. We do the first one here, so that you know what to do and what to expect. After that you take your supplies and go… If that's your choice, would you like to step into the room next door?'

'Your name is terribly familiar, Mr Styne,' Dr Davidson said cheerfully. 'It's been nagging away at the back of my mind all the time we've talked . . .' Frank felt the needle slide in. 'I know—you write those books. Is that you? I must say I've been a fan of yours for years. Would you sign one for me when you come for your check-up?

'Takes about ten minutes. Put your things back on. You'd be surprised, Mr Styne, at the number of famous people—actors, sportsmen, TV personalities and so on, even royalty—who have sat where you are sitting now. Along with quite ordinary people as well. Confidentiality is, of course, absolute. Do you feel anything?' Frank nodded, preoccupied. It was growing. It ached.

Very occasionally, the consultant said as he counted out the syringes, the erection didn't subside, in which case there was a remedy, another injection, which, however, must be administered by a qualified medical professional. The best thing was not to use it the first time, but to wait downstairs, or at the very least not to go too far away for an hour or so until de-tumescence occurred.

Frank emerged, dazed, from the clinic's cool atmosphere, clutching his supplies. The light was over-bright, the city air smelled of burned dust. Nothing seemed quite straight or parallel; the bright white lines of sills and window frames appeared to fight with each other, broken suddenly into two halves that didn't quite meet. Traffic sped past nose to tail and the whole of London seemed to rumble as if there were a slow, steady earthquake running on and on, night into day. He had missed lunch to make the appointment which, he thought, might explain how shaky he felt . . . The erection burned between his legs. It felt separate from him, like something clipped on. Feeling very conspicuous, he crossed the road carefully and passed through wrought-iron gates into a small park. He thought he would sit there a while, sit very still, on a green painted bench under a plane tree, in deep shadow with his eyes closed.

He squeezed his legs together and felt the sensation shift, increase. The contact of skin on skin, the pressure, was real enough. So now he could do it . . . A syringe and a length of washing line. Pressure on nerves, travelling to the brain. It almost hurt. He could, Frank thought, visit a prostitute now, as a trial run. Though he had no desire to. Somehow, he just wanted to be on his own. He tried to think of the picture taped by the telephone, but his mind kept wandering away.

After a few minutes other sensations appeared. Tears began to ooze from behind his lids. He didn't touch them, but felt their slow tracks creeping down over the contours of his face, and somehow this made him very aware of the difference between inside and outside. Outside—on the sur-face—he felt the slow trickling, the coolness of evaporation: sensation which was real, physiological, yet felt unimportant. Outside was the thing between his legs, burning. Inside was a great hollowness, an empty and expanding space contained by something infinitely elastic which ached and ached. A seeming only, not really there; just a feeling which was, how-ever, much more compelling than the sensations of tears or arousal. And as well as this he was afraid that everything—that he—might burst. He breathed shallowly so as to pre-vent the aching space inside or the erection from growing any larger.

He felt he would never be able to move from that bench, until suddenly there were voices somewhere close and he found himself on his feet, striding in the opposite direction with the tears drying and the inside feeling at least temporarily gone. He took a taxi to the station, and by the time he arrived he was, physically at least, back to normal.

The train rumbled sedately through the endless suburbs. He'd brought his work with him.

He wrote about Sandra. Her legs were swollen, her belly pressed her to the bed. Besides, Dr Villarossa said, exertion would not be advisable. She spent her days lounging in her bathrobe, listening to the radio and watching television. The husband carried her meals up; Dr Villarossa supplied special supplements to her diet, and visited her at home every day . . .

'I should have had it last month,' he made Sandra say.

Her face too was swollen, reddened, heavy. Her roots had grown out. Her eyes were bloodshot. She'd become lazy, ate with her fingers, was always hungry, had no sense of time. Thick blue veins pounded on her thighs. She had bedsores. Her husband had to help her to the toilet and shower. She disgusted him.

'Everything is as it should be,' he made Dr Villarossa say.

'Please,' she begged, 'let me see another doctor.'

'That won't be necessary,' Dr Villarossa replied.

'It was what you wanted!' the husband said to his wife. 'You've got what you wanted, so stop complaining.'

'Always lock the door,' Dr Villarossa instructed. She and the husband talked as if Sandra wasn't there. 'Give her a little alcohol if necessary. It will do no harm now. You're doing an excellent job. Keep the curtains drawn; light may be harmful.' Downstairs the carpets were thick with dust. They passed through the sitting room. Dr Villarossa made no comment about the filth in the kitchen where she washed her hands. She shook the husband's hand in hers.

'The time is almost come,' she said.

The movement of the train sent Frank's pen on strange jerks across the page. The other people on the train were mainly commuters, ashen-faced. No one else was trying to do anything, they just sat there, staring. Here and there a woman made a splash of colour, like some escaped tropical bird, glimpsed among the sparrows and starlings. Covertly, he watched them.

What would Katie Rumbold be wearing, he wondered, when she opened the door that led straight into his front room? The telephone would be disconnected and hidden in a drawer. The blinds would be down. The washing line would be under the cushion on the settee. Unnoticed, he would lock the door behind her. Should he serve her some wine and a light meal, chat a little beforehand? Or should he just grab her as soon as she came in? He closed his notebook and felt his lids sinking slowly over his eyes. Sleep. There was always, and would be in the end, merciful sleep.

Three weeks were left until the award ceremony on 9 May. Steadily it converged to a point, every minute of each day, as he wrote, cooked, slept, as the train rattled on down the line, past the sidings where Liz Meredith once used to live.

And across the city, Annie Purvis had returned to work after her sick leave. Her future was still uncertain, but things had moved on in her absence. Clare Moat was in care. Brian Farrar was on remand. She wasn't doing abuse work, but she was working hard and doing everything she was advised to do and it made her feel better. Once a week she went, because Mandy suggested it, to see a counsellor, a Dr Simpson. She always arrived early and waited in a conservatory smelling of lemons and damp. It was very hot, but the door to the garden, which she tried several times, was locked. The many potted plants were beaded with water and her skin felt the same.

She talked to Dr Simpson and fidgeted with the chain around her neck. The humidity reduced her to a state of almost vegetable content, yet at the same time it was not quite possible to relax when every wall was glass. Most of the conservatory ran in front of a sitting room with French doors opening into it and broad windows around which grew some kind of vine. She sat, keeping her back straight. Often the other Simpsons were preparing their evening meal and she could hear laughter from somewhere deep in the middle of the house.

She went there and sat in a glass house and cried a lot. She talked about work, because she knew that Sim didn't like her to do it at home, even though he had been marvellous when she told him what had happened. She wanted time to move on carefully, evenly, in the regular doses of the working day, passing forever through her fingers like beads. She lived in terror of dropping them.

Liz's restlessness carried her to the swimming baths. At the cinema, earlier in the week, they'd not been allowed in. You just can't, said the man behind the glass whose eyes were hidden each behind their own window—powerful lenses which made them so big they seemed to be hanging in front of his face rather than a part of it, images on a screen, holograms—You just can't take a baby into an over-eighteen film.

He's asleep, Liz had said, though she had been intending, once inside, to wake him up. Very few people had come to see *Damned in Space,* and it would be easy enough, in the dark, to pretend they were on their own. He ought to be in bed then, the man had replied. At this hour. Suppose he wakes up? He'd be terrified out of his wits, wouldn't he? No, he wouldn't, Liz had said. He'd scream his head off, asserted the man. I know he wouldn't, said Liz, because he wouldn't *understand.* She'd felt, as she said it, that she was betraying Jim. It's against the law, the man said. Suppose he was blind and deaf? Liz asked. I said, it's against the law; you're the deaf one, the man had said, looking over her shoulder at the customer behind . . .

She half expected the same thing to happen again at the baths, despite it being advertised as the morning for mothers and babies, but the woman smiled and Liz pushed through the turnstile, followed the arrows into the changing room.

She hoped Jim would take to the water. We've got to have something, haven't we? she thought. So we'll just see. We'll just see first if I can get into this . . . The costume was from Oxfam, the thick fabric of a former era, smocked in two panels down the sides. Room for two! Easy, she joked at Jim, easy as pie. She piled their things into the locker, fitted Jim with the swim diaper, then hitched him onto her hip and made her way through the showers and footbath. She pushed through the strips of opaque plastic that divided the changing rooms from the pool, out into the sharp tang of chlorine and turquoise blue that made her gasp. The swimming pool was set beneath a glass roof, with windows open all along the sides. She stood a moment, taking it in. There were two pools, the smaller of which was used for the mothers and babies.

About fifteen women crouched or stood thigh deep in the bright water, supporting their babies so that they appeared to float. In fact, one or two actually were floating, more or less of their own accord. Like another world, she thought at Jim. Is there water where you come from? Perhaps, she continued, you'll be able to swim straight away, underwater and all? She imagined him, arms by his sides, feet kicking, eyes open wide, a stream of bubbles coming from his nose.

The water was warm. It made her legs a very pale blue. Silly-boy, she mouthed at him, I like this, I like this, do you? She held him close to her as she sank down into a squat, lowering him gently up to the neck. The reflected blues made his eyes seem even more brilliant than usual. She crept slowly across to the other side of the pool without taking her eyes from his. She tipped him onto his back, feeling the water lift him slightly from her hands. She thought: if the world was underwater, if we lived at the bottom of a lake—whole cities—because of the tendency to rise, we'd have to sleep on the ceilings.

'Excuse me,' a woman with a very fat baby tapped her on the arm. 'I always like to do a couple of lengths in the big pool, don't you? If you mind Timothy while I go, I'll do the same for you.' Liz glanced at the other pool. A whistle had just blown for change of session, and all the swimmers were making their way towards the shallow end. She watched how they moved, the steady rhythm of the strokes, the heads dipping up and down. It was almost possible to imagine herself doing it, although she never had.

Soon the pool would be all but empty. She would never have thought of it on her own, but as she looked at the huge expanse of water, just moving and catching the light, her heart suddenly ached.

'Okay,' she said to the woman. Suppose I can't? Suppose I sink, drown? Jim floated at her side, his head just cradled in her hand.

Carefully, the other woman slipped her baby into a blow-up seat and pushed him towards Liz. He really was very fat. 'Timothy loves the water. I've done this before. He won't cry.' She launched herself towards the other pool. It was just a question of letting the water hold you up, Liz thought, watching her.

Despite his bulk, Timothy seemed in some way younger than Jim. He had fat cheeks and a dimpled chin, not such a huge head. Jim's eyes were wider, his face stiller, more like a grown up. He had more hair too. Timothy's mouth was busy, opening and closing. His whole face contorted with the effort of producing sound. His head twisted constantly, up, down, around. He patted the yellow arms of his blow-up seat. Meanwhile, Jim almost floated, moving his legs and arms, but not his face. His blue eyes slipped in and out of focus. Occasionally he blinked. For a second she took her hand away from the back of his head, lowering it just a little in the water.

'Brrpt,' said Timothy, then, 'omom.'

'I don't much like Timothy,' Liz thought at Jim. 'None of them are special like you.'

'Okay?' The woman in the bathing cap emerged beside them, glistening, rubbing red-rimmed eyes. 'I keep thinking to get some goggles, but it doesn't seem worth it for the amount of swimming I do.' She held out her arms, slipped one around each baby, and pulled them close. 'What a pretty boy!'

Liz turned her back quickly and made for the side. Leaving Jim with a stranger was harder than she would have predicted but she made a point of not looking back.

Deliberately she walked along the length of the main pool, right to the deep end. Then she looked back down the expanse of blue. The figures of the mothers and their babies looked very small, and the sound of their talk was muffled, strange. She stood with her toes curved over the edge. The water lapped inches below them. She was aware of her heart beating frantically in her chest, and when she bent her knees and tried to fill her lungs with air they seemed to have shrunk. Silly-boy, she thought desperately, help! And then, before she knew it, she had dived into a shock of coldness, splitting the water cleanly with her outstretched arms.

She opened her eyes. It was very beautiful, the endless blue, the feeling of moving forwards under the momentum of her leap, the rushing sound in her ears. She pointed herself upwards, broke the surface, gasped and pushed down again. She was doing the breaststroke: there was nothing to it. She swam deeper, then followed the upwards slope that divided the shallow from the deep end. Something was lying there on the tiles, and she grabbed at it as she passed. A pair of goggles. She slipped them around her neck to give to the woman. Because this was something, really something.

She turned, paddled her feet to keep afloat and was gripped by a desire for speed. She propelled herself back up the pool, flinging her arms forwards as fast and hard as she could: a very free kind of freestyle. She grasped the rail and kicked off again, pointing herself like an arrow and using all her strength, though it didn't seem enough, or as if it could ever be enough, to go as fast as she wanted, which would always be faster, faster. The water's resistance, its thickness, almost angered her. She screwed her face tight as she flung herself through it, smashing it into spray—she would have liked to do away with it entirely, to be in the air, and she would have liked to be an engine, to be a spaceship launched at the Cape, shooting out beyond the confines of gravity and all the things of Earth, carrying a cargo of human beings, to whom anything could happen and would . . . Come on, she thought at the water, come on, I want to *move*.

The woman was waving at her from the other pool when she reached the shallow end for the fifth time. She levered herself out and stood, suddenly heavy, on the narrow tiled strip between the two pools. The woman held Jim up so that he could see her coming. The brightness of his eyes and the paleness of his face all but made Liz gasp. Her legs shook as she made her way down the steps towards him and the woman in the bathing hat, grateful for the warmth of the little pool.

'I found these,' she said, holding out the goggles. The woman smiled, accepting them, then passed Jim back to Liz.

'Sorry to cut you short. I've got to pick my others up from school.' She hitched Timothy up out of water. 'He was ever so good. Do you mind me asking—is there something the matter with his foot? Or is it my eyes? It doesn't look quite straight.'

Liz's heart flipped, but she smiled. 'Born like it,' she said. 'It's nothing much.'

'Oh dear, what a shame . . . I'm sorry . . .'

'They'll be able to straighten it later on,' Liz found herself saying. 'But at the moment he's growing too much, you see.' She held him to her chest, sunk down, and kissed the middle of his forehead. The lying words had skipped out, just like Alice's.

But it was all right. It was to protect them both. He would understand . . . The woman waved as she disappeared between the polythene strips.

Thanks, Liz thought at Jim, thanks Silly-boy, for teaching me how to swim. What a Silver Lining, to have you to show me how. To make me know.

She felt very warm afterwards, and the bus that carried them as far as the ring-road was peopled with dreams. They would move, quite soon, to somewhere warm by the sea, completely on their own. There, on the beach, as a reward for her efforts, Jim would initiate her one by one in the practices of the Zone, so that by the time he was full grown physically she too would have grown in other ways to match them. The price of abandoning human language—not just speech, but also the words that passed through her mind unbidden and the words people said on TV—would be as nothing, for she would learn telepathy, and the power to move objects by thought, and levitation, and how to overcome the need for air; she would be able to know what fish, crabs and whales, even the plants that waft at the bottom of the sea, thought and felt. They'd need nothing from outside, be beyond the need for food and drink. Slowly, perhaps, others would join them as they did at the railway carriages, which had been in a sense a rehearsal for this, as well as its beginning.

When she got out of the bus, Onley Street looked cheerful, almost foreign.

'Hiya!' Alice called. 'What's happened to your hair?' Don't spoil my day, Liz thought at her, screwing her anger into a kind of steadiness. Don't ruin my day. Don't—

'Can't stay,' Alice said. 'I'm off to a session. Counselling. We're going twice a week, and I'm taking every vitamin on earth. He puts them out for me at breakfast time. It shows he cares, doesn't it?' She waved and climbed into the car.

Wow, Liz thought, closing her door. She unstrapped Jim and lifted him in the air, which seemed to bristle with light.

'What have I done to deserve you?' She set him in the bouncer and unlaced her boots. Putting them by the door, she saw the envelope. It was from Purvis.

'Oh God, no,' she said aloud.

> Dear Liz,
>
> I am terribly sorry not to have been in touch sooner, and that there seems to have been some misunderstanding about the telephone. I'm a little worried that you haven't contacted me either; also, I understand you have missed an appointment at the clinic. Recently I have had to take some time off sick, and our meeting is now well behind schedule. I shall visit next Thursday at 10:00 am and we can have a good long chat.
>
> Annie Purvis.

Liz sat on the floor, and leaned back against the wall. She breathed deeply, in and out. Okay, Silly, she thought at him hard; we could piss off for the day, but that means she'll try again, so there's really only two choices. Listen, Silly, and tell me which: we piss off for good, or we try and face it out, and somehow *hide* at the same time as being here.

Which, Silly-boy? Which? She went on breathing, in and out, repeating the thought, waiting. But nothing happened. The two possibilities hung there, equal. Jim twisted his head to look at the window. A thin worm of spittle ran from the corner of his mouth and hung in the air beneath his chin. I'm on my own with this, she thought.

'Are you hungry?' she asked aloud. She stood again, feeling very heavy, just as she had when she emerged from the pool. Then she picked up the boots and hurled them one after the other at the opposite wall.

THE UNIMAGINABLE REAL

'Styne here.'

As Frank switched off the answering machine and answered his telephone for the first time in weeks, he realised that since that last evening at the Three Compasses he had spoken to no one, other than Dr Davidson and people in shops. The days and hours had seemed to fold themselves on top of each other silently and seamlessly. He had purchased a replica pistol, with which to ensure Katie Rumbold's co-operation. He had experimented with washing line and two types of sash cord, deciding on the latter, unwaxed, which was rougher and easier to tie. He had practised on his own ankles several times, cutting himself free with the knife. He had obtained an ample supply of sleeping pills for afterwards. He was waiting only for the call from the hospital which would enable him to complete the final scene of *The Procreators* in good time.

He needed to see a Caesarean section or a forceps delivery and had made an unofficial arrangement with the maternity unit at the local hospital. The person he'd dealt with wouldn't give his name, and had made him swear secrecy. The first donation was to be made as a sign of goodwill, then, in due course, he would be contacted by phone. Following his attendance at the procedure he would make the second donation. His cheques were to go towards the eventual purchase of an ultrasound scanner. His name would go on a plaque but they certainly didn't want to be thanked in the front of *The Procreators*.

There was to be no further contact following the first payment, and absolutely none afterwards. When they did eventually call, he had almost given up on them.

'A suitable case has arisen, Mr Styne. Please hurry.'

Frank stepped from his taxi and followed the signs at a brisk walking pace. The hospital was vast and only recently completed. It looked rather like a housing estate except for the abundance of direction signs, the uniforms, and the quantity of people being pushed in wheelchairs or carried on stretchers. Hundreds of windows gleamed and outside, small plants bristled in newly set out beds and borders. Immured in his house these past weeks, he had forgotten how interesting the world was... But if—when—he won, he would see no more of it.

He followed his escort, a balding man of about his own age, along a series of windowed walkways to the operating theatre. There he was asked to change into mask, hat, gloves and robe so that only his eyes and a thin segment of his forehead showed. The uniform made him feel invisible; for once he looked the same as anyone else. And the others in the theatre all looked the same as each other too, men and women virtually indistinguishable—the only obvious woman being the one lying down. She had no idea who he was; of her he knew only that she was single and alone, the absence of concerned relatives making it easier for him to be smuggled in.

The woman on the bed looked nothing like his Sandra. It was hard to judge her age. Her face was ashen, her exposed belly huge. Her breasts swelled beneath the cloth that had been draped over them, but her collarbone jutted and her wrists were thin. She had been given something that stopped her feeling pain, though she was still in some way awake, her glassy eyes fixed on the ceiling, flickering occasionally from one part of it to another. A screen arranged across her ribs cut out her view of what was happening below.

Protracted labour was as near as you got to hell on earth, Frank's mother had told him. She was a small woman, not five feet three, with huge eyes and brittle bones. She shrank even smaller as she grew older. He came from inside her, but eventually weighed three or four times as much as she ever did. It was unimaginable, but here he would see it for real.

Someone beckoned and led him to a chair by the woman's side. Someone, the anaesthetist, it turned out, was already seated on the other side. Perhaps the person who seated him knew who he was, or perhaps, uninformed as to the nature of his visit, they thought that he must be the father. As indicated, Frank took the woman's hand. It was damp, limp and very small; her dark brown eyes glittered and fixed themselves on him when he did so. He adjusted the place of the chair slightly to ensure a good view around the edge of the screen.

'The baby,' he was informed in a hurried whisper, 'is lying with its back to the neck of the womb.' Her body had been willing it out, but to no avail and it was thoroughly stuck. Apparently they had waited some hours trying to get it to turn. The woman's face was unnaturally still, motionless but for a slight movement about her lips. She stared at him, unwavering and unnerving. It was almost as if she knew he wasn't supposed to be there. The hand that held hers grew damp inside its glove.

He leaned back slightly, so as to better see around the screen. Two gloved and masked figures were bent over the woman's swollen abdomen, but he couldn't see what they were doing. He let go of the woman's hand and stood, just as the scalpel bit into the skin above her pubic hair. The incision was about five inches long, but it gaped, red-edged, then filled with a gush of fluid which ran over the body onto the table. The sides of the cut were pinned open, stretching it to more than double its size. One of the doctors reached in until the gloved fingers of both hands were inside the woman's body. Well, there was something in there. Lumps and bumps and blood... Bile rose in Frank's throat and his legs felt weak. Suppose the anaesthetic stops working, he thought, looking back at the woman, whose eyes were still fixed on him. He sat down quickly, took her hand again, and at that moment he felt, or imagined, her hand twitch in his. It was as if something dead had suddenly moved. Suppose she was just paralysed, a device he'd used in his very first book? Suppose she was in agony, trying to communicate, trying to tell him, begging for help? Suddenly everything seemed far too quiet and too controlled—this quietness was not calm, it was the very opposite, because in it he could imagine the most heart-rending scream, and behind those eyes he could imagine any nightmare he chose, brightly lit and searingly painful—

As if aware of his thoughts, the masked figures standing at the other end of the woman looked briefly up and then back again. They were easing her baby out, pulling it whole from her stomach. Its skin glistened with bloody fluids. Its eyes were closed. It was very thin. Was the baby even alive? Suppose—

The room spun. Frank wanted to run away—out of the room and out of the hospital, but he was held there by the woman's hand, which seemed to burn in his. She turned to look at the baby, held up so that she could see. At the same time, behind the screen, one doctor removed a huge liver-like thing from the woman's womb, while another mopped her insides with sponges and cloths. Then, at last, someone was sewing her up.

'Come on now, please . . .' Without saying goodbye, Frank placed the woman's hand carefully on the sheet, and was ushered quickly from the theatre. Divested of his gloves, mask and robe, he made his way slowly towards the exit. After the muffled closeness of the theatre, he was very aware of the outside air, brushing against his skin, and how all around him the sounds people made leapt suddenly into being, then died.

As he stood at the gates waiting for his taxi, new words began to write themselves in his head. Even though time was converging to the final point, he now knew that he was going to have to make a radical change that would necessitate an almost complete rewriting of *The Procreators:* it must be the husband, not Sandra, who would become pregnant and have to be locked in the upstairs room with something growing bigger and bigger inside him, day after day. It must be the husband who was forced to give birth.

It would be far more shocking, far more original, far more difficult to do—it was very risky, given the way the days seemed to run after and into each other until now there were only a few left. But the idea of it had started to grow inside him, putting on flesh and developing a will of its own. He would race the clock, write and rewrite until he caught himself up.

The answering machine was broadcasting Pete Magee's world-weary voice when he arrived home: 'Just thought I'd let you know, old chap—there's some sort of fuss about *TTS.* A group of women, feminists or loony lesbians or something, protesting outside WH Smith. All to the good, I say.'

Barely registering the news, Frank went straight to his manuscript. Sandra, attentive, efficient, concerned, would wind washing line around her husband's rib cage, under the table, back again. There would be no anaesthetic. The incision would be made with a kitchen knife. Strangled sounds would emerge through the gag. The kitchen table would jerk, making a noise like blackboard chalk on the kitchen tiles. The kitchen would be spattered with blood. It was huge, what had grown there and stuck; stuck inside and it didn't want to come out, not at all. Sandra would be pushing with all her might, whilst Dr Villarossa, gloved in blood, would pull . . .

WHAT YOU WANTED

I t was Wednesday, the night before Purvis's visit. Liz sat, cross-legged, with the light on and the gas fire blazing. Her Indian-print skirt was stretched tight across her knees, the excess tucked beneath her, forming a taut surface to serve as a table from which to eat her paper of chips. She sat with her back to where the television set would have been. Jim was strapped in his bouncer. She blew on a chip and held it out, but he ignored it. One day, she told him. Food of the gods. She was ravenous from swimming again. Even though the usual woman hadn't been there she'd managed to get someone else to look after Silly and she'd done fifteen lengths. She was aiming for twenty by the end of the month, and as well as that, a class for mothers and babies was starting up in three weeks' time. 'Our names are already on the list,' she told Jim. 'They say babies can swim naturally. It's impossible for them to breathe in water, because until about a year old they have this reflex that protects them, and of course they tend to float anyway. There was this picture...' It was hard to describe, but she tried: the turquoise-blue water, the huge head of the smiling baby, its blue eyes wide open, a stream of bubbles emerging from its nose. The little arms paddling away. Blissful was the word that came to mind. 'All underwater!' she said, and just then, a man shouted outside, an urgent sound, all the more compelling in a street normally so quiet.

She stood, and taking the chips with her, looked out through her front window. In the house opposite an upstairs window had been flung open, showing the shape of a figure against the yellow light. Below, in the shadow of the hedge in front of the house, some kind of fight was taking place. It was hard to see, but there were two men, both elderly. What on earth could that be about? Filling her mouth with chips, and peering through the unwashed glass, she recognised one of the men as the owner of the house opposite, who Alice had told her was called Captain Stevenson, though she wasn't sure if he really was one, or if, being so straight-backed that he looked as if he was standing to permanent attention, he just looked like one. Captain Stevenson had some kind of stick or truncheon and was swinging it repeatedly at the other old man, who sprouted an unruly beard and wore a coat and boots that were clearly too big for him. 'Get off! Get off me!' he yelled as he tried to dodge or ward off Stevenson's blows.

Some kind of elderly love triangle, perhaps? It ought to have been almost as good as TV, but Liz could not help but feel sorry for the old man with the beard. She'd met plenty like him. She had even sat around the fire with one or two and heard how they started out like her, running away from trouble at home, then never settled down again, never left the road… How she should go home and make things up with her parents while she still could, *et cetera*. It was not advice she was going to take but you could tell they were sincere and meant well, and you could see how every bit of them—back, feet, hands, head, skin—every bit of them hurt, down to the pores. And now, as she watched, Captain Stevenson kicked at the other old man's legs, legs that already hurt him, and thrust him to the ground. 'No!' the old man yelled, 'Please!' It was not a good situation to get mixed up in but at the same time it was just too much.

'Silly!' Liz said. 'Sorry. I've got to go. She dropped the chips, pushed through the front door, and strode across the street.

By the time she arrived, the whole scene was frozen, a tableau. The bearded old man knelt on the pavement; Captain Stevenson stood behind him, the stick held across his captive's neck. Both were breathing hard; the kneeling man moaned faintly, almost mechanically.

'They said they're coming!' Captain Stevenson's wife called from the upstairs window, her voice halfway between terror and excitement.

'What happened?' Liz asked. The kneeling man, so far unaware of her, groaned. Captain Stevenson tightened the stick.

'Been prowling around the area all week,' he said, breathing heavily. 'Scaring people out of their wits. Caught him trying to get in through my window.'

'Only knocking—' the kneeling man managed to spit out. His filthy coat was torn in several places. Liz bent to see his face. It was shrunken and wrinkled, the right temple freshly grazed. He looked ill, and hungry. His bloodshot eyes darted about in the dark, as if still hoping for escape. It seemed like some grotesque acting of fear—or fear coupled with a terrifying sense of the absurd. What next? What else will rain down on me? There was a smell of spirits and very old clothes.

'He's just a tramp,' Liz told Captain Stevenson. Though at least in his sixties, the captain was a fit-looking, broad-shouldered man.

'Mrs Nelson saw him in the passageway.'

'You're—mad,' the tramp spat out, struggling to turn his head, trying to cough against the stick. 'You're ab-solute-ly mad!' The stick tightened again.

'He doesn't look dangerous,' Liz said. Her heart was pounding, but she felt calm. Solid. She knew what she was talking about. 'He isn't. Look, I'm not scared of him.'

'He should go back where he came from.'

'Can't, can he, like that?' Liz said.

'Let me go, you bastard! I'll bite your hand—' the tramp's choked voice rose then stopped dead. He began to growl, like a dog. 'I've got a disease.'

'Let him go!' shrieked the woman upstairs. Captain Stevenson glanced up at her, then kicked the tramp twice in the back, released him and stood, stick at the ready, as the tramp picked himself slowly up. A second later he was running, the loose soles of his shoes slapping unevenly on the pavement like a pair of extra feet.

'Go back where you came from!' Captain Stevenson shouted, brandishing the stick.

'And she should do the same!' the voice from upstairs hissed. 'Stan, don't you see? It's that girl from opposite! Don't live much better than a tramp yourself, do you! Ever heard of curtains? That tip of a garden ruins the whole street!'

'You've no right to beat people up,' Liz said.

'I've every right to defend my family. Get off this pavement.' Captain Stevenson raised the stick another inch or so. Light from the window showed the sweat on his face, his bulging eyes. There was no point in contesting his dominion over the pavement. In fact, Liz thought, he was welcome to it. She turned and walked back towards her house.

The blotched-faced man had his blinds down. Alice and Tom's curtains were closed, too. But she could see right into her own front room, where Jim, suspended in his bouncer, faced the fierce glow of the gas fire, his diminutive chair set on the dusty floor. She saw the pine cones on the mantelpiece, the pile of cushions, the dusty floor which she must clean before Purvis saw it tomorrow. As soon as she got in, she turned out the light and the fire and took Jim in her arms.

The remaining chips were cold, but her appetite had gone.

'That was a stupid, vicious old man,' she muttered into Jim's hair. She could feel her heart pumping. Next door, Alice and Tom were watching TV. No one else had seen what happened. I'm not going to cry, she thought. What would be the point?

'TV without sound is OK,' she said conversationally in the dark, 'but TV without pictures does nothing for you.'

There was classical music playing on the other side.

'You know, we could still go on the road,' she said. But she went on sitting there, unable to move at all. 'Catch up to Mr Tramp and have some company for a mile or so . . . Even now. I still could. We'd wrap up warm and just take the essentials. A sleeping bag, knife, camping stove and such. A lot of the time you can sleep right out under the stars. Though I must say it would be a good idea for you to be potty-trained. You don't see many people on the road carting around giant bags of disposables . . . I guess I should have learned to drive . . .

'We *could* do it, if it wasn't for *Purvis,*' she said eventually. 'She'd call the police. They'd look harder now, and two of us would be easier to spot. She's coming tomorrow.

'I would lie low if I were you, Silly. Sleep through it.' She replaced the cold chip she had been going to eat and pushed the package a little further away. Jim's face was slack: you'd almost think he was bored. On the newspaper wrapping under the waxed paper bag of chips her eyes slid over the racing results, across the photograph of a jockey falling from a pale-coloured horse to the column of racing results and the last-minute news to the left of the page: Toxic Waste Found on Beach; Hospital Closed Despite Appeal; Mysterious Fire on Barracks Road; Woman Cautioned; Lorry Overturns; Man Pleads Not Guilty to Murder of Wife.

'There's no point in drawing her attention. Might zap us with her ray gun,' she said as she screwed the chips into the newspaper and threw them into the corner of the room.

Annie Purvis lay on her front, her head twisted to the side, one arm thrust under the pillow. It was 2:00 AM.

'Annie,' Sim said, shaking her shoulder. She heard him as from the far end of a tunnel stuffed with wool. Her mind answered, but her lips and limbs wouldn't move. 'Annie—wake up!' Slowly she propped herself on one side.

'Was there a noise?' she tensed, listening.

'No,' said Sim. 'I just want to talk.'

'Now?'

'I'll wait until you're awake.'

'Don't put the light on,' she said, struggling to a sitting position. 'Well . . .?' she said after a minute or two.

'Annie—I think of things going on forever and ever like this and I just can't stand it.' His voice seemed to fight with itself—it broke like a boy's, recovered itself, became over-strong. She was afraid of what was to come, but so was he. There was nothing to do but listen.

'Day in, day out, what we do—it's somehow become all wrong. Like being here, in this flat, jumping every time a bottle breaks. Going to school every day. Being sarcastic. Hating people because I'm not where I want to be and they're part of it. Sitting behind a mound of marking at home. Waiting. Waiting for things to mysteriously improve. I don't like any of it. You and your work, the way it sucks you away—'

'But—'

'It's an addiction. You swear off for a bit and then you're back, inching up again. It's all about other people's lives—'

'I've got to have something—'

'You haven't got anything!' He was shouting now, and she wanted to stop him anyway, but even more in case someone heard. When had Sim ever shouted before? Ever? If so, she couldn't remember it, not like this: 'Nothing! It's all other people's lives!

'Sorry,' he said after a few moments. She felt how she imagined she might feel if he had ever hit her: a cold, unforgiving sting, then nothing. Shock, she supposed—a barrier against the guilt that would follow. That he felt so terrible, and had to tell her like this…She looked straight ahead at the window and the darks shapes of the flats beyond. None of the windows were lit. She turned back to look at Sim again but he too was looking out.

'I'm sorry, but what you do or don't do about the way you work,' he said calmly, softly rubbing the stubble on his chin, 'well, right now it's my business because we are married. If we weren't it wouldn't be. What I want to do about my situation is to change it. Drastically. That is your business, again because we are married; again, if we weren't it wouldn't be.

'It's been like this a long time,' he said. 'I wanted to wait before saying it. I wanted to wait until you were completely over what happened with Jackie. Until it was all settled. And perhaps I was hoping that then you'd be glad to get out of the world you're in. But I'm thinking now—there isn't an edge or an end to what happened, and there isn't a getting over it. It's endless and ongoing. That was an extra big wave in a choppy sea. And I just can't stand it anyway.'

'What is it,' she said, still searching the blind windows opposite, 'that you are saying?' Sim reached across. Her shoulder itched and she pulled her hand away from under his to scratch it with, although she could have used the other one. She could feel him willing her to look at him, and in the end she did. Her eyes had adjusted and she could see the hollows and planes of his face, the faint glint of his eyes.

'I am saying that in six months' time I want to be somewhere else or on the way there. Not just want. I will be. Together, or on my own, I will be somewhere else. But I really want it to be with you.' He stroked her back.

'I see,' said Annie woodenly. His face was a moonscape of shadow, a strange thing. 'Well, that's clear.'

'I'm sorry to be handing out an ultimatum. But there's time,' Sim said, 'to think about it all and talk things over. Six months. I'm sorry, but this, now, just isn't what I want. It can't go on.'

'The baby was enormous and even heavier than it looked,' Frank Styne wrote. He adjusted the Anglepoise lamp, which didn't seem bright enough even in daylight, rubbed his hand over the four days' growth on his chin. Exhausted cups of espresso stood on the table in a row, their dregs dried to thin crusts. He pressed his pen hard on the paper as he moved in to describe the delivery. His gorge rose and he felt waves of pain cross and re-cross his lower abdomen. He could only write a little at a time. 'It was a small hard man they cut out of him, covered in hide-like skin. It had been growing for twenty-two months and could already stand and speak . . .'

The husband felt weak and soft, without edges. He looked at the baby and was afraid. It was hideous. It was his. He was its. He couldn't move.

'"Hungry," it said, grasping at his leg. Its hooded eyes glared at him, angry and needful. "Feed me on something soft and solid, something fine and warm, raw."

The husband looked helplessly at Dr Villarossa, who looked back at him, then at Sandra. Her expression was one of patient concern, forehead furrowed, the ghost of a smile on her lips. She pushed the child towards him. The husband's stomach heaved.

'"It was what you wanted," Dr Villarossa said. "At my surgery, everything can be arranged," and she laughed, thumping the table with her fist.'

Frank filled the space between the last line of *The Procreators* and the bottom of the page with an arabesque. He exhaled and clicked the outworn pen into its cap for the last time. He went to his sitting room and checked the equipment. He lay on the sofa. He set the alarm on his watch, took two pills and closed his eyes. He would sleep now, sleep until just before the Hanslett broadcast came on the television. It was almost dawn and his light was the last in the street to go.

EXPLORATORY SURGERY

Liz opened the door to Mrs Purvis, smiled, and answered that she was fine.

'Have a seat,' she said. She had spent several hours cleaning the floors, and the house had a strong lemony smell, though some of her footprints seemed to have soaked indelibly into the wood. Mrs Purvis knelt, groped behind herself, and settled awkwardly on the green cushion: the narrow circumference of her skirt meant that sitting on the floor was difficult. She had to spin her legs around and sit with them sticking straight out in front, the way dolls sit. I'd never wear a thing like that, Liz thought as she plunked down opposite her. You couldn't run.

'You *have* put in some work outside!' Purvis said.

'Oh?' said Liz, surprised.

'And how are you doing for adult company, Liz? Are you seeing any of your old friends from the carriages?' A loaded question. It was a matter of making the story come out how Purvis wanted it.

'No,' she said, which was both true and correct. It was not, Liz thought, as if she even knew where any of them were. Mexico perhaps. Mars. Maybe some of them were dead. And by now the carriage dwellers' traces would be completely grown over, if the weeds beyond the stuck back door were anything to go by.

She glimpsed last night's packet of chips in the corner, missed when she cleaned, but it was too late to pick it up now. She smiled at Purvis, to distract her from her surroundings.

'Your life has changed a great deal, and very suddenly, hasn't it, Liz?' Mrs Purvis said. 'But perhaps that's a good thing on the whole. What about the street? How are you getting on with the neighbours?'

'I see a lot of the woman next door,' Liz told her.

'That's good.' While it was impossible to assent to this, Liz found it easy enough to hold Mrs Purvis's gaze. The other woman smiled and leaned forwards a little. 'I imagine there's quite a sense of community around here. You know, I really miss that, where I live. Flats aren't the same. I was born on a street like this, Liz. In Halifax. So intimate. People in and out all the time. And talking over the fence in summer . . .'

Perhaps, then, Liz thought, Mrs Purvis would want to go out the back next, through the door that had to be kicked open, into the waist-high grass, the piles of builder's rubble and old plaster slowly returning to earth, the collapsing fence. She quite liked it herself, and sometimes took a chair out back to sit in the sun and watch the wind in the leaves, but she sensed Purvis would disapprove. Perhaps she should offer tea now, to divert her. But Mrs Purvis continued.

'Liz . . . I wonder if you'd thought lately of making contact with your family? You'd be surprised how often, even when things have gone terribly wrong in the past, a family will rally around at times like this.' Liz noticed for the first time that there was a faint echo in the room. *At times like this.*

'No,' she said very softly, so as to escape it. 'Not yet,' she added. There was a moment's silence. The two of them looked at each other. Purvis was thinner and very pale, Liz noticed. She looked oddly fragile—and it was unlike her not to pursue the family question, not to say how all families were imperfect in some way, but that over time, et cetera, but simply to respond, 'Well, bear it in mind. May I have a look at Jim?' She struggled up from the cushion, Liz offering her hand just too late. Purvis's shoes clattered on floorboards.

'Shall I take them off, Liz?' she asked, and did so without waiting for an answer, setting them by the door. Now she stood in her stockinged feet. Pale beige tights. Climbing the stairs, she gripped the banister and talked over her shoulder.

'Liz, I'm very sorry I didn't get around sooner, but the department's been in crisis. And I've been under stress at home, too . . . Left or right?'

Jim lay sleeping on the middle of the bed. Liz had fed and changed him half an hour ago, and as luck would have it, he was on his side, the way Purvis had recommended. His hair was quite long now and his face, relaxed, looked more babyish than it normally did.

'What a cherub. You don't use the cot?' Mrs Purvis asked in a low voice as she pulled back the blanket. 'Co-sleeping does carry a risk. You really should... He's certainly grown,' she commented. 'Looks very healthy. Well done, Liz. Any problems?'

Liz shook her head. 'He cries if there's something wrong, and I just work out what it is and fix it.' She felt sick saying this because underneath the babygrow was the foot, perfectly healed, but not quite the same as the other one. The way he had cried that night! She felt sick mainly because of what she had done, but also because of lying: she'd rather not. The ankle was still stiff, though she hoped it would get better in time. And the woman in the pool had noticed it. But Purvis seemed to be looking at Liz more than at Jim, and liking what she saw.

'Have you been to the mother and baby clinic?' she asked.

'Well, last time it didn't work out. I missed the bus.'

'Make sure to go to the next one.' Purvis sat down on the bed and patted the space next to her.

'Liz, I think it's time to look ahead a bit. At this stage I suppose what you have to do is pretty much the same as with any baby. But it'll go on and on, and it is bound to feel harder, without the progress you might expect. Later on, you might start to feel . . . trapped.' As she spoke, Jim turned, opened his eyes and stared at the ceiling, spellbound. *In the Silent Zone*, Liz thought. *Take me with you, please.* 'You must tell me, Liz, if you do get to feel that way,' Purvis said. 'May I?' Liz nodded, dumbly, as Mrs Purvis reached over and scooped Jim up.

'Oops, there you are. So heavy now! Did you read the leaflet I sent about the George Meridel Centre?' She stood and began to sway and jog as she spoke.

'Haven't had time yet,' said Liz, still sitting on the bed. Mrs. Purvis patted Jim's back and sniffed the top of his head with her eyes half closed. It was bizarre to see her do that. As if he was hers! But all in a good cause. Liz smiled some more.

'Well, George Meridel is a place where they teach you how to give a special baby like Jim proper stimulation. So that he reaches his maximum potential...' So this was it: more people telling them what to do. A whole other level of it. 'Now you've settled in here,' Purvis continued, 'I think it would be a good time to contact them and set up an assessment. If you like, I can call—'

'But,' Liz cut in, 'Mrs Purvis, I talk to him all the time. He's always with me. Never apart. We're fine how we are.'

'I'm sure you do the best anyone can *on their own*, Liz,' said Mrs Purvis. 'Of course you do. But the thing is, with a baby like Jim, just talking in the ordinary way may not necessarily be the best thing.'

'It's *not* the ordinary way!' Now, Liz wanted Mrs Purvis vaporised, and failing that, for her to put Jim down. She stood and held out her arms, but Purvis ignored the gesture.

'Of course, of course. He's very attached to you,' she continued, approvingly. 'I'm just saying that you may need to work out other ways of communicating as he gets older. So that at least he can tell you what he wants, express his feelings and so on. And of course some of these children really are very special, you know. Despite how it seems at first, they can be very talented; certainly they can be happy. You'll want to give him—'

'Mrs Purvis, we are already happy,' said Liz. 'We do communicate.' And it was the absolute truth, sometimes at least. In the swimming pool or the bath. Sitting together on the back step. Walking. With effort Liz kept her face loose, the smile hanging there: *Hide. Look them in the eye.* If only Silly could back her up.

'At the George Meridel, you see, they'd watch the pair of you together and then work out an individual programme for each family and their child. They can see things you or I might not notice. It's even possible that some of the things you naturally do even hold him back, Liz, and they could show you, if so. And of course you'd meet other mothers with babies a bit like Jim.'

It was even more people telling her what to do and asking her to agree with it and tying her down.

'We're fine now!'

'But perhaps a little later?' Purvis asked.

'Perhaps.' Liz managed to say. We should have gone last night, she thought. But still, even now, there was—wasn't there?—always the possibility, the dream of escape. The hope that they might reach the Silent Zone first. At the last possible moment, bliss. As soon as she's gone . . .

'Nothing happens overnight. There's quite a waiting list,' said Mrs Purvis. Jim had fallen asleep in her arms and she lowered her voice. Then she stood and settled Jim into the cot Liz had never used, and covered him with the spare blanket that hand been airing on its side. Straightening her back, she looked around the room: empty bar the bed and cot, an upturned box for a nightstand, beside which stood an ancient pair of

Dr. Martens boots. Light poured through the windows and caught the motes of dust in the air. Opposite, the neighbour's windows were veiled in net.

'You could claim for some furniture, you know,' Mrs Purvis said, 'and carpets. A vacuum cleaner. Maybe even a TV. From the Trust.' She reached in her bag. 'I have the application form here. Let me know if you need any help with it…' At the bottom of the stairs, she said, 'Liz, I think I explained that I'm under pressure at work. I wanted to ask you how necessary you feel my visits are? Liz, I'm not trying to cut you off. I just wanted to check as to how often—'

'We're doing fine,' Liz said. 'I don't need anything.'

'Perhaps every six months, then?' Mrs Purvis slipped her shoes on, hesitated by the open front door, then touched Liz awkwardly on the shoulder.

'Please don't hesitate to get in touch at any time if you do need something. It's been lovely to see you getting on like this. There are plenty of mothers with normal babies *and* a husband who don't manage half so well. I'm really pleased. And Liz, it's meant a great deal to me to work with you. I'm proud of you.' Proud? Liz overrode her reaction, nodded. It was almost over, yet Purvis was not leaving. She stood there, smiling. Waiting? What for? Then it came to her.

'Thank you,' Liz said, and Purvis leaned in and hugged her close. She smelled of a laundry, laced with a whiff of sweat; her blouse was damp, and the clipboard, still in her hand, dug into Liz's back. But a moment later it was over, and Liz watched as Mrs Purvis stepped into her car, wrestled with her skirt, then propped her clipboard on the steering wheel.

'Another form,' Liz muttered. 'Thank you and fuck off, then, why don't you just fuck off, form-face!'

Mrs Purvis's hands shook as she turned the ignition key. The engine spluttered, then failed. She felt dizzy, remote. It was as if she too was a machine going wrong, but on the third try, the car started and she glanced back at Liz, lifted her hand, and mouthed something halfway between goodbye and good luck. Breathe, she reminded herself, breathe.

It was all out of proportion: the way she felt giddy with panic now that she had seen Liz and Jim and knew they were doing well, and yet when Sim had presented her with his ultimatum in the middle of the night she'd felt nothing, nothing at all.

She glanced in the driving mirror for safety's sake but saw only her own eyes, brimming with tears. 'I'll go back to the office and talk to Mandy,' she thought as she set off. Acid churned in her stomach, rose briefly and seared the back of her throat. She changed into second gear and felt for the chain around her neck. The car swerved, she righted it, then she was around the corner and into third. The road was wider; she put on speed. Trees and other vehicles flashed by in a lurid blur.

Liz watched the red car disappear and then, without warning, burst into tears. Through them, she saw her garden. No wonder Purvis had commented. It had been transformed. Transformed. A new gate had swung closed after Mrs Purvis; to the left of it a strip of freshly turned earth was planted with marigolds; to the right the tiny lawn had been edged and cut exposing a narrow border of herringbone brickwork on all four sides. In the centre was a small lavender bush, already in bud and wilting slightly.

'You're lucky with that brickwork. It's original,' Alice leaned over the fence, grinning. She was wearing yellow rubber gloves. 'We did it first thing this morning. Tom's got a day off. He did the gate and I did the rest. Another day we'll help you with the back. It's like an Amazonian rainforest out there. What's the matter? Are you okay?' Despite all that she knew, Liz shook her head. 'Come around,' said Alice. 'Come around for a chat . . .'

'No,' Liz tried to say. But though her lips moved the sound wouldn't come out.

'Come on, now. Bring the little one, or will he be all right for half an hour or so? I expect the baby alarm would still pick up over here.' Alice's voice was firm and she reached for Liz's arm. She'd removed the glove from one hand, and it hung limply in the other, like an empty banana skin. The exposed hand was pale and bluish, looked to Liz like something out of a film: some subtle nightmare where people mustn't touch, where their hands burned, sunk through others' flesh like acid—and to take off the rubber coverings could only be malice. She stood, spellbound, waiting to feel the bite.

'It's okay,' said Alice softly, and smiled. 'Come for a chat with me and Tom.' It seemed to Liz that there was triumph in that smile, but she'd become an automaton: obedient to Alice's will, she returned to her house, climbed the stairs. Jim's face was pressed into the cot mattress. She could see the rise and fall of his breath, hear the faint wet sound of it. The hair on the back of his neck was damp.

'Silly?' she whispered. He didn't move. She pulled the covers down, and left the room. She closed her front door, and walked down the newly revealed path, which wavered slightly in the tears still seeping out. She continued through the gate, which clicked resoundingly behind her, then through Alice's gate, up the other side's path, and just as she'd sworn she never would, she crossed the threshold of number 129. She wiped her feet on the bristle mat that said 'Home.' The place looked oddly familiar because all the rooms were the mirror image of hers.

'Straight on!' Alice called gaily, but Liz knew, anyway, where the kitchen was. In it was Tom in jeans and his maroon track suit top. A glance passed between him and Alice, over Liz's head.

'No need to make a big deal of it,' he said, pouring water into the coffee maker. 'It's only our old gate, painted up. And the plants were left over from ours.' He and Alice stood next to each other, leaning on the kitchen cupboards. They wore the same style of jeans in different sizes. Liz seated herself at the table, and kept very still. The kitchen was bursting with stuff. It bristled with jars, packets, utensils, crockery, cutlery. She felt that if she moved even slightly all the things, the jars, kettles, mugs, pans, racks and machines, could come flying off the walls like in *Poltergeist*.

'Besides,' said Alice, 'it's so nice having you next door. It's helped us both, having a chat with you now and then . . . You must need company, too, being on your own. In adult terms, I mean.' She pushed a small plate towards Liz. 'Do take some of that banana bread. I made it yesterday. Go on.' Liz took a slice, but even though she was hungry she couldn't quite bring herself to break off a piece and put it in her mouth. The coffee machine burbled and spat, then made a horrible sucking noise… The thing could be almost be alive. It could liquidise you and spatter you around the room, Liz thought, as she wiped her face with a tissue from the box Alice had pushed towards her.

'You already know a fair bit about our problems, so we might as well tell you we've decided to have exploratory surgery,' Alice said.

'Even though they *say* there's nothing wrong physically,' Tom added. 'Of course, because of that we're going to have to pay for it. *Costs an arm and a leg*!' No one laughed.

'The thing is . . .' Alice began slowly.

'The thing is,' Tom interrupted, grinning, 'Who's going first?'

Alice frowned. 'We want to do everything we can. It's been so difficult to tell what the real problems are: whether it's something emotional that's stopping us, or whether it's the strain of not conceiving that's making us argue.' She nudged Tom, who set out three cups. Conversation was paused while he decanted some coffee and handed it around. Drips fizzed on the hotplate.

'Thanks,' Liz said as she took her cup: the second time that day. And being there was still, right now, far better than being on her own.

'We've been seeing Dr Howatch,' Tom said, 'Twice a week. The hypnotism we tried before was just too slow. And the homeopathy. And that woman Alice went to see.'

'She said it might take years for me to know what I really felt about all this,' Alice said in a rather puzzled tone of voice. 'And that accepting my real situation might be very painful. But then, at the end, I'd feel better for knowing myself.'

'Very airy-fairy,' said Tom. 'Howatch does trend analysis. It's much more business-like. You plan out what's possible in order of preference, and go for them all; really go for them, one after the other, working down. But the trick is to timetable it, and never go over on what you've given each option. If nothing shows up medically, we'll try sperm donation, IVF and then adoption, in that order. Looking at eighteen months or so, I suppose.' Alice and Tom looked at each other, then moved closer, slipping their arms behind each other's waists. Only two days ago Alice had asked Liz to keep an eye on number 129 in case Tom brought anyone home while Alice was at her exercise class, but Liz had forgotten about it, and so, it seemed, had Alice, because she never asked.

'It's very practical. What do you think, Liz?' Alice's gaze seemed to waver and struggle for focus reminding Liz in a strange way of Jim. So much inside—a whole world—and such an effort to bring it to the surface for someone else to see. A dangerous thing, too. She raised her coffee cup.

'Best of luck,' she said, but she only pretended to sip. She'd never much liked coffee. What do they want? she wondered. There was something, for sure.

'Feeling better, Liz?' She nodded, half-smiled.

'The point is,' Tom said, 'if you do what Howatch says, at the end you can say you've tried . . .' Again, Alice and Tom exchanged a glance.

'You know . . .' Alice began again, 'we've been think-ing . . . don't take this wrong–'

'It's just an *idea*,' Tom interrupted, 'you mustn't be offended.' They both hesitated. Are they going to ask if I'll have a baby for them? Liz thought. Screw him and then hand it over? Thank goodness she hadn't touched the coffee: suppose it was laced with crushed sleeping pills.

'But you do hear these things about mothers on their own who can't cope—you know, terrible things—but not their fault.' Alice looked quickly between Liz and Tom as she spoke. 'And you're so young! It might not have been the best thing for you to have a baby. I mean, you could go to college. You could get some qualifi-cations and a good job where you met people your own age. You must be lonely! And a baby doesn't make meeting people easy . . . Well, we just wanted to say that we know you're in a tough situa-tion. If it ever got like that for you, if the strain was too much for you, well, we are thinking of adopting, if nothing comes . . .'

'Well' said Tom, 'we contacted the agency already, because it does all take so long, with tests, interviews, all that. Funny really, it's not as if they give them to people who have a kid in the normal way . . .'

'Jim's such a sweetheart. It'd have to be all legal and proper, of course, but we'd make sure you were all right. Tom earns a good salary. And we've got savings . . . I mean that's only *if*. A *double* if, really.

So this was it: they wanted Jim. Liz wanted a ray gun. Shoot the bastards down! Leave them in a bloody heap on the floor, then steal the TV. Failing that, tell them Silly was going nowhere, stand up and get out of the kitchen. But their torrent of words, seemingly unstoppable, pushed her back and down onto her chair.

'We'd rather, you know, that it was a baby we knew about and I expect you'd feel the same, knowing who he went to.'

She took a huge breath, held it.

'As for seeing you all right,' Tom said, 'was, well there'd be all those things like moving, of course, we'd be the ones that had to move, I can go anywhere, really in my line of work, and it'd be best anyway—'

'Because of the memories here.'

'But the thing is, if you wanted to make a clean break as well, we'd make sure you had funds to tide you over. And anyway, even if you stayed in the area, something to give you a bit of a start finding your feet, to buy a car or something like that . . .'

'Of course, it's only a thought. At the moment, we're still trying for our own. That's absolutely our first priority. You don't need to answer, or even think about it right now.'

'No,' Tom agreed. 'Maybe we shouldn't have mentioned it, because it might not happen. We wouldn't want you to feel let down. Just file for future reference. Let's change the subject! What do you fancy? Babies or babies?'

'I've got to go,' Liz said, lurching to her feet. 'I think he's crying'.

Annie Purvis sped on around the ring road, feeling that the moment she left it she'd lose herself in a tangle of one-way streets and dead ends. Near the end of the circuit a jam had built up at the roundabout; she decelerated to meet it and then leaned back against the headrest, feeling the faint vibration of the idling engine. She had absorbed the events of the morning, and felt calmer now. 'Liz is coping very well,' she told herself. Maybe it was crazy to talk to one's self in a car, but there were only strangers to see it. 'Jim is thriving. And so,' she added brightly, 'I can have a baby. I can be a mother, and I can give Sim what he wants. What happened in my own family is just that, and it won't be repeated. I will make something—some-one—new, and everything will be all right.'

The traffic inched forward, then stopped again. She was almost at the front of the line, and any minute now, the light would change to green. She thought of Sim, standing in front of his class of thirty students of whom only one or two would ever love math. She thought of what he had said in the night and how brave it was of him to say it. In some way, Sim now seemed a rather distant figure. Bulky, but cast in shadow, and yet quite soon she and her child could be calling him *Daddy*... She had no qualms about him, though, more a kind of curiosity. And now that she had come to it was such a relief to change direction, and to want such a sweet and simple thing as a family of her own.

Behind her, someone tapped their horn; she raised her hand, and slipped her foot from the brake.

In 125 Frank lay on the couch with his eyes closed. And if I win, he thought—*You will, John, I'm sure of it, I can feel it in my bones* Katie Rumbold had said, and soon she'd be feeling it there, up there—and when he won, if anyone said, the thing about Frank Styne, the thing about Frank Styne is ... And they certainly would, oh yes, they would: they'd certainly have to analyse a bit, and they'd certainly have a bit to say when someone pushed open that door and found him dead and her, tied and bound, trussed. But he wouldn't be there to hear it.

'Katie here. I have made excuses for you. I trust that at least you'll watch it tonight on TV? If you win, Pete will speak on your behalf.'

'This is Brian Williamson of the Hanslett Trust. I understand from your agent that you are seriously ill. I am terribly sorry and wish you all the best for a speedy recovery ...'

'Michael Frean on 344567 ... I'd like to interview as to your stance in the censorship debate ...'

If it was possible to laugh from beyond the grave, he would be, oh yes, on both sides of his face. Frank couldn't remember ever before having slept through the morning and into the afternoon. He stretched and sat up and decided that he felt good.

He was surprised, then, that the imaginary radio chose that moment to return. It was different, the words pronounced with a soft carefulness that was almost sympathy. It was worse, because it seemed yet more intimate. 'The thing about Frank Styne is not, as one might think, just the outer ugliness of the man . . .'

He thrust his fingers in his ears, but he could still hear it.

'The real thing about Frank Styne, the man and the work, is ugliness, yes, but not of a physical kind.'

'Metaphysical?'

'No, Gordon. It is a moral ugliness, barrenness, I think, that gives these books their terrible power. Reading them, one is aghast that Frank Styne can bear to live. Here is someone who does not belong to the human race. A monster like Grendel, he haunts the hearth of common humanity, drooling. Indeed the name itself tells us: Frank Styne, you know, was born John Green . . .

'Can one make such claims on the basis of a work of fiction? To do so, to me, would seem to violate an important distinction. One must not—ha—attribute to Styne himself the actions that take place in his books. Yes, they are his creations, but they are not real. Frank Styne has not put a woman's eyes out, nor sawn her arm off . . .'

'But surely you know that he tied the wrists and ankles of his agent, Katie Rumbold, with washing line, then raped her?'

'You're saying that because of events in his personal life, we should look askance at what are arguably some of the most—'

'The thing about Frank Styne,' Frank said loudly to the room, 'is that he wrote pulp, simple pulp, right up to the end. His life was pulp. Pulp, pulp, pulp, and nothing more or less.'

It shut them up all right. He took the picture of the trussed woman down, folded it in four and slipped it under the answering machine. Soon he might be seeing the real thing.

He switched the television on.

THE SILVER MAN

Jim, too, had slept all afternoon and then through the first dusk, as if Purvis's touch had bewitched him. Liz took him out of the cot and set him, still sleeping, back on the bed. She put her hand on his tummy and shook, felt her fingers dig in a little too hard, stopped herself. 'Wake up, Silly!' She couldn't bear silence, nor her own voice without him to listen. 'I know!' she hissed. 'I'm supposed to sleep when you do but I can't. I need to let off steam. Wake up! Wake up!'

Slowly his eyes opened, the right slower than the left. She bent over till their noses almost touched. 'An hour I was, next door this afternoon! They can't keep their hands off. Nobody'll leave us alone! Purvis wants us in some centre, the neighbours want to adopt you—what d'you think of that?' She picked him up and clutched him to her. Her voice kept breaking out of its whisper. It was an animal in her throat.

'I haven't told them about your special advantage in life, Silver-boy. It'll be a while before they notice anything—years I should think, they're that fucking stupid . . .' One word dragged the next after it. She couldn't keep still, felt herself fighting the air she breathed the way she fought the water in the swimming pool. So much of it, everywhere. She carried him downstairs to the front room. It was gloomy, but she didn't notice, or bother with the light.

'Pair of them haven't much more fucking brain than you, you know. Just enough to be a nuisance . . .' Her arms, holding him, were alternately over-stiff and non-existent.

'Between them, that is,' she added, stabbing her foot into one of the cushions. Suddenly she was afraid of crushing him. She set him on the floor, face down. That's what it said to do in the book, *Infant Care*. His arms flexed and reached, flexed and reached; his fists clenched and opened, clenched and opened; his legs kicked, kicked—his muscles were growing. He would crawl one day and then walk: the doctor had saved that for last, like ice-cream. *Walking and so on? No problem there.* She breathed hard. She wanted to punch something, and tried the wall. Her torn knuckles stung and burned, but still it was not enough. She stopped, breathing hard.

The soft flesh on Jim's arms wobbled slightly with each movement and he made a rhythmical sound, half song, half grunt, in time to his effort. Infinitesimally, somehow, he was inching towards the wall. 'We two were made for each other,' Liz proclaimed. She bit her lip, tasted salt. Beneath his song, she could hear Jim's knees making soft thuds as he began to move his legs in time with his arms. His head strained forwards, eyes set on the wall, sank, lurched up again. She crouched down. 'Aren't we?' she said into the whorls of his ear, very loud. The head jerked away as if it hurt, down, up again.

'Tell me, are you human?' she asked quietly as his hands made contact with the wall, slid up it, fingers spread. Then she found herself shouting again, right in his ear: 'Answer! For fuck's sake, answer me!' Her skin pricked, flared with heat. She drew a deep breath and thought hard of thick, untrodden snow, glimpsing it, just.

'Sorry, Silly,' she said after a few moments. 'Not fair at all . . . Not that I mind anyway . . . I suppose that the answer's yes *and* no. Maybe more no than yes . . .' He pushed against the wall, shuffling his knees closer at the same time. It was almost, she thought, as if he were already trying to *stand:* though *Infant Care* said that wouldn't happen for months and months. It was a landmark, a thing to look forward to. 'Well, definitely you're alive and kicking,' she said, closing her eyes.

There were noises everywhere. Outside, a group of women walked by in high heels, laughing. Someone was knocking on Alice's door. Even the quiet man on the other side had his TV on.

Inside, the tiny thuds, the catch of cloth on wood and Jim's breathing seemed to grow both faster and louder until it drowned everything else out. 'A living thing, Silver-boy. A living, growing thing,' she said and then, suddenly, she saw him: full-grown, taller than her, stronger, his blubber turned to muscle, his skin coarse, pitted like cast metal, glistening. A silver man. He stood before her naked, bald-headed, stiff shouldered, his genitals hanging from a nest of silver-wire hair. A silver man, speechless, invented, beautiful. But when he took a step forward the boards beneath their feet, the whole house shook as if a train were coming down the line.

On Frank's television screen Gavin Millay, a thin-faced man in a very loose suit and a turquoise shirt unbuttoned at the neck, threshed at the air as he spoke: 'The book chosen is one the judges were proud to select for the first Hanslett prize. It is controversial, and no doubt there are many who will find it offensive, but none who could call it slight . . . The Hanslett isn't a prize that panders to the squeamish or the effete. This is a book for our time and for the future, dealing as it does with the dark underbelly of the modern psyche, exposing the ugliness of humanity with refreshing candour and triple-edged wit. It is a shocking and an exciting book: a cross-genre novel that combines ingredients of the fairytale and horror story, then binds them together with the new realism of the nineties . . .'

Like mayonnaise, Frank thought. He felt his heart thumping steadily. The description was ludicrous, but he could see how it might be applied. Millay's voice faded as the camera moved in on a copy of *To the Slaughter*, which he brandished at shoulder level. Applause rang out.

Frank poured himself a small whisky. The programme cut to a discussion, a pile of copies of the book in the middle of a glass-topped table and others open at different places, set like dinner plates before the three men and one woman seated in the corner of a living room that could almost have been that in *The Procreators*. Their eager voices faded up.

'I mean, put like that, the plot is ludicrous, but that would be to miss the point—'

'I couldn't agree *more*. The great strength of it is the language. I just love his language. On the face of it, cliché after cliché, and yet so honed and polished. I could read it till my eyes fell out, Gavin. I don't know how he does it—it's like some kind of miracle—the irony is ravishing—I'd beggar myself to be able to craft a sentence the way Mr Styne does.' The woman speaking closed her eyes when she emphasised a word: 'I'd *die* for it, literally *die!*' she concluded. Frank snorted.

Gavin Millay leaned suddenly forward. 'There's been much dispute about the ultimate meaning of this book,' he said, 'with feminists, for instance, complaining that—'

Immediately the woman revived. 'I don't think a book like this can be *reduced* to a single *meaning.*' Reduced? Like making stock, Frank thought, sipping. 'I think to do that would be to *commit murder.* This is a *huge* book.'

'What do you think, Ian?' said Gavin, staring fixedly at a man in large round glasses.

'Indeed, I think the whole censorship debate that this book has revived is indeed one of the things Styne has, albeit obliquely, addressed within it, so to speak. With a great deal of subtlety. Naturally, he cannot be expected to come up with any answers...'

'Professor Green?' said Gavin Millay. 'This is your field, isn't it?'

'I agree with Ian Rushcroft here. I think the Hanslett has to be welcomed as an antidote to the tedious moralism that has beset other awards of late. The Hanslett looks all set to put the flavour back into contemporary fiction. We live in a complex world and what we need is a multitude of mirrors, not a narrow vision . . .'

'The point is, that this is not a book we are supposed to take literally,' said Ian Rushcroft.

'No?' said Frank. He was, he realised, enjoying himself. Gavin Millay beamed and nodded, leaning back in his chair, the tips of his fingers pressed together to form an arch. A big watch with no numerals on the face glinted at his wrist.

'And yet at the same time,' Professor Green rejoined earnestly, 'naturally, one cannot escape doing so. It has a tremendous viscerality, at times produces reactions more akin to *watching* than reading, wouldn't you say?'

'Oh yes. It's a tremendously clever and even frightening book, but one which also gives immense pleasure to those with the courage to read it.'

'And given Styne is an author who already had a popular readership, this is a book that dissolves the distinction between the popular and the literary, the exploitative and the exploratory. It is a book which *everyone* will be talking about . . .'

'And *reading!*' said the woman, closing her eyes again.

'Well, there you are!' Gavin Millay filled the screen so that even the pores of his skin came into focus. '*To the Slaughter.* Our choice for the Hanslett prize.' I am only sorry that the author of *To the Slaughter* cannot be with us tonight, but—' Applause rang out again. The camera pulled away and panned across the audience. Frank saw Pete Magee, twelve inches high in his living room as he navigated through a sea of tables and glassware towards a dais. The back of his jacket was crumpled and he stumbled slightly.

'I've known Frank for almost twenty years,' said Pete Magee, breathless, a sheen of sweat on his forehead. His glasses flashed briefly in the lights. 'He will be deeply honoured to receive this prize, and I would like to offer heartfelt thanks on his behalf.' The camera panned around the tables again, lingering on Katie Rumbold's smile. She looked flushed, but perhaps it was the colour on the set. Perhaps, thought Frank, the viewers would assume her to be his wife. The other, losing, authors all seemed to have wives, or, in one case, a husband. He poured himself a little more brandy.

'I well remember the first time he came into my office—' Frank could bear it no longer, shrank Magee to a dot and the sound of tiny dust falling down. After, eight minutes passed, one by one. Suppose she didn't ring? It was a weakness in the plan, yet he had felt so sure she would call. He was sweating worse than Pete Magee; he felt as if he was watching a film, wanting the suspense and wanting it over at the same time, the music winding him up, until at last the telephone rang, and it was her.

'Congratulations, John! You must be absolutely delighted. I do hope I'm the first to call?'

'You are, Katie, actually,' said Frank. His voice was warm, hers paintbox-bright.

'Are you feeling better now?'

'I'm feeling pretty good,' said Frank.

'I thought so. We really have to sit down and have a good talk, don't we? I've got a string of people asking for you. It can't go on. We've got to sort it out.'

'Yes,' said Frank, 'but not on the telephone. Why don't you come and see me in the morning?'

'I'd be delighted—'

'Get the early train. Arrives just after nine. You must ring me, please, if you'll be late,' he said. 'It's important.'

'I won't be late, John. Congratulations.' Tomorrow, he thought, I think I'll make you call me by my real name.

Now the room waited, clean and calm. Nothing would move. Each item of furniture stood as if bolted to the floor, its shadow etched beside it. The disc was ready and waiting in the player; he pressed the remote and then music began to seep into the air. He would listen to it until she came.

The face of the silver man twisted, unreadable. A sound, half song, half grunt, emerged from his throat. He was trying to speak, but Liz couldn't understand. Her insides liquefied. Ants were crawling on her skin. 'Are you real?' she tried to say, her throat shrinking tight. The silver man took another step towards her. She backed towards the door, half stumbled. His hands were outstretched, grasping or beseeching, she couldn't tell. He might weep or hurt her again, she couldn't tell. There was no meaning. 'What do you want?' She glanced behind her, because she knew there was a precipice. She'd seen that, too, in a film years ago; how the body tumbled in space, a roaring cry coming and going, sudden quiet, then an echo, like here.

Fear clogged the words in her throat. 'What do you want? What am I supposed to do?'

It was a mistake, like telling Purvis her name, like telling Alice Jim was a boy; it would lead on and on, unstoppable.

From the silver man himself there was no reply. He just took another step. He raised his arms. 'Stop! Stop, please!' There was no defence. And then, with immense effort, a trick learned from television all those years ago when she lay beneath the plaster vines in the Grapes, she managed to open her eyes and make the silver man go away.

She saw that Jim had pushed his arms almost straight. One of them buckled as she watched, and he slipped sideways to the floor. 'Silly,' she muttered, checking beneath the down on the back of his head. Though of course, she thought, at least brain damage need not be my concern—and there's another Silver Lining. Then he began to wail.

'I am sorry, Silly,' she said as the cries swooped and fell. 'I am going to let you down. I am going to fill the laundry bag and then we are both going around to Alice and Tom's to do the washing and watch television in their front room. That's all—don't worry—just that.'

Tom answered the door, still in his work clothes: grey suit-trousers, braces, a candy-striped shirt undone at the neck. He held the door wide open as if for her to pass, but said nothing. Behind him, Liz glimpsed the hallway, doubly familiar now: the 'Home' doormat, a pinkish carpet scrupulously clean, an old-fashioned coat stand on which hung the jacket to match Tom's trousers; a pine table with a drawer, a vase of dried flowers, bunch of keys, the soft light from a frosted glass fitting set in the wall.

She hadn't expected it to be Tom. But really, what did it matter? She adjusted Jim on her hip, pulled a smile and pushed the words out.

'Hello. I just wondered if I could put this in the wash and watch your television while it does?'

'Like Alice offered,' she added when he didn't reply. Both the bag of washing and Jim seemed inordinately heavy. 'I brought the baby, too,' she said and smiled again.

'Oh.' Tom didn't blink. Tom's face looked, she thought, as if it had been slapped and got stuck.

What was wrong with him?

'Please,' Liz said, 'It would be a big help.'

'Oh—well. You see the police are here.' He said this quite naturally, matter of fact, as if he knew Liz knew why that must be. He inhaled sharply, then let go of the door and slipped both hands in his trouser pockets like an older man taking the night air.

'Andrea's lost her baby,' he continued. 'She's in hospital, and she's decided to press charges against Alice. Grievous bodily harm! They want to take a statement. We haven't had supper yet. I think I'm in shock.' He was, she now realised, on the verge of tears.

To his left a door opened briefly on a blaze of light. A police officer emerged. Liz stiffened—a habitual reaction. Jim squirmed and she shifted him from her hip to a front hold.

'We will have to take your wife to the station I'm afraid, sir,' the officer said in a low voice. The door behind him opened again. Accompanied by a WPC, Alice stepped into the narrow hall. All of them were crammed together and everyone's face was in someone else's shadow. Alice looked like someone else. Her make-up had gone; her curls seemed to have thickened, darkened, grown wild. Her jaw was set hard, her eyes puffed and narrow.

'Is there anything you want to take? Toiletries?' the WPC asked.

Alice ignored her and turned instead to Tom. 'Thanks. You were a lot of help,' she said dully. 'You're glad, aren't you? They'll lock me up and you can rush around to the hospital and hold her hand. Screw her as well, why don't you, while you're there?' Tom looked at the floor, didn't answer. Then Alice noticed Liz, standing in the shadows at the threshold of the house. For a moment or two, she just looked. The hairs on the back of Liz's neck and arms rose and stiffened.

'You,' Alice said, 'you haven't the first idea, have you, you and your stupid bloody baby, that you probably got without ever trying at all!' Her voice was deeper and hoarse, her hands clenched into fists: this was another Alice. Did Alice even remember, Liz thought, that she'd gone with her that day to look at Andrea's house? They'd retuned by different routes and that must have been when it happened, when this version of Alice last emerged. A few words, the flung fist, giant strides as she burned her way home...

'*And* I'm pregnant!' Alice added, as if it was Liz's fault. 'Found out this morning. Joke! What made me think I wanted a *baby*. I want someone to look after *me!* So why am I the one being arrested here? Who started all this?' Jim began to moan, a thin sound.

'Let's keep calm, Mrs. Foster. If there is anything you want to bring, please get it now,' repeated the WPC, while her colleague positioned himself to restrain Alice if required.

'You can't stay,' Tom said. And Liz wanted to leave, but she couldn't quite because Alice was still staring at her, speaking out her rage as if she was the only person there, the one who could take it away—

'Goodbye,' Tom hissed at Liz, then slammed the door.

She paused with her hand on the latch of her new gate. Why the hell am I crying? She thought. This is pure TV, she told herself. Not the best TV, soap, really, or one of those cheap detective series, or even a bad zombie movie, but still, TV. 'But the thing is, Silly,' she said aloud, 'you watch TV. You don't want to be in it.'

She wished she had said something to Alice. She wished, as she had while the tramp flapped down the road the night before, that the words would come easier and quicker when she really needed them. She should have given some advice, as she'd stood there dumbly watching. Alice, run! she should have shouted. Run! Leave! You'll be fine on your own! This is your last chance! But she hadn't, and it was too late.

The police car, which she hadn't noticed before, was parked a little way further up the street. Any minute they'd come out: Alice and the two officers. Tom would stand at the door and watch them go. Then he would climb into his own car, drive off, turning the lights on as he approached the junction. She didn't want to see it. And she didn't want to spend the night, after such a day, alone with Silly in a house without the gravity of things to pull them in, hold them down, to muffle them, without a carpet to pad them against impact, without a curtain, a television set or even a telephone to dial 999. The place was miserable and empty. She hated it. She was afraid of the silver man, and afraid of herself.

She gripped Jim with one arm and heaved the bag of washing into her front garden. She could ask the writer man if she could watch his TV, she thought, but using his washing machine might be going too far.

There was an old-fashioned bell-push on the door, and she pushed it hard. Sssh, ssh, she said, and kissed the top of his head. Best behaviour. The man was taking ages to come to the door.

HARMLESS FANTASY

'Oh,' Frank said when he opened the door. He stood with his arms hanging at his sides and stared at her. It took him a few seconds to remember who she was.

'Ah—yes . . . Did you read the book I gave you?' The words tasted thick in his mouth, stuck to each other. He had been looking through the pile of unopened mail, and he had made the mistake of opening an envelope, a small white one typed with a worn-out ribbon . . .

'No,' said Liz, jiggling Jim up and down. Ssh, she thought at him hard, or he won't let us in.

'A good thing too. Now, tell me—what kind of man do you think I am?'

'What? I don't know,' said Liz. 'I—'

'Oh, come in, come in—why not?' said Frank. Inside, he gestured at the sofa. Music was playing, a requiem, solemn and resonant; the speakers were fixed to brackets on the wall so that the sound travelled freely, filling every inch of the room. He lowered the volume and sat opposite her, slumped in his chair. Between them on a low table sat the bottle of cognac and the sleeping pills. The sash cord was under the sofa cushion. The syringe was upstairs, in the bathroom. The letter he had opened was on the coffee table. It said:

Mr Styne,

We the undersigned have read your book *To the Slaughter.* Whatever the literary establishment tells you, we think it is misogyny of the lowest order. It expresses and sanctions a violent hatred of women and a will to degrade and destroy them . . . One of the consequences of this kind of 'literature' is the inability of its consumers, mainly men, to see women as properly human. Living under such conditions, it is scarcely surprising that many women, living in any case as second-class citizens, accept and internalise a view of themselves as lesser beings.

Either directly (see below), or indirectly (see above) it also leads to extreme physical violence, sometimes death, carried out against women by men.

A newspaper cutting had been glued to the letter.

Women in the idyllic village of Westhampton are being warned to lock their doors and windows at night after the body of Mandy Simpson, 22, was found in her bathroom by a friend, who grew worried when she failed to turn up for a yoga class. Her face, police said yesterday, had been horribly mutilated around the eyes.

'The type of motiveless crime involving an obviously unbalanced killer is particularly worrying and seems to be on the increase,' a police spokesman said. Police are appealing to the public for descriptions of anyone seen in the area, a stranger, or someone acting suspiciously.

It was his Annie Smith. His page 154. The letter continued:

We wish that *To the Slaughter* had not been written or published, but given that it has been it should certainly not be honoured with a literary prize. We are angry that such a litany of mutilation is earning praise, and that we are expected to live our lives in an atmosphere of threat and intimidation. We will take direct action wherever we see it sold.

Have you ever considered what exactly you are doing, Mr Styne? How does it make you feel?

Pretty ugly.

Frank reached out for the spotlight fixed to the bookshelf and twisted it so that it lit his face.

'Well?' he said with his eyes screwed shut. 'Am I an ugly man. Yes or no?'

'I suppose so,' said Liz. The voices from the speaker grumbled, low. The words were Latin, a steady beat. She felt Jim relax in her arms.

'I'm ugly inside as well,' Frank said.

The letter had left him feeling weightless, as if the words he'd just read had picked him up and deposited him on another planet, or as if he'd just woken from an operation: exploratory surgery that had delved below the distracting skin, the insulating fat, and touched a hard knot of something, left it there, rawness nudging through the anaesthetic. It was not, in the end, fair, he thought, to blame him for some lunatic acting out things read in a book. But that other word—indirect—it was possible, he saw, that he was part of a larger plot. That what was outside became inside and then outside again—that people soaked things up, like soft white bread dipped in sauce, and then released them into the digestive system, where they became flesh. Possible that they went into shops and bought spectacles—just as he himself had studied magazines in connection with the plan—through which they afterwards saw, or by which they were blinded without knowing it.

It was, when you considered it, a vision of hell, and it could have been a story all of its own if he had the time or the will to write it, but at a time such as this he would rather not consider it. *To the Slaughter* had just won the Hanslett prize. He'd written it. Upstairs, the syringe. Under the cushion was the washing line. He remembered Brian Farrar, that night in the Three Compasses. How he, Frank, had drunk a pint of beer to keep him quiet, and gone to hide in the toilets. That was what the letter called 'an atmosphere of threat and intimidation.' Fear explained many things. And complicated them.

'Actually . . .' Liz began.

'My book—the one I gave you—has just won the Hanslett fiction prize. Thirty thousand pounds. Is that a lot or a little, considering? My whole life has been shaped by the ugliness of my face, and its consequences, direct and *indirect.* It's the only subject matter, direct or *indirect,* of my books. To win a prize for it! Utter humiliation. And now, I've heard that the book has caused a murder. Someone copied it in real life.' He paused, twisting behind him to reach the row of glasses on the shelves. It made him short of breath. 'A woman died. Others are afraid.'

'Say something,' he said, filling a glass with brandy. Liz wiped some thinnish sick from Jim's chin. Frank set the glass down in front of her, and waited while she took a sip, and then another.

When she looked up she said, 'Well, you didn't actually do it, did you? I suppose you could give the money to the victim's family, if she's got one.' A lone tenor soared above the grumbling bass of the requiem.

'What?'

'It might make a difference,' said Liz. 'They could go on a cruise, to get over it. You could do something like that . . . Please, I only came to ask if I could watch your TV for a bit. I can't get one till next year: they want you to live in the same place for a year, if you're unemployed. I just tried next door but they were busy.'

Frank pushed the remote to her across the table, keeping his eyes on her, as if she were a sudden apparition that might vanish if he looked away.

'I thought of copying something from a book myself,' Frank said. But he understood already that he would not be having Katie Rumbold. Rather, she would be having him. He prised the lid from the bottle of sleeping pills and swallowed one with a sip of brandy. It was best, he had read, to do it slowly.

What would Katie Rumbold do, when she opened the door that led straight into the front room? The letter would be on the table. Maybe the corpse would be sat on the floor with his legs splayed and his back propped against the settee, his head jerked sideways. Would she drop her bag and run over to kneel by his side? Press her head against his chest? His shirt would be tight and the buttons undone. His jaw would have dropped. Perhaps he would have vomited, his mouth still full of it, like melting ice-cream in a cone. His flesh would smell chemical and rank. Would she scream? Would she reach for his hand, hold it briefly, feel how cold it was, lift his arm, let it drop— unbalancing him so that he slipped a little further to one side?

Would she stare down at him, dry-eyed, and give him a little sharp kick, and then another, so that the well-fed flesh that had been him hours before slid slowly sideways down the sofa, and banged its head dully on the floor?

Liz investigated the channels, flicking from one to the next. One image blended into the next. Faces, explosions, blood, doctors, animals, all to the soundtrack of Frank's weird music. She already felt better. But then the music stopped.

'I deserve to die,' he said.

'Why?' she asked. 'Did you do it?'

'I'm not going to—'

'Well it doesn't matter that much then,' said Liz.

'But . . .' She was clearly not listening, so he abandoned the sentence. The baby lay on his back across her lap, her legs in lotus position in the chair. Her eyes, the only part of her face which looked alive, darted greedily from control to screen. She sat very still, the changing pulses of light throwing her face in shadow, then illuminating it. She pushed a stray tail of hair behind her ear.

'Where's the volume?' she said, without looking away.

'At the top.' On screen, a woman was taking a shower. The music, yelping strings, indicated alarm, but the woman was smiling as she soaped herself under the arms. Frank felt nauseous, looked away.

'He's a very pretty baby,' Frank said, loudly. She nodded, without taking her eyes off the screen.

'It's a big advantage in life,' he said. 'Well, what's your baby's name?'

'I call him Silly,' Liz said, staring hard at the screen, where a shadowy figure waited behind the semi-opaque curtain of the shower.

'Why?' he persisted. Liz turned abruptly to face him.

'Because . . .' And he watched as her face began to change: muscles around the jaw quivered, tightened, the strings in her neck pulled taut, quite pluckable; her nose flattened, her forehead seemed to be trying to gather itself into one spot just between her eyes. Her mouth stretched, fighting itself for up or down, her eyes—it's awful, Frankie thought as he stepped over the table, his foot catching the brandy bottle, horrible, must be stopped—her eyes had become slits in flesh, filling with water, which crept, then coursed, down her puckered cheeks. She couldn't breathe—the baby was in the way. Crouching awkwardly, he knelt, lifted it off her lap and onto the rug, then pulled the girl to him.

One hand cradled the back of her head, holding her face to his chest, the other settled in the small of her back. Her shoulders heaved, breath shuddered through her. Frank closed his eyes and let his chin rest lightly on the top of her head. Her hair smelled rich, musky. Not perfume, but the real thing. Her right hand plucked at his shirt which was already damp; the other gripped his shoulder. It was as if every nerve in him ached; even when he opened his eyes the sensation didn't fade. It was something he'd never known before, not even listening to music.

'He won't talk—ever,' Liz said with her mouth still pressed against the wet cloth. 'I don't know what's—' the words felt like hairballs in her throat. She pulled suddenly back to help them out—'inside? Nothing! Nothing! He's a moron.'

Frank loosened his grip. Keeping one hand in the small of her back he twisted to pick up one of the glasses and gave it to her. His hand shook. She held it without drinking while Frank Styne rubbed the small of her back.

'I used to be free,' Liz said. 'Now I'm stuck with him. I wish at least I was on the road—I used to go wherever I wanted, now I'm in that fucking house. And those fools on the other side want to adopt him. They said so this afternoon.'

'Well, why not?' Frank began, 'it might be—'

'They don't *know*. I've only told you. Besides...' Her face was swollen, her eyes crazed with red. A clump of hair was basted to the side of her face. Her upper lip glistened with mucus. 'I love him,' she said.

'You should get one of those trucks,' Frank said in a voice he didn't quite recognise. 'Diesel, with a cooker and stove and everything inside organised like a ship.' Liz, holding her glass, looked at the man kneeling in front of her. His face glowed like a beacon, even the scalp beneath the thinning hair.

'I can't even drive!' she said, and it was half accusation, half laughter. She continued to stare at him and the corners of her mouth turned up in a smile. She was waiting, he sensed, for more.

'You could learn,' Frank said softly. 'It's not so hard. Like that, you could park it anywhere you fancied, and move on just the same. You could go all over the world, with or without the baby. You could get a special seat to strap him in while you drove. He'd probably like it: a different view every day if you chose. Lots to see, but somewhere safe to sleep at night . . .' It was a lovely idea, Liz thought.

'I like you,' Liz said, 'who cares about your face.'

Frank reached for the brandy and took a slow, small mouthful. His eyes watered. After the sound of his swallowing there was silence, but it had, for him, the feel of music: something about it both taut and melting, rapt and yet flowing too. The brandy pressed its path to his stomach, and it was as if its effect were spreading further, slackening the muscles in his back and arms, warming the inside of his thighs, melting, sinking, gathering in his groin. Long after the brandy-effect had gone, that feeling stayed and grew, something he wanted to be touched. It took Frank a little while to realise what was happening, all on its own, and then he didn't understand. That seeing someone broken, ugly could—

'But would you kiss me?' he asked bitterly.

With Henry Kay, Liz thought, startled, nothing was ever *said*. It was almost out of surprise she leaned forwards (also, it seemed fair enough—he had cheered her up). She did it the way she had used to like, when it happened by accident with lean, half-dead Henry Kay, in the abandoned railway carriage on the other side of town, what seemed like half a lifetime ago.

This is not what I imagined, Frank Styne thought. He was looking at her face from just a few inches away—it was still swollen, but somehow not ugly—and he was feeling the kiss with his whole body. He hardly wanted to move, in case the moment changed or slipped away.

This could be, Liz knew, as she felt Frank's hands move over her skin, a tie that bound. Sex was worse even than talking, she'd told Jim, in its potential for misunderstanding, deceit and harm. But Jim was asleep.

AFTERWARDS

THE END OF A ROAD

Liz long ago gave up carrying Jim in a sling. Instead she pushes him in a pushchair, two woven shopping bags hanging from the handles, a striped shade fixed over the top. It is approaching midday and very hot. Both of them are dressed in the cream-coloured cotton sold locally and Liz is wearing a straw hat. She's beginning to learn. She knows the words for bread, cheese, oranges, no and yes. She knows husband, brother, sister, wife, child, petrol. She knows which, where and when, tomorrow, sometime, stars, the verb to work, the numbers to twenty and the adjective beautiful. The women in the village say Jim is beautiful. They whisper questions in his ear, and afterwards slip coins into his hand.

Liz has told them in sign language that Jim will never speak—has widened her eyes, tapped her forehead and pressed down her tongue. It is beginning to show now, anyway: a lostness in his eyes. But still they whisper, brushing their lips against his ears, and sometimes Liz can understand a word or two: work perhaps, or child, the intonation of a question. Perhaps, she thinks, they believe that one day Jim will wake up with perfect answers, having thought hard and deep for many years about their questions, their wishes and nothing else. Or he could be seen as a transmitter, beaming the questions to a far wiser planet, years away. Or perhaps they believe that the words they whisper fade and are lost somewhere between his ears, and so, as a result, the questions themselves and the feelings that prompted them will vanish—just as warts disappear if you rub them with fat and then bury it.

Actually, Liz believes, she could answer many of their questions herself. When she is more fluent, perhaps she will. She has a great urge to talk. In another language: it's different, she tells Jim, without moving her lips. Doesn't count. She walks slowly down the dust-white path, her limbs soft in the heat.

The truck took a month to find, and it took two more to pass her driving tests. This achieved, she drove slowly, with no plan. She arrived here and parked, two months ago.

It's a strange thing to come to the end of a road. After all, most of them simply join seamlessly on to other roads, going to elsewhere and back. In this instance it happened gradually, the surface rendering growing thinner, as if the builders had run out and tried to make it last, but failed. The road grew uneven, pitted, became a track, a crust gleaming with nuggets of flint, dusted with sand. It turned a corner, then finished, still half a mile from the sea. Liz didn't know this, when she took it for the first time, driving just anywhere.

There is a house to the left of the road's end. The people in the house let her use their water pump. To the right is an orange grove and the truck is parked by one of the older trees. Her washing is suspended on string lines between several of the others. Two breeze blocks support a plywood table-top.

The cab of the truck is brand new, gleaming with chrome and painted rich maroon. Behind it, bolted to the chassis, is a wooden structure rather like a garden shed, though the roof is convex rather than pitched and the windows on each side are less than a foot square. Green-painted steps lead to the door in the back. From the road she can see that there's a letter jammed under the handle of the door to the cab. She sits in the shade to open it. She knows there will be a money order inside; she'll cash it and put it in the tin with the rest. *Just ask if you want more*, writes Frank, in careful longhand.

When Katie Rumbold did arrive, dressed for out-of-town in a cocktail of beiges, Frank shook her hand and led her through the whisky-smelling front room where he had plotted her rape and his own death, and into the kitchen. There, Liz Meredith was feeding Jim and at the same time sipping a mug of hot milk with sugar and a dash of espresso. Katie Rumbold stood a few moments, taking everything in: the soft but immaculate room, the smells of coffee and a baby's sourness. The curious, strong-looking girl with her tatty purple skirt, faded leggings and rather grubby feet; the silver-haired child, who looked nothing like either of them. Then she sat straight-backed in her chair and smiled at all three of them.

'I had no idea,' she said, 'no idea how you lived.' Her shoulders relaxed. She looked interested.

'No,' Frank said, slowly, after a pause. He went to fetch her coffee. When he looked at Katie he felt nothing other than relief. But when he so much as thought of Liz Meredith he was helpless. He had much, he thought, to learn. He was glad he wasn't dead.

'What are your plans?' Katie said, looking at both of them. Liz ignored her.

'Really, I don't know,' Frank had replied.

'He bought this truck,' Liz tells Jim.

If you ever want company, Frank writes, *I will join you. I would like to see more of the world. On the prize money and the proceeds of the house we could live simply, all three of us, for years. Perhaps we could stop somewhere, in the end. I think what I would like to do eventually is open a restaurant . . .*

The truck's engine is well-maintained. If it hasn't been used Liz turns it over once a week and checks everything, the way

Frank showed her to. The sheet of plain paper in her hand slips a little. The writing is small and neat with large gaps between the lines. Her eyes are heavy as she reads on: *I have begun to write poetry. It is not very good but I enjoy doing it. Perhaps some people stay the same all their lives, but I am changing, I feel it inside . . .*

Strange, Liz thinks, lazily. To feel the tug of ties that bind. . . Even if they are still easily snappable: one to a baby that will never speak, another to a man with a blotch on his face, and both of them stretched slight by distance. Beyond the trees' stippled shade the light is very bright, sky and earth faded and powdery like old paint. Despite the heat it makes her think of that first winter in the carriages. The only sound is Jim's pushchair, inching forward and back on the stony ground despite the brake.

Any time she likes, Liz thinks, she could strap him up in his special seat and drive the truck away, leaving nothing but the ash from her fire, some faint tyre tracks and the things village women say and think about her and Jim. Or she could drive away quite alone, leaving Jim in the village square. Because here, no one would call the police. Here, they would know how to look after him, do it easily, and no form-filling would be required . . . She could arrive at a new place, and not even tell Frank Styne where it was . . . He knows it, she thinks. He gave me the truck, put it in my name, the driving lessons, the pushchair, the money. Not because we fucked. Or not *exactly*. For lots of reasons, including that he hopes for something back. But he'll send it anyway, because it's the best thing he can think to do at the moment. Freedom of movement, money, quick fingers, a sharp knife. Sun, the beach, my little TV . . . do I need anything else?

Avoid, Grammy said, sitting upright in snowy sheets that were slurry and brown slush underneath, avoid the ties that bind. Her eyes burned, her finger jabbed the air and hairs used to rise on

Liz's legs and arms . . . But now she feels a lump in her throat: something's gone, and Grammy has become rather sad. She is an old woman who sat in her own shit, fearful of discovery and recrimination, a person who lost all but the last shreds of her power years before she died, so that only a child could feel what was left. The commands and prohibitions: simple, strong, unchanging, unambiguous, physical—etched, embossed. Small fingers could feel them, even in the dark.

ABOUT THE AUTHOR

Kathy Page's writing has been described as "compulsively read-able" (*Time Out, London*) and ranges widely across genres. Her story collection, *Paradise & Elsewhere*, was nominated for the 2014 Giller Prize. She is the author of seven novels, including *Alphabet*, a Governor General's Award finalist in 2005, *The Story of My Face*, longlisted for the Orange Prize in 2002, and *The Find*, shortlisted for a Relit Award in 2011. She co-edited *In the Flesh* (2012), a book of personal essays about the human body, and has written for radio and television. Born in England, Kathy has lived on Salt Spring Island since 2001. For further information, please visit her website: www.kathypage.info.